MW00083101

Embers

by

Philip Soletsky

Embers by Philip Soletsky

Cover Artwork: Rachel Carpenter Artworks

Copyright © 2014 Philip Soletsky

ISBN-10: 1497565286

ISBN-13: 978-1497565289

To my mother

Who loved reading stories.

And my father

Who loves telling them.

One

It all began with a call for an ordinary house fire, at least to those of us who consider house fires at two in the morning ordinary.

"Fallon, tank up!" Russell Burtran, a grizzled forty-year veteran of the fire department shouted at me over his shoulder from the officer's seat. "As soon as we get there, you're with me on the hose line."

"Right." I hooked my arms through the straps on the air tank built into the seatback and lifted it from the clips. Snapping my facemask onto the regulator, I tightened the straps so the tank rode snug against my back.

Paul McNeil, a kid so new to the department that he wasn't certified on the breathing gear yet, sat across from me, watching me with wide eyes as he struggled to close the spring clips on his jacket. "What should I be doing, Jack?"

1

"Just get your gear on. Russell will tell you what to do when we get there."

He swallowed; I saw his Adam's apple bob. His face was thin, his cheeks almost adolescently smooth. He was what, nineteen? If he stuck with it, he'd have forty years in the department someday. I had a moment's doubt about the wisdom of joining the Dunboro volunteer fire department at the age of thirty-five.

The house was a two-story colonial with grey clapboard siding, white trim and a hip roof. The right side of the first floor was fully involved. The front bay window and side patio door had both blown out and were pouring columns of thick dark smoke and occasional licks of orange fire into the night sky. So far the second floor appeared uninvolved. As we drove up we could hear the shrill of the smoke alarm going off inside the house. A blue Nissan was parked in the driveway. Russell relayed his observations of the fire scene into a handheld radio as he climbed down from Engine 2.

I jumped out of the back and pulled out the speedlay line, 150 feet of hose and a nozzle folded up in a rack underneath the pump control panel for quick deployment. Running to the bottom of the front porch steps, I fed the line out as I went. Tom Schmitt, the driver, got down from the cab and climbed onto the back deck of the truck to activate the pumps.

"Paul, get a ladder set up to that top window on the left and clean out the glass." Russell pointed at it, "We find anyone in the house on the second floor we're taking them out that window."

"Will do," Paul nodded once and ran off around the side of the truck.

"Tom, when Engine 3 gets here, I want them to get lines into the first floor."

"I'll let them know," Tom shouted over the throb of the big diesel engine.

Russell joined me on the line just as the pumps started, water rushing down the hose at one hundred pounds per square inch. I spun the air tank valve with my facemask on and took my first breath of canned air – cool, dry, and tasting a little rubbery.

We lifted the hose and dragged it up the three steps onto the porch and to the front door. It was like wrestling with a 150 foot boa constrictor.

"We'll hit the fire on the first floor and then head upstairs to look for people." Russell exhaled with a hiss from the regulator reminding me of Darth Vader. I knew as well as Russell did that the presence of the car in the driveway indicated someone was home, most likely in bed at 2:15 in the morning, and possibly overcome by smoke.

I put a hand on the doorknob but it wouldn't turn. I rattled the knob and the door felt loose in its frame. It was probably only locked at the knob without a deadbolt.

"Locked!" I shouted, putting my helmet against his to be heard over the roar of the fire.

It took three tries with my shoulder before the door popped open. We both ducked down as flames rolled over our heads and puddled in the underside of the porch roof. I hit the nozzle while crouched and drove the fire back. Russell put a hand on my shoulder and pressed me forward against the force of the water. We duck-walked into the house.

Even with my flashlight off, I could see well enough in the flickering orange light of the fire. To our left was a dining room with six chairs around a large oval table, bare except for a pair of crystal candlesticks which reflected the firelight onto the table surface. A china hutch stood against the far wall. To the right was the living room: sheets of flame instead of walls, burning couch, burning love seat, the entertainment center a small inferno, the television and stereo components already reduced to shapeless lumps of metal, plastic and glass.

A large patch of the woven rug in front of the couch was burning, sluggishly, like a guttering candle. That struck me as peculiar and I filed the observation away for later. A stairway going up was in front of us. The shrill of the smoke alarm mounted directly over our heads was deafening.

Russell pointed to my right, and I opened the nozzle all the way, throwing a few hundred gallons of water into the living room. The backwash of steam into our faces blinded us. I fumbled with my flashlight and turned it on.

"Leave it for Engine 3," Russell shouted in my ear. "Let's get upstairs."

I closed the nozzle and put the hose down. We crawled up the stairs, the smoke becoming thicker with each step, until visibility at the top was reduced to nothing. When Paul took out the window we could get some ventilation and clear the smoke out. Of course, that might take too long to help anyone who was in the house. We pressed our faces to the floor and groped our way down the hallway.

My questing fingers found a door on the left. It only opened partially, coming up against something solid. I squeezed my upper body through the opening and found a cardboard box wedged behind the door. I felt another half dozen boxes within arm's reach; the room was full of them. Rather than search the room further I backed out, figuring I wouldn't find anyone in a storage room in the middle of the night. I realized that wasn't perfect deductive reasoning, but it was the best I could do since time wasn't, as the Rolling Stones claimed, on my side.

I heard the thump of Paul setting up the ladder against the house. I didn't know what Russell was thinking, but I was wondering how we would get a victim past all the boxes to the ladder if it came to that.

The next door along the hallway was open, and I crawled into the room with Russell right behind me. I bumped into a desk and a chair before finding the bed. I climbed on top and swept the surface looking for the telltale lump of a body, finding nothing but sheets. Russell crawled underneath– not an easy thing with a tank on his back– and also found nothing.

I climbed off the bed and ran a hand along the wall until I found the closet door. When caught in a house fire people have been known to become disoriented and crawl into the closet when they think they're escaping the room. I opened it and reached in and discovered only a vacuum and bucket. We made our way back out and down the hallway.

At the next room the flooring changed abruptly at the doorway from the rough carpeting of the hallway to the hard smoothness of tile.

"Bathroom," I shouted over my shoulder.

I quickly swept across the tile floor and felt inside the tub. Instructors at firefighter training had told me that people in house fires will sometimes seek refuge in the tub, though I've never seen that happen and never personally known a firefighter who has. The homeowner I guess hadn't either, because the tub was empty.

I heard the shattering of glass. Paul had taken out the window. Perhaps it was my imagination but it seemed instantly the smoke was thinner. I could just make out the shape of my glove in front of my face.

The last door on the hallway opened into a room that somehow felt large and open. The master bedroom. We had been crawling around in this house for more than five minutes on top of our response time plus whatever time it had taken for the fire to be called in. I was all too aware that the chances of someone surviving much longer in the smoke were slim.

Quickly we found the bed. Russell scooted under, and I again took the top. Immediately my arms slid over a dead, no, make that inert, shape that could only be a person. My adrenaline level, already pretty high to begin with, shot through the roof.

The person, a woman, was lying on her back, above the covers and even through my heavy glove I could tell was completely naked. I heard myself panting rapidly into the respirator and fought to control my breathing.

I patted Russell on the shoulder as he came out from under the bed. "I've got one!"

Russell got on the radio. "We have a victim. Second floor, end of the hallway. We'll be coming down the stairs. Have EMTs meet us on the lawn." He moved away from me, vanishing into the smoke in less than a foot, probably towards the stairway to make certain our escape route was clear.

I slid my arms underneath her and lifted, the body only coming up a couple of inches off the bed before she bowed backwards and I was forced to put her back down. I ran my hands up her body, a moment's embarrassment as I brushed past her breasts, up her arms to her hands which were stretched over her head. I felt metal rings on her wrists, and a chain. She was handcuffed to the headboard! I grabbed the loop of chain in my gloved hands and heaved. The slats of the headboard creaked, but held firm. I let go and felt back down to her feet. Heavy links encircled her ankles and the solid wooden frame of the footboard.

I rocked back on my heels to think for a second. I'd need a bolt cutter to get her loose, or maybe a chainsaw would be quicker. A hacksaw? An axe?

Russell came back to my side and yelled over my shoulder. "What the hell are you waiting for, Fallon? Get her out of here!"

"I, that is she, I'm going to need . . ."

"What?"

"She's chained to the fucking bed!" I yelled.

Two

It was the next evening, and I was at the fire department working at the long steel table which rested against the back wall of the apparatus bay. I had the facemask off of my breathing gear and had been spending the last half an hour trying to clean it. Typically that's not a big job; clean the sweat out of the inside and the soot off of the outside, rinse the filters, sanitize the whole package, and put it back together. Whatever I had gotten on the faceplate in the house fire wasn't coming off. It was smearing around like some kind of heavy grease.

Tom Schmitt had come up behind me while I was working on it. "What did you do to your mask?"

"I don't know. Something got on it in the fire last night."

"Let me see that."

I handed him the mask and he ran a thumb across it, then rubbed the residue between the ball of his thumb and his forefinger. He brought the fingers to his nose and sniffed. "It smells like tar."

"Tar? Where would I have gotten tar?"

Then I remembered seeing the strange way the rug had been burning in the living room and felt an idea start to come together.

Before it could fully form Max Deaks, the deputy fire Chief, called us from the doorway leading upstairs, "Guys, the Chief wants to talk to us."

Tom handed it back to me. "Good luck with that."

"Thanks." I looked across the various cleaning supplies available to me on the shelving over the table. I couldn't see anything that would take tar off without etching the plastic of the facemask rendering it worthless. Maybe I could call the manufacturer later and see if they had any ideas. In the meantime I wrapped the damaged mask in a plastic bag and set it aside and took a new mask from the storage locker, put it with my equipment, and then ran up the stairs.

The meeting room was long and narrow, situated above the rear equipment bays. The blue-grey industrial carpeting on the flooring was clean but worn thin in spots, the room furnished with old plywood tables which swayed unsteadily on rickety legs. They were a good match for the battered folding chairs that we used. The furniture came out of the same budget as the rest of the equipment in the firehouse, so we bought what we could from salvage companies and garage sales, anything that could be had cheaply.

Groups of firefighters clustered around each table, the electric buzz of their conversations filling the room. John Pederson, the Chief of the Dunboro Fire Department, stood at the front of the room talking with Max. John was tall and lean while Max was on the short side and rounded. Whenever I saw them next to one another I couldn't help but think about Laurel and

Hardy.

I took an empty seat near Paul McNeil who looked a little green around the gills.

"You feeling OK?" I asked him.

He swallowed, "I couldn't sleep last night. I kept thinking about that woman."

"We did everything we could."

"But she's dead."

"It'll be alright," I replied, but realized as I said it that it sounded asinine even to my own ears.

"How is it going to be alright?" Paul whispered fiercely, "How?" He was clearly freaked by the whole thing.

I didn't have an answer for him, in no small part because he was saying exactly what I was feeling, only I guess I was better at hiding it.

During my two plus years in the fire department I had already seen a couple of dead bodies, but both of those were car accidents. Not in any way to minimize how ghastly car accident fatalities can be. My very first was a pedestrian hit by a log hauling truck. After impacting the radiator grill he had been rolled and tumbled under the wheels down the entire length of the trailer, eighteen heavy-duty, deep-tread tires in all, his body parts and blood smeared down a quarter mile of asphalt. It was an image which still caused a shiver up my spine whenever it surfaced in my mind. My second fatality had been no more pleasant.

But this woman, naked, chained to the bed, her wrists bloodied by her struggles, added an entirely new dimension to the horror.

I hadn't managed to sleep last night either.

John put two fingers in his mouth and whistled, sharp and piercing, then shouted over the din, "Could everyone quiet down now? I'd like your attention."

The silence in the room was instantaneous and so complete that I could hear the slight rasp of Paul breathing through his mouth next to me.

John began, "As you probably heard on the news this morning, the Sheriff believes the woman in the fire last night was murdered."

I heard Paul next to me make a 'Heh' sound, like someone had hit him in the stomach or he was thinking about throwing up. When I had heard the story on the news my response had been very similar in feeling, if not sound.

"Did someone send Barney Fife a telegram?" a firefighter named Fiske called out from the back of the room.

"Someone must have. I don't think our esteemed Sheriff figured that out all by himself," Russell Burtran muttered from his seat next to Fiske.

This got a small round of grim laughter from several other firefighters.

John slammed his hand down on the table hard enough to make half a dozen firefighters jump in their seats, and it's not easy to startle firefighters. "That's enough of that," he said loudly. "Like it or not Bobby Dawkins is the Sheriff in this town and it's up to him to figure out what happened to that poor girl."

"If he can," Tom Schmitt blurted out.

That earned him a black look from John. Tom shrank a little in his seat.

"And it's up to us," John continued as if without interruption, "to give him whatever help we can. Is that understood?"

There were some sullen noises and a few weak "Yeahs."

"I said, is that understood?" John repeated firmly.

This earned him a few more "Yeahs," perhaps with just a smidge more enthusiasm.

Not the response he had been hoping for, John looked like he was going to say something else, but at that moment the Sheriff entered.

Bobby Dawkins held a thick stack of papers in one hand as he strode into the room, every eye upon him. It took several seconds for him to reach John's side and during that time no one uttered a single sound.

I felt a harsh tension in that silence, a volatile mix of barely contained anger and frustration radiating from the other firefighters. It made no sense to me. What made them think the Sheriff was so incompetent? I was a relative newcomer to the town, so they must have known something about him that I didn't. But what?

I had never before seen the Sheriff in person, and was shocked by how large he was. John was about my height, a little over six feet, but he was a half a head shorter than Bobby Dawkins who must have been six-six or a taller. Max looked like a small, chubby boy compared to him. And it wasn't just that he was tall, but he was huge, with a bull neck and heavy shoulders and a broad chest, and thighs that strained the fabric of his uniform pants. He looked to be about twice as wide as John who was no string bean himself.

The Sheriff stepped into the space at the front and center of the room that John vacated for him. "I have the written witness statements from those of you who were at the fire last night," he raised the hand which held a thick sheaf of papers then let it fall to his side again. "I'd like to talk individually to some of the firefighters, especially those who were first on the scene, and go over your statements with you. If you have any details you didn't write down because you didn't remember them or thought they weren't important, I'd like to hear about them. Any questions?"

No one had any, or at least none they chose to ask.

"I'd like to start with the officer of the first truck."

"That would be me," Russell Burtran raised his hand from where he sat slouched in a chair near the back of the room.

"Come with me, please. For the rest of you, I realize you have other places to be so I'll try and get through this as quickly as possible." He and Russell left the meeting room.

That unsteady silence continued for some time after they had left, but quietly whispered comments grew and spread until the buzz of conversation again filled the room.

"Oh man, oh man, oh man," Paul breathed as he rocked in his seat.

"Relax, Paul, it's going to be alright," I said, finding that it sounded only slightly less asinine the second time I said it.

"But what do I say to him?"

"We're witnesses, not suspects. Just tell him what you saw."

A pretty easy task really, because what I had seen was going to stay with me for a very long time.

Three

Three hours later I was still sitting there, literally the last person waiting to be interviewed. I had been on the first truck and had found the woman in the house, so why hadn't I been among the earliest? I didn't know.

The only other person in the meeting room with me was John. He had been interviewed hours ago, but probably felt that it was his duty to be the last one to go home. We sat at a table together, me slouched back in a chair with my arms folded across my chest and John leaning forward with his elbows on the table, desultorily staring into a Styrofoam cup with a half inch of lukewarm coffee dregs in the bottom that he was swirling around.

I felt like a clock with its spring wound too tight. Inside my guts were thrumming, and yet at the same time I also felt spent, as if just holding up half a conversation was almost more than I could handle.

"Do you know how the town of Dunboro was founded?" John asked me, or perhaps his coffee cup, out of nowhere.

I had no idea what he was talking about, but threw him a shrug anyway.

"It was a mistake."

"What?" I replied, my ragged mind trying to pull together bits of what he was saying.

"Some land grant cartographer missed when the lines were drawn for Brookline and Milford, New Hampshire. There was a gap between their borders, and in 1745 the Fifth Earl of somewhere or other noticed it and claimed it as his own. He named it Dunboro after his favorite polo pony."

A part of me had always wondered how a town as small as Dunboro had been founded, though admittedly not enough to actually look it up. It's a little less than six square miles and as of the last census had 937 residents. Were this the movie *Arthur*, Dudley Moore would likely make a joke about having the whole place carpeted. In 1770 a similarly-sized town named Monson had been divvied up among its neighbors, but somehow Dunboro had endured.

Likewise our fire department is small, I thought as I looked around at the empty chairs that had held our twenty-eight members. Our police department is even smaller: the Sheriff, two patrolmen, and a secretary.

"What the guys were saying about the Sheriff earlier, the Barney Fife cracks. What's that about?" I asked John.

He didn't answer me at first, staring into the cup he held as if it contained great secrets, then he sighed heavily. "I knew Bobby Dawkins as a kid. He grew up here in Dunboro. Some of the younger guys on the department went to school with him. Give him a football and he could break a defensive line easier than a farmer plowing a furrow in a field, but no one ever accused Bobby Dawkins of being the sharpest tool in the shed. Do you know how he was elected Sheriff?"

I shook my head.

"His uncle, also named Bobby Dawkins, had been the Sheriff for about forty years. A good man, a solid cop. The year he retired Bobby squeaked through UNH with a criminology degree; his family planned it that way. He ran his election using his uncle's campaign posters, and it was entirely possible many voters didn't even realize they were not voting for his uncle."

Small town politicking at its best and exactly the kind of thing that makes people from the city label us as bumpkins. Still, the man deserved the benefit of the doubt. "That doesn't mean he's not a good Sheriff," I commented.

"No, it doesn't," he agreed, "and for a town like Dunboro he really is a pretty good Sheriff for most of what we need. He's affable, fair, and simply too big to fuck with. I've seen him stop a drunken brawl just by walking into the room. You need someone to write a speeding ticket or deal with some vandals, he's your man. But a murder?" He frowned.

"How many has he solved?"

John gave a hollow laugh. "How many has he had to solve? None. Just like his uncle before him. I can't think of a single murder that has happened in this town in my entire lifetime, and I asked my dad and he couldn't either."

Ernest Pederson was the second oldest person in town, nearly ninety-seven years old. I wondered if a town that had gone almost one hundred years without a murder was some kind of record.

"But he'll have help solving it, right?" I asked.

"From who?" John replied with a question of his own.

My hometown was in the wilds of northern New Hampshire, a town so small that it had had no police force of its own whatsoever. My recollection was that it had worked some kind of deal with the Staties for coverage. I had no idea how small town police departments worked, but I had to believe that there was some mechanism either at the county or state level that would prevent an inexperienced Sheriff from bungling a murder investigation. "From the arson guys," I ventured.

"They'll investigate the fire, but they don't solve murders, not unless how the fire was started leads them to it."

"What about the State Police then?"

"Dawkins can call them in, but he's trying to fill his uncle's shoes. Calling in the State boys would be the same thing as admitting he can't solve it on his own."

"Which you don't think he can," I interrupted

John closed his mouth and looked away, the muscles of his jaw working. When he continued there was tension in his voice. He wasn't any happier about this than I was. "What I think doesn't matter. The case is his and his alone until he calls for help."

He placed his hand on my arm. For an old-time New Englander like the Chief, and a guy who wasn't touchy feely, that modest contact meant a great deal. "Look, Jack, this one has gotten under your skin. I can see that. And Lord knows someone should pay for what happened to that poor girl. But Bobby Dawkins," he shook his head sadly. "You did everything you could in that fire. You found her fast and you tried to get her out. I don't want you thinking for an instant that there was anything you or any of us could have done better. You did what you were supposed to do. What happens next is not our job."

17

I was surprised by a momentary flush of anger that surged through me at the thought that the person responsible for her death would never be caught. Then it passed, leaving a raw ache in its place.

John lifted his hand from my arm and slowly leaned back in his chair, his eyes watching me steadily as if he sensed I might be about to do something crazy.

The Sheriff came into the meeting room. "Jeff," the Sheriff said.

"Jack," I corrected him.

"Jack," he checked the papers in his hand, as if somehow I had been wrong about my own name, "You're next." He turned and left.

I glanced at John as if there was more to our conversation hanging in the air. He looked at me with concern and said quietly, "I've heard people in this town say that Dawkins is as much a mistake as Dunboro was when they founded it. Even though they might be right, you'll be better off if you just let this go."

Four

John had loaned the Sheriff his office to conduct the interviews. Bobby Dawkins opened the door and ushered me inside. As I stood next to him in the small room I had a *Jack and the Beanstalk* meets the giant moment, but he had a wide, kind face and calm, hazel eyes which belied his imposing physical size. The hand that swallowed mine whole was rough, but the handshake squeeze was gentle as if he had learned long ago to gauge his strength to keep from hurting people. I looked down at his feet and wondered if some company actually stocked work shoes in his size, or if he had to get them custom made.

He took the Chief's chair and gestured with a hand that was full of papers to the other chair in the office, so I closed the door behind me and sat down. Placing the stack of papers on his lap, he fumbled with them for a moment and then pulled a blank pad from the bottom of the pile and placed it on top.

"I've read your written statement," he began, referring to the incident report I had completed upon returning to the station last night, "but I'd like to hear about it again now that you've had a chance to sleep on it, see if anything else may have occurred to you since the report."

So I told him.

First bolt cutters had been used to try and free the woman from the bed. While they made quick work of the chain on her ankles, the hardened steel of the handcuffs proved beyond them. A paramedic came in, moving awkwardly in the unfamiliar fire gear he had borrowed from someone outside, and began to administer CPR to the woman while she remained chained to the bed.

It was like a nightmare; the sounds of the fire, the noises of the crew fighting it, the cursing of the EMT and the rapid shush and click of his breathing regulator as he gave CPR. At some point a vent fan was set up and the smoke slowly dissipated which if anything increased the eeriness of the scene as the thinning smoke, like some kind of cursed fog, first obscured and then gradually revealed dark, shadowy figures moving about.

The thing I remember, the thing I first saw clearly as the smoke dissipated, the thing that is going to stay with me for a long, long time, was the sight of her hands. They hung limply from the handcuffs as if in resignation, the skin coated with soot making them a far darker grey than the usual color of death. She had struggled, the metal bracelets tearing into her wrists, rivulets of dried blood streaking her forearms and dotting the pillow around her head. Her right thumb was broken badly at the joint where it joined the hand, and it canted off at a crazy angle.

Someone brought in a chain saw, and I first thought, sickly, that her hands would be severed to free her. The headboard slats were cut, and the woman was carried out on a stretcher with the handcuffs still on her wrists.

Additional crews arrived to continue to search the house.

Initially we had believed that we were looking at some kind of sex scene, and no one was thinking murder; at least I know I wasn't. We had expected to find another person, her lover, somewhere in the house. That might sound odd to someone who has never been in the fire service, but after you've been called in to help free a four hundred pound man in a pink leotard who has gotten his head stuck in an old-style brass and glass diving helmet, which had happened to me just three weeks after I had joined the department, you become less surprised at what goes on inside your neighbors' houses.

When the search was completed we determined she was alone. The apparent origin of the fire, the living room, was far away from the action in the bedroom. The mood changed as we realized this was likely no innocent sex act.

I had run down to the truck and retrieved the digital camera from the glove box of Engine 2 and taken pictures of everything – the living room, the bed, the chain wrapped on the footboard, the padlock used to secure it, the orderly pile of her clothing on the floor of the bathroom. There was a folder of prints in the stack on the Sheriff's knees; I could see the edge of the photographs from where I was sitting.

While I spoke Bobby listened, but took no notes. That wasn't surprising as my witness statement had covered three pages, on both sides, in small, dense print.

Once the fire was out and the woman was in the ambulance, that was it. We packed up our gear and headed back to the station.

When I came to the end he asked, "Did you see any other cars there that night?"

"Just the blue Nissan. That was hers, right?"

He nodded. "And no other people?"

21

"Firefighters. And later some neighbors showed up at the end of the driveway. And the police. And as we left a news van was setting up; I think it was Channel 9. But no, nobody particularly suspicious if that's what you're looking for."

He jotted something on the corner of the pad, but instead of trying to read it I hung my head and closed my hot, grainy eyes. A vision of her hands floated in front of me and I felt somehow close to exploding, as though I just wanted to sweep all the shit off the Chief's desk and tear the posters off the walls and rip the books from the shelves. Infused with a righteous fury, I knew that if the person responsible were in front of me I would have gotten violent. The power of the sensation, the hair-triggeredness of it, was frightening.

Bobby's voice came to me as though from a very great distance. "Notice anything unusual at all?"

Unbidden that anger flashed to the surface. My head snapped up and my voice climbed in volume, very nearly to a shout. "Unusual? You mean *besides* a woman chained to a bed?" The Sheriff merely blinked at me. I took a deep breath and let it out, trying to envision the stress inside me as some kind of toxic black smoke I could just exhale and expel from my body.

I felt a razor's edge of control return and lowered my voice. "I'm sorry, Sheriff. I've been through Homeland Security training: be observant, the criminal sometime likes to watch so look for him thing. Honestly, I'm completely vapor locked. All I can think about is her hands, when the smoke started to clear and I could see her hands-" I choked a little and swallowed, pressing the heels of my palms against my eyes until splotches of color burst behind the lids. "I suspect when I start sleeping again at night, and I'm not sure when that's going to happen, I'm going to dream about it."

"I'm sure you did everything you could," he said softly.

I let my hands drop and felt my mouth form into a twisted smile. "The Chief said the exact same thing to me not five minutes ago. It doesn't change how I feel, though. How does a person chain someone to a bed like that to suffocate on smoke?"

"Not that it makes it any better, but what makes you think the smoke was supposed to kill her and not the fire?"

"It's . . ." I began, but at that moment I remembered and understood the fire guttering on the living room rug and the residue on my mask. "Just a second," I got up, opened the door, and bolted from the room. I returned with the bag containing the damaged mask and handed it to him.

He looked at it through the plastic. "A respirator mask?"

"That's the one I was wearing that night. I tried to clean it today and there was something on the faceplate which wouldn't come off."

He opened the bag and took out the mask. He sniffed at the residue and dug at it with his fingernail. "What is it?"

"The rug in the living room was saturated with heating oil or diesel fuel, something like that, and it was set on fire. When I came through the door and hit the fire with the hose, the backwash of steam carried droplets of it which stuck to my mask."

"So the fire was started using diesel fuel?"

I shook my head, "Diesel fuel doesn't burn like that. Neither does home heating oil. Both have to be atomized to become flammable."

"Then why pour it on the carpet?"

"The carpet fibers would act like wicks for the fuel. The whole thing would smolder for hours, making a lot of smoke, filling the whole house with it. It would kill the woman on the bed upstairs, but do it slowly."

He gaped, looked at the mask in his hands and then back up at me. "You're serious."

"Completely. A rug that size saturated with fuel would have smoked for a long time, and never set the rest of the house on fire."

"But a fire did start," he pointed out.

"The rug was too close to the couch, or maybe it was the entertainment center. One of those started burning and it went on from there. But up until then the rug acted like an oil lamp, and she was upstairs chained to the bed, maybe for hours, maybe for a whole day. Did she show up for work yesterday?"

"I don't know."

"Ask her employer, but if she didn't I'd guess she was already sucking up smoke. It was a big house; it would have taken awhile."

Bobby wrote that down almost word for word.

Another thought occurred to me. "Have you checked if she had an ex-boyfriend or ex-husband?"

"No. Why?"

"Because whoever killed her went to a lot of trouble to make sure she suffered while she died, and she took a long time doing it. That's not something a stranger would do."

I watched as the Sheriff took notes rapidly, in a curiously flowing and artistic script.

I was just spitballing here, murder investigations 101, and

nothing that you couldn't pick up from watching The Rockford Files reruns on television. Yet here he was writing it all down verbatim as if I was channeling Sherlock Holmes. The Chief had said that his criminology degree was from UNH. Did they even offer a degree in criminology? I didn't know, but the fact that I was posing questions he didn't seem to even know to ask was depressing the hell out of me.

Five

The woman on the television screen squinted slightly in the camera lights. She ran her tongue along her lower lip, pressed a manicured hand to her earpiece and then nodded at something she heard. Her heavily frosted and moussed hair never moved. She raised the microphone to her mouth. "I'm in Dunboro, New Hampshire where last night in the house behind me," she paused and glanced momentarily over her shoulder down the driveway at the house, "police say a young woman lost her life in a fire they are calling suspicious at this time." The bright wash of the lights just reached the structure revealing melted and soot-streaking vinyl siding, the glassless upstairs windows like eyeless sockets. She continued, "The victim has been identified as twenty-four year old Patricia Woods, a dental hygienist in Nashua who was originally from Vermont. She leaves behind her parents and a younger sister."

"Diane, are the police saying why they consider the fire suspicious?" The voice of the anchorman cut in from off camera.

"No, but they do ask anyone who has any information to contact the Dunboro Police Department." The phone number appeared at the bottom of the screen. "And we will continue to watch this story as it develops. I'm Diane Ridgely reporting for Channel Nine news."

The scene cut back to the newsroom where the anchorman shuffled some papers on the desktop in front of him and looked up at the camera, but before he could say anything the screen when dark.

Valerie, my wife, put down the remote control. "Honey, don't torture yourself over this. I'm sure you did everything you could."

"I've been hearing that a lot," I replied, my eyes still drawn to the blank, glassy stare of the television.

Standing next to me at the kitchen counter, she hugged me from the side, fitting her head into the curve of my neck. Her blonde hair tickled my cheek and smelled of jasmine.

I put one hand on her waist, feeling the slick surface of the blue silk robe she wore. It was quite short and very sexy, but soon, as fall dwindled down and winter started to take hold, she would be wearing her yellow terrycloth one. She looked great in that one too; she looked great in everything, but it wasn't the same.

"Come to bed," she murmured.

"Soon," I said.

She took my chin in her hand and turned my head to kiss me on the lips. There was a lingering to it, a half promise that if I came upstairs quickly, before she fell asleep, there might be more to follow. She broke the kiss and headed up the stairs. Tonk, our English bulldog, scrambled to his feet and followed her, his nails clicking on the wood of the stairway treads.

A part of myself, a very large part, wanted to follow her, but I instinctively knew I wouldn't be able to sleep that night.

After a big fire, a big car accident, a big anything, I've always found myself too wound up to get much sleep, and I suspect I'm not alone among firefighters in that regard. There's too much adrenaline churning through the bloodstream, and it's hard to get your brain to shut down as you replay every frame of the action that is often too fast to follow while you're doing it. My typical solution has been to drag ass around the next day, try to get to sleep early the next night, and get myself back on track. As I was entering my second sleepless night since finding Patricia in that house, I had the feeling my traditional solution wasn't going to cut it.

My initial fear was I would relive the incident in my dreams, distorted through a nightmare lens into endless, winding, smoke-filled corridors with the screams of the dying ringing in my ears. As I leaned against the kitchen counter looking at the blank television screen, I wondered if the nightmares or not sleeping at all and continually seeing her hands every time I closed my eyes was worse. I was beginning to think the latter.

I breathed and closed my eyes (her hands!), repeatedly rolling my fingers into fists and then relaxing them. What I felt most of all, along with a sort of consuming anger at the brutality of the murder, was a type of restlessness, a feeling like I should be doing something. It was a feeling that wasn't entirely unfamiliar.

I knew early on in my life that I was different from my peers. The New Hampshire town I grew up in near the Canadian border, a place so small that to this day even Google can't get a handle on it, was grooming my classmates to take their father's places in the paper or lumber mills. It was a process that to me felt uncomfortably like lining cattle up in a chute for a long, particularly brain-deadening slaughter. I fled, a word I do not choose lightly, to Manhattan, where I embroiled myself in the most intellectually demanding major I could find – physics.

I met my wife Valerie at Columbia University while I was in graduate school and she was an undergrad in need of tutoring. In a graduate physics department which was at that time completely male, the big draw in tutoring was the women. It certainly wasn't the four dollars and forty cents an hour it paid, I'll tell you that.

The intensity of our relationship, the perfectness of our fit, left us both breathless. My graduate research into a new method to administer chemotherapy drugs using advanced fluid flow models looked like it was going to be a breakthrough. I was already filing patent disclosures and had visions of fat licensing fees eight weeks before I graduated, when we were married surrounded by friends and family.

If I had to put a finger on the last time in my life that everything felt absolutely right, that would be it.

Two weeks later a grey and humorless guy in a very serious suit marched into my lab, dropped a two-hundred-page legal document in my lap and marched out. I've always marveled at the fact that someone delivered the document by hand, like FedEx wasn't good enough. I took the document over to a friend in pre-law who read it through and boiled it down for me. The government was seizing my technology and classifying all of the patents in the name of national security, but at least I turned out to be right about the licensing fees. Valerie took one look at the numbers and acted as though we had won the lottery, which in one sense we had, but almost a year later I realized what the government wanted the technology for, and in retrospect I felt naïve and stupid that it had taken so long.

They were using my chemotherapy technology to build bioweapons, off the books, unacknowledged, remarkably specific, and extraordinarily hard to detect. As easy as flipping a switch it would be possible to kill one particular man standing in a crowd of thousands, or ten particular men, or a specific half of the crowd. Or all of it while leaving the city around it untouched. Or the government could decide to go nuts and wipe out a given city, like the Roman soldiers of old burning crops and salting the Earth, and my research was at the root of it all. I could end up being responsible for killing more people than Josef Mengele.

I was given my PhD without any thesis defense by a perplexed graduate committee who was told to do so by the President of the University, who himself had probably been told to do so by a guy in a very serious suit. But despite the PhD, physics was done for me, like if the inventor of the hypodermic needle had suddenly found out his invention was being used exclusively to give lethal injections.

The government money gave us freedom. We traveled, bounced around the country, aimlessly and with a sort of unhinged pleasantness. When we decided to settle down Valerie wanted to return to Manhattan with its restaurants and theaters and museums, but I had small town living on my mind, where people actually knew your name and genuinely cared about you.

I couldn't go back to my hometown; I no longer had any connection to the people there, and in comparison to any real city it would have driven Valerie insane inside a week. Shades of *Green Acres*, we settled on Dunboro, which featured small town living within reach of Boston. Valerie built a circle of friends and discovered fulfillment in volunteer work, but I remained restless.

I took continuing education classes in sushi making, blacksmithing, weather forecasting, maple syrup boiling, and woodworking. After erecting a workshop next to our house I started doing some furniture building and serious carpentry, joining local construction crews and rapidly becoming known as an exacting, hardworking, and reliable guy who was peculiarly adept at math. The wood felt good in my hands, the smell of sawdust sweet, a planned and measured joint that perfectly fit was a thing of beauty, but it didn't fill some undefined need within me. I found the woodworking to be an enjoyable pastime but I didn't want to be a woodworker.

When I saw an article in the local paper that the Dunboro volunteer fire department was looking for new members, I joined, perhaps hoping that by helping people it would in some small way balance out the deaths my invention had caused, was quite probably still causing, on an almost daily basis. Yet my restlessness, accompanied by the feeling that I needed to atone, continued to nag at me.

Alone in the kitchen with the television dark in front of me, I relived the fire in my mind, the heavy smoke, the press of heat around me. I remembered trying to lift the woman from the bed, felt the muscles of my shoulders bunch at the memory of the way she had bowed backwards, a small adrenaline spike to my heart when I recalled discovering the handcuffs on her wrists.

Our Sheriff was a good old boy, his election engineered by his parents and his retiring uncle. That was what John had told me. The other firefighters thought Dawkins was a joke, and I valued their opinions; they knew him far better than I did. I had caught a glimpse of his investigative capabilities during my interview, and saw nothing there to inspire confidence.

If left in his hands, her murderer would never be caught. Even the slightest possibility of that happening was unacceptable to me.

I retrieved a pad of paper and a ballpoint pen, and then sat down on one of the stools with the blank page in front of me for some time. I ran a finger along the depressed lettering stamped into the barrel of the pen. *Reliable Towing Service.* I cleared my mind.

At one point when I was a kid I had become obsessed with how memory worked. How did people remember things? What formed the interrelations between stored memories? Like your body, was it possible to improve your memory through exercise?

I tried an experiment on myself, staring at a random page in the Concord phone book for one minute, and then seeing how much of the page I could recreate from memory. After just a few tries, I found I could memorize the entire page, and so shortened the time to forty-five seconds, then thirty, then fifteen. I envisioned the process as taking a photograph of the page, and then just looking at it later with my mind's eye.

I found it fascinating, because on the one hand it became almost automatic. Show me a page and without even trying I would remember it. And it didn't matter what was on the page; numbers, a page of text, a crossword puzzle. Yet fifteen seconds was the absolute fastest I could ever manage to memorize the whole page no matter how much I practiced or what tricks I tried.

Once the nib of the pen touched the paper I wrote in a flurry, without pause, line after line spooling out of my memory. Two minutes later I was done and I looked at what I had written.

In the three seconds it had taken the Sheriff to pull the pad from the bottom of the stack of papers on his lap and cover the top page I had memorized a little less than a quarter of it. It was from a cell phone bill with the name Patricia Woods across the top. She had made three phone calls the evening of her death, and now I had those numbers.

Six

The miracle of the internet yielded all the information I could have wanted to know about the phone numbers.

The first call, at just a few minutes after five o'clock, probably just after she had walked through the door from work, was to Ruth Woods, who at forty-nine years of age was married to Arnold, fifty-two, and lived in Rutland, Vermont. She had two children: Rachael, twenty, and Patricia, twenty-four. How long would it take for the internet to catch up and list her as deceased?

The second call took place just after she got off the phone with her mother, and went to a phone registered to a Michael Carston of Amherst, New Hampshire. He was thirty-three years old and married to Samantha, thirty, with two daughters, Mary, ten and Alice, eight.

Out of curiosity I looked myself up, and found that indeed I was thirty-seven years old and living with my wife Valerie in

Dunboro, New Hampshire. She would probably be unhappy to learn her age was listed as well. Furthermore I found my Masters thesis online, the notice of my graduation with a PhD, and a picture of my own wedding. I wondered, not without a little hostility, when we as a society had decided it was perfectly alright to have our privacy violated by companies who bought and sold our personal information like they were stock prices or sports scores.

Patricia's last phone call of her life had been to Antonio's Pizza in Milford.

I ran it through in my head: she got home from work, she called her mom, she called some guy, and she ordered a pizza. I recalled the neat pile of her clothes in the bathroom. Maybe after dinner she had gotten in the shower and the killer had caught her there. Michael Carston was probably the last person to talk to her, discounting for the time being the pizza guy who had taken her order. I wondered if Michael Carston was perhaps a coworker, but another search told me he worked for an investment firm in Bedford, New Hampshire.

So, not a coworker.

My mind made a colossally ludicrous leap of illogic and whispered 'her murderer?'

I closed down my computer and checked that I had my keys as I went outside. The night was clear and the temperature was creeping downwards. My breath plumed in front of my face.

I started my pickup truck, a maroon F-150, and pulled out, telling myself that I was just going to cruise around a little and let my thoughts percolate, but then wasn't the least bit surprised when I glided past Patricia's house. I made a U-turn at the end of the block and cruised by it again, then one more time for good measure. The next house down the road on the right had a 'For Rent' sign by the curb and long weeds in the gap between the wheel ruts of the driveway. I shut off my lights and turned in,

parking at the very end in front of the empty house with the nose
of the truck pointed out in case I had to make a quick getaway.
The driveway was so long that I was invisible from the road.

I was on the edge here, about to do something incredibly
stupid, all because I thought that the Sheriff couldn't do his job.
My veins felt filled with ice and my heart trip hammered in my
chest. I opened the truck door, the dome light went on and
startled me, and I quickly closed it again. I reached up and
flipped the switch so it wouldn't come on, and then reopened the
door.

I sat there unmoving, late season mosquitoes finding their
way in to buzz and whine around my head. Crickets sang loudly
from the nearby woods.

There are decisions in your life you make which you can't
take back, and I knew that this was likely one of them.

I put on a pair of rubber gloves from the box I keep in the
truck for handling patients at accident scenes, removed a
flashlight from the center console, and got out, closing the door
softly behind me. I made my way carefully back to the road
without using the flashlight, then up the driveway of Patricia's
place. The builder had cleared the trees back from the house for
fifty feet in all directions, the waning quarter moon bathing the
lawn in pale light but leaving the surrounding woods
impenetrable and black. In the gloom the glassless windows
looked more like eyeless sockets than ever.

Police tape stretched across the posts of the front porch and
a notice stapled to one of them warned trespassers to stay out,
that the property had been sealed by the Dunboro Police
Department and the New Hampshire Arson Investigations
Division. Technically the Arson Division is an offshoot of the
fire service of which I was a member, which meant absolutely
nothing – I had no right to go back into the house at all and I
knew it.

I ducked under the police tape, climbed up the porch stairs, and opened the front door, the lock still broken from the night of the fire. The interior of the house, the walls now darkened with soot, was near pitch black inside. I pushed the door closed behind me and thumbed on the flashlight, illuminating the burned and broken sheetrock walls, the insulation that spilled from the stud spaces firefighters had broken out chasing after the fire. I climbed the stairs, experiencing a strange dislocation as I did so, seeing the stairway and upstairs hallway as it was today in the meager beam of my flashlight, but at the same time reliving crawling through it on my knees, my face pressed to the carpet, the heat of the fire surrounding me. With the cold fall air coming in through the broken front windows it was probably forty degrees in the house and I wore no jacket. Nonetheless I was sweating profusely.

When I came through the doorway into the master bedroom I was startled by the sight of a body on the bed, then my flashlight revealed it was just the sheets and blankets bunched to one side. The pillow was still there spotted with her blood. The ends of the cut and splintered slats of the headboard glowed whitely like broken bones. The chain that had held her ankles was gone; presumably the Sheriff had come and collected it.

I stood in silence looking at the bed, I couldn't even tell you for how long. What the hell was I doing here?

Then I had a sudden idea, maybe the one I had come here for all along, and my brain was only now letting me know about. I went back down the stairs, walked through the dining room into the kitchen, and opened the refrigerator door. Because the electricity was off, the little light didn't come on inside.

The flashlight quickly reflected off of a large clear plastic salad takeout container with 'Antonio's' stenciled on the cover. I took the container from the shelf and held it up to the light. Inside was a small pile of lettuce leaves, some crumbles of feta, and a few black olives rolling around. Most of the salad was gone. I put it back inside and looked around some more, but didn't see any pizza. I closed the refrigerator door.

A doorway out the back of the kitchen opened into a mudroom with a second door beyond that which led into the backyard. Pegs on the wall held a few coats and an umbrella. On the floor was a pair of yellow rain boots. Leaning against the wall near the door leading to the back yard was a pizza box with Antonio's logo on the cover. I picked the box up and shook it – empty.

The box was the size a medium pizza, I think fourteen inches, comes in. I can't eat an entire fourteen inch pizza alone, no matter how hungry I am. Plus there was the salad, and Patricia was smaller than I was. When I had tried to pick her up off the bed she felt like she had weighed no more than a hundred and twenty pounds.

A medium pizza and a salad were about what Valerie and I would eat together.

Patricia had had someone over for dinner the night she was killed. Michael Carston?

At the sound of a car in the driveway my heart leapt into my throat. I quickly turned off the flashlight and crouched low, moving back through the kitchen into the dining room. I peeked out the bay window.

A police car was coming to a stop with a slight squeal of its brakes, the moonlight reflecting off the plastic lenses of the lights on its roof. The silhouette that opened the door and got out could be none other than the Sheriff; no one else on the police department was that big.

Had someone seen me drive by several times before pulling in next door and called the police? Maybe someone had seen the beam from my flashlight in the house. Or was he here for some other purpose?

He turned on a flashlight he was holding, a big, powerful unit like a spotlight, and swept it across the front of the house. I practically flew back through the dining room, barking my shin on one of the chairs, through the kitchen, and into the mud room. The heavy footsteps of the Sheriff as he crossed the gravel walkway and climbed the porch steps pursued me.

I tried to open the door to the backyard but it was stuck. I tugged on it. The goddamned door wouldn't budge.

The Sheriff stopped on the porch, and I stopped trying to open the back door. I think I also stopped breathing. Perhaps my heart stopped beating. I crouched down and waited.

He stayed on the front porch. I couldn't imagine what he was doing.

I looked down and saw the glint of a slide lock on the bottom of the back door. I reached down. It was stiff but yielded slowly as I wiggled it. When it was free I eased the door open, stepped out onto the back stoop, and closed the door softly behind me.

I ran off into the woods behind the house as quickly as my legs would carry me.

Seven

Not willing to risk turning on my flashlight, I stumbled blindly through the woods, my face whipped by small branches, making only slightly less noise than an entire herd of deer. I was trying to circle around, come back at Patricia's house from the side to see what the Sheriff was doing and if he had left, but my sense of direction was a little fuzzy from my initial panicked flight into the woods and my shin was a throbbing distraction. After half an hour of crashing through the brush, sure at any moment I would catch sight of the house or the driveway only to find more woods, I became concerned I was actually lost.

An hour later I realized that, favoring my injured leg, I was very likely walking in circles, and made a concerted effort to track a straight line. I broke out of the trees soon thereafter a little ways down the street.

I quickly hurried back to Patricia's house and cautiously peered down the driveway. The Sheriff's car was still there, but there was no sign of him. I waited, hoping to see the light of his flashlight, either in the house or in the surrounding woods.

Nothing.

I became concerned that maybe he was somehow tracking my path through the woods silently in the dark, and he would come up behind me at any moment. I lost my nerve and I ran back to my truck, got inside, and was just about to start it up when I thought that if he were anywhere nearby he would surely hear my truck start, and see my license plate as I drove away. I pulled my hand away from the key as though it was hot.

Was I better off being caught here, or caught fleeing, or caught later at home? Maybe if he caught me here I could pretend to be drunk. He'd take me down to the station; I'd blow the breathalyzer and score a zero. Then where would I be? I thought about getting out and removing my license plates, but I had no tools to do so, and even if I could the light package on the roof would still mark it as a firefighter's truck. He could find his way to me through a simple process of elimination; all of the other firefighters were at home in bed. Would Valerie lie for me and say I was at home too? What would be my reason for asking her? 'No big deal, honey. I was just poking around in the house of the woman who died in the fire, trying to find some clues and solve her murder, and the Sheriff saw my truck. Just tell him I was in bed with you, OK?'

Strung out from lack of sleep, desperate, my head filled with crazy half thoughts.

I could leave the truck and walk home. I could say it broke down here and just walk home, but then could come up with no excuse for why it would have broken down here. And it would of course still run just fine. Unless I did something to the engine so that it actually was broken down. That led to the thought that maybe I could set fire to my truck, though plenty would remain after the fire to identify the truck was mine, and I didn't want to burn my truck. But it could work. I could say someone had stolen it and set fire to it here. Fishy, but it had a pleasant air of plausible deniability to it. I then thought about setting fire to the rental house instead. I could wait for the fire call, and then say I had responded to it, though I always responded to the fire station for calls and had no idea what reason I might give for coming directly to the scene in my own truck.

In the end I sat paralyzed, drenched in sweat, sifting through and rejecting dozens of ideas, my dilated eyes darting about wildly at any shadow that moved. And so the night passed, and as the first glimmers of dawn lightened the sky I decided waiting forever was not an option either.

I turned the key slowly as if that would somehow make the truck start more quietly. The starter caught and the engine cranked and roared to life like any full-throated Detroit V-8. I jammed the truck into drive and floored it, the rear wheels spinning plumes of gravel that stretched three yards behind me. Just as quickly I banged on the brakes and slid to a stop, not wanting to appear suspicious by fishtailing out onto the road at forty miles an hour.

I tried again, pressing my shaking foot gently onto the accelerator like the greenest of teenage drivers. The truck crept forward. I wondered what I would do if suddenly the Sheriff's car poked its nose down the driveway as I was trying to leave. I had the fleeting insane thought if that happened I would ram it.

I made it to the road and there wasn't another car in sight. On impulse, I risked taking a right, slowing slightly as I passed by Patricia's driveway. The Sheriff's car was gone. It had left at some point during the night; I had no idea when.

I drove home almost pathologically, making certain I came to a complete and absolute stop at every stop sign, holding precisely at the speed limit, and centering the truck as perfectly as possible within its lane at all times.

Dawn was fully broken by the time I put the truck away. I pulled off the rubber gloves I had been wearing and stuffed them way down inside the garbage can in the garage, carefully piling other trash on top so that it looked undisturbed, and then went inside. I found Valerie sitting at the kitchen counter in the blue silk robe drinking tea from a Lake Winnipesaukee mug. Tonk jumped to his feet and mashed his face against my shin in his weird way of displaying doggie affection, right on the same spot where I had hit the chair. I gritted my teeth and tried not to wince.

"Where have you been?" she asked with concern.

"I went out. Just drove around. I couldn't sleep." I pushed Tonk away, trying to keep him from battering my injured leg.

"All night?"

I looked out the window at the new dawn. "I guess so," I answered quietly.

"Oh, honey," she stood up and came to hug me. "Ugh, you're soaking wet, and your clothes are a mess."

My clothes were damp with sweat and there was dirt on my shoes, and leaves and grass clung to the legs of my jeans. "Yeah I, uh. I need a shower."

I darted past her before she could ask another question, ran upstairs, stripped in the bathroom, and jumped into the shower. I cranked up the water hot and basked in the luxury, feeling the sweat if not the stress wash away and spiral down the drain. Our shower is a big open concept thing realtors sometimes call a human car wash with lots of nozzles and a partial glass block wall instead of a curtain.

Valerie came into the bathroom. She leaned against the glass block and I turned away from her to face the water spray, pretending I was completely focused on showering.

"Jack, look at me. Where were you last night?"

I turned around again, the water sluicing my back and sides.

"Oh my god, what happened to your leg?"

My first glimpse of my injury in good light impressed me. The bruise on my shin was world class, as big as my palm and dark blue trending towards black.

In the seven years we have been married I have never lied to my wife and rarely even evaded, and I'm not good at it. "I can't tell you," I replied.

"You what?" she asked, as if she hadn't heard me correctly.

"I can't tell you. Don't ask me to."

"But why?"

I stepped out of the water to the edge of the shower and clasped her hands with my dripping ones. "Do you trust me?"

She flinched a little. "What?"

"Do you trust me?" I asked again more firmly.

"Of course I do, but what-"

"I will tell you, but I need some time. Just let me work it out and I'll tell you everything."

Her eyes bored into mine, then clouded over and looked away. "OK," was her only reply.

Eight

Valerie and I conspicuously avoided one another for the rest of the morning. While I toweled off and got dressed she was downstairs reading the newspaper. While I was having breakfast she was out in the garden doing what was likely the last weeding of the season before bedding it down for winter. When I settled Tonk with a rawhide bone, she was in the shower.

That was especially painful, as often when one of us is in the shower the other would get in as well. You know, to save water. But when I had been in the shower earlier she had walked away, and here she was showering and I was leaving. Not good.

I had considered several times during the morning approaching her, trying to explain to her what I was doing, but I had to admit I was a little uncertain of that myself, and became even less so as I drove my truck to the investment firm where Michael Carston worked. Was I there on a fishing expedition? Confronting Patricia's killer? I didn't know.

I reasoned that there was no harm in talking to Carston, provided he agreed to see me at all. Doing so was not nearly as reckless as, say, breaking a police cordon to bumble about the scene of an active murder investigation, and I had already done that.

I parked in the small lot in front, got out of the truck, and headed towards the building, which looked to be a home that had been converted into office space when the surrounding area had gradually transitioned from residential to commercial. It had originally been a modest farmhouse, I guessed, with black shutters and white trim, a jumble of rooms to the left had likely been bedrooms, and a larger boxy room on the right that had been the family room. A small farmer's porch was in the middle and the door off of it opened into a small reception area, the receptionist's desk right about where I figured the dining room table would have been.

"Can I help you?" the woman behind the desk asked me pleasantly.

"I'd like to see Michael Carston," I said. I delivered this with a mild New Hampshire lilt. Between growing up in the North Country and living in Manhattan I had learned to chameleon myself, adopting either the clipped, all-business tones of a harried New Yorker or the soothing, easygoing 'ayuh' of a New Hampshire farmer with nothing but time on his hands, as the occasion warranted.

She didn't ask me who I was or what business I had with him. Part of that was probably because I had dressed in business casual, trying to project the image of a fellow investment guy or maybe a mid-level businessman looking for some financial advice, and also because of my New Hampshire accent and demeanor. It also was likely due in a large part to the fact that this was a small freestanding business off the main drag in Bedford, New Hampshire and had very little problem with aggressive solicitors.

A low tech office, she got up from her desk and went to one of the doors off of the reception area. She knocked, and then opened the door and leaned into the room. "Someone here to see you, Mike."

"Send him in," was the reply from the man in the office.

She leaned back from the door and gestured me inside, closing the door behind me after I had entered. This was going easier than I had anticipated.

Michael Carston got up and came around his desk which looked like a stock executive model from some soulless office supply catalog. He was a little shorter than me, with dark brown hair and eyes. He wore a dark suit, kind of old-fashioned, with the vest and a watch chain with a Phi Beta Kappa key dangling from it draped across his flat stomach.

"Michael Carston," he gave my hand a firm pump.

"Jack Fallon," I returned the shake.

This building had definitely been an old farmhouse. The walls of his office were uneven horse-hair plaster and the floor was wide pine planks aged to a warm, beautiful honey color, many with the original mill strakes visible on their face. There was a stone mantelpiece over a sealed fireplace on the left. The old hominess clashed with the six high-definition wide-screen flat panel displays that had been hung in a two-by-three matrix on the wall and showed a dizzying array of stock data updated continually.

"Jack," he pointed me into one of the two visitor chairs on this side of his desk and then perched himself on the edge, "What can I do for you?"

"Well," I began, a little uncertainly, "I'm with the Dunboro Fire Department, and I'd like to ask you some questions about Patricia Woods, a young woman who died in a house fire recently."

He frowned, "I saw it on the news." He paused there. It was almost as though I could see the wheels turn in his head. Finally, he added, "What does it have to do with me?"

"She made a call to a phone number registered in your name the night of the fire."

His eyes narrowed, "You're with the fire department. This sounds more like something for the police."

Had the police not already been here? How was that even possible, given that Dawkins had had Patricia's cell phone records before I did? One more piece in the mounting pile of evidence that maybe the firefighters were right about our town Sheriff; he was out of his depth.

"We're calling the fire arson," I replied, hoping to form some connection in his mind between my role in the fire department with an official arson investigation, though in reality no such connection existed. He seemed to swallow it.

"Oh, OK," he nodded, "I knew her. She was my dental hygienist."

"On the night of the fire she called you and then ordered a pizza and a Greek salad. Antonio's Pizza in Milford. The two of you ate it at her place."

He worked his jaw but said nothing.

His response made me feel as if I was watching one of Valerie's soap operas. Suddenly, I realized that in digging for clues to Patricia's murder, I had just inadvertently uncovered an affair. This bitter realization made me feel dirty, unjustified in my prying into other people's lives. I furthermore understood, as Michael watched me warily, he knew that I knew.

A spectrum of emotions flitted across his face: guilt, sorrow, and after another moment, anger. His gaze hardened. "I want you to leave."

This was not the way I had thought this would go at all. I tried out a number of different responses in my mind trying to salvage the situation, convey to him that I didn't care about his marital problems. When run forward in time, I found they all ended with him calling the police and me in a shit heap of trouble. I was done there, and I knew it.

"Thanks for your time. You've been a big help." I said dryly, and headed for the door.

"Wait," he said, and I stopped, my hand on the knob.

"You're not going to talk to my wife about this, are you?" he said.

I looked back at him. His eyes managed to meet mine for only a moment before they ashamedly slid away.

A young woman was dead, a woman he had supposedly loved, or at least fucked, and that his foremost desire was to cover his own ass disgusted me. I opened the door and left without responding to him, not bothering to close it behind me.

Nine

I spent the rest the day throwing myself into the framing job, hoping it would leave me completely exhausted, praying it would let me get to sleep that night. I worked so hard and so fast that Paul Shaley, the building contractor, told me to slow down before I had a heart attack. It was likely the first time any man on one of Paul Shaley's crews had heard him tell someone to slow down.

That night, the third night after the fire, was worse than the first two, by which I mean to say it was the same: sleepless. I spent much of it sitting in the dark kitchen listening to Tonk snore where he lay on his bed in the corner and thinking about Michael Carston. Would he have had anything to tell me if I had approached him differently? Was that bridge truly and finally burned, or could I go back and try him again? Should I approach his wife, as he had feared I would, and what trouble might I pull down on my head by doing so?

As a homespun sleep aid I considered trying a glass of

warm milk, then opened the fridge and found we were out of
milk, and somehow a glass of warm blueberry pomegranate juice
just didn't sound as appealing. When did Valerie start buying
that? Every so often I would go upstairs and lie in bed for
awhile staring at the ceiling and listening to Valerie's slow, even
breaths beside me, give up, and go back downstairs. In the
living room I turned on the TV and found a re-airing of that
day's Red Sox game highlights. Did I mention I'm not a
baseball fan?

After a couple of hours of that Tonk and I went out to my
workshop. He flumped down on a makeshift bed of sawdust and
started snoring again almost immediately. Particles of sawdust
made little dervishes in the vortices of air from his nostrils.

Sitting on my workbench was a block of burled walnut,
about two inches thick, ten inches wide, and two feet long. It
was the remainder of a custom wood order from a shop up north,
a gift from a friend who worked there who knew of my desire to
try my hand on many different wood types. This block was
going to be the basis of my next woodworking project; I just
didn't know what I was going to make out of it yet.

For weeks I had sat and communed with the wood, waiting
for a sort of a Michelangelo moment. What was trapped inside
this piece of wood waiting for me to free it? This piece
presented an interesting challenge given its peculiar dimensions.
There was not enough wood to make a table top, but far too
much to make something small like a clock face or a picture
frame. I suppose I could make a dozen picture frames, but it
seemed like a shame to cut such a fine large block of wood into
so many little pieces.

The idea came to me to rip the block into ornamental panels
for use in a china hutch. I took some measurements and laid out
plans, marking the cut lines on the wood. I was all set to go but
the problem I faced was that, as wired as I was from lack of
sleep, I was starting to doubt my ability to safely operate power
tools. There was no way I was up to any framing work that day.

Heck, another night or two of this and I wouldn't even trust myself to drive.

I got up from the stool and left the workshop. Tonk scrambled to his feet from the pile of sawdust and trotted behind. If my midnight wanderings were upsetting his sixteen hour-a-day sleep schedule, he was bravely not letting it show. He stopped long enough to shake himself, a motion that started with his head twisting back and forth, jowls flapping, which rippled down his whole body ending at his tail. With the particles of sawdust flinging from his coat in a shower, he momentarily looked like a snow globe without the globe.

As I brushed the residue from his flanks, Tonk misunderstood my rubbing and rolled onto his back with his feet in the air, hoping to get his belly rubbed as well. He wormed around, and then looked at me, his lips sagging back to reveal his one-inch long canine teeth. Unable to resist my upside-down vampire dog I knelt at his side and scratched his stomach, which caused him to worm some more and thump his tail on the grass.

As long as I wasn't sleeping, I couldn't think of any better way to spend the sleepless time.

When the newspaper hit the end of the driveway, Tonk abandoned the belly rub and rocketed down to check it out, hoping perhaps the passing car had flung a pizza out the window. He sniffed at it, found it was not a pizza, snorted in disappointment, and trotted off to pee in the woods. Life goes on.

I took the newspaper inside and unfolded it on the kitchen counter. A few small column inches were apparently all Patricia warranted, and I found her on the second page of the Local section. There had been no arrest or announcement of possible suspects in the murder, but Sheriff Robert Dawkins was quoted as saying that the police were working on 'many promising leads.' I wondered wryly what those might be, if not talking to the guy she had called on the phone and eaten dinner with just hours before her death. The article furthermore noted her funeral would be on Saturday in her hometown of Rutland, Vermont.

I flipped to the obituaries, feeling a little ghoulish as I did so. I'm not usually much of an obituaries guy, though I remember my maternal grandmother reading them religiously in her later life, tsk tsking whenever someone she knew had died. I also remember driving with my grandparents in western Maine one summer when she made my grandfather pull the car over so she could walk around some cemetery we were passing. She didn't know anyone buried there; she sometimes just liked to walk amongst tombstones. My grandmother was one creepy lady.

The first thing I noticed when I found the obituaries page was a photograph in the lower right hand corner of the page of a little girl in pigtails, the caption underneath read 'Our baby Alice. It's hard to believe it's been 5 years. You'll always be with us in our hearts. Mom, Dad, Jenna, and Muggins." There was enough depression in that two by three inch rectangle to last me the whole day.

I scanned around the page past pictures of people, old and young, men standing proudly in military uniforms, teenagers at the peak of immortality smiling out from yearbook pictures, one man bordering on ancient, clearly in a hospital bed with a tube up his nose and the collar of a jonnie visible in the picture. I found Patricia in the fourth column of the lost, two obits down from the top.

She only had a couple of column inches here also, listing her graduation from the Vermont Technical College in Rudolph, Vermont with a dental hygienist degree, her love of Ansel Adams photography, and that she was survived by her mother, father, and a younger sister named Rachael. The funeral was scheduled to take place at the Evergreen Cemetery in Rutland at 3PM on Saturday. The accompanying picture looked like maybe it was from her graduation, but shrunken down to near microfiche proportions it was a little difficult to tell.

I heard Valerie behind me just a moment before she wrapped her arms around my waist and kissed me on the back of the head, a small but significant peace offering.

"Not now, Britney!" I whispered, "My wife is sleeping upstairs!"

She let go of me and slapped me on the shoulder blade, "Ew, Britney Spears? Seriously?"

"No, but I just saw the VH1 *Behind the Music* show on her life, and it was the best I could come up with on short notice. I also watched a rerun of yesterday's Red Sox game. They clinched a wildcard slot, by the way."

"Since when did you become a baseball fan?" She crossed the kitchen to the pantry door and opened it.

"At three o'clock in the morning, I'm a fan of anything not an infomercial or a test pattern."

"Ah, the TV of the damned and the insomniacs. You want coffee?"

"Caffeine, that's what I need."

She turned around holding the can of coffee grounds cradled against her stomach, "I'm sorry, Hon, is there anything else I can get for you?"

"I don't know, let me make a phone call and we'll think about breakfast."

I pulled my cell phone from my pocket and went into the living room, speed dialing Paul Shaley as I stared out the front window at Tonk sitting on the front porch looking out into the woods, ever vigilant. When Paul answered I told him I wouldn't be able to make it to the house framing today.

He told me that was okay, they were just doing roof trusses. "But I want you to promise me you'll be in to do the staircase next week. I'm sure we both remember what happened when I let the Duggan kid do a staircase without you."

I remembered. No two steps the same height, like a staircase as drawn by Escher. Joe Duggan was good with a tool, but not with a calculator. We both laughed at the memory.

"I'll be there."

"Hey, you see the Sox yesterday?" he asked.

I told him that I had, which was probably a mistake on my part because he launched into dissertation of Wakefield's knuckleball against left-handed batters, and it took several minutes before I could manage to excuse myself and hang up the phone.

When I got back into the kitchen the coffee maker was trickling along and Valerie was mixing batter in a bowl, "I decided to make waffles. That OK with you?"

"That sounds super."

I went and got the syrup out of the pantry. It was good stuff, locally made. Every spring Valerie and I would make a pilgrimage up into the hills over Marlborough in the truck, wheels churning in the mud of unpaved backcountry roads. You could almost hear the strains of *Deliverance* banjos twanging in your ears. There was this shack in the woods, a big mushroom cloud of steam venting through hatches in the roof that had been winched open. Inside an old man stoked an even older cast iron boiler, blackened by age and use, while an equally elderly dog curled into a ball looked on from the seat of a sprung and faded couch. That old man boiled up New Hampshire gold second to none.

Valerie poured batter onto the lower plate of the waffle iron and closed it. It sizzled, and narrow filaments of steam shot out the sides. She turned her back on it and leaned against the counter.

"Are you sleeping at all?"

"I don't know, not much."

"But you don't feel tired?" She took a blue ceramic mug down from the cupboard and poured herself a cup of coffee from the decanter underneath the drip filter. I smelled the hazelnut from clear across the room.

"I feel tense. I feel like every time I lie down in bed I can't get my brain to shut off. I feel like I should be doing something to help her."

"The girl from the fire?"

"Yes. Patricia."

"What can you do for her?"

I shrugged. "I don't know."

"What would you like to do for her?"

"Bring her back to life? A little laying of the hands maybe," I waved them in front of me, "and presto!"

Valerie gave me a weak smile, "Seriously, Jack."

I frowned, looking at the syrup container on the countertop as I twirled it, "It's going to sound stupid."

"Try me."

"I want to find her killer."

She didn't answer immediately. I could sense she was formulating her response with great care. "No," she placed a hand gently under my chin and lifted, bringing my eyes up to meet hers. "I don't think it sounds stupid. It sounds extremely reckless and dangerous." I opened my mouth to object but she continued talking so I closed it. "What makes you think you could even solve a murder? You're not a cop; you're just a volunteer firefighter."

Ouch. That 'just' hurt.

"Honey, you're a very smart and caring guy and I appreciate you want to help, but can't you see dwelling on this is hurting you? You haven't slept in, what, two nights now?"

I heard myself say, "Three, if you count the night of the fire," though I wasn't helping my own case any.

"Three nights, Jack." She paused, and then a little light bulb went on over her head. "Was that what you were doing last night? How did you hurt your leg? Where were you?"

I shook my head stubbornly; I wasn't willing to go into it.

"You're not thinking rationally, Jack. You need to get some help."

I have always had a sort of aversion to all things psychiatric. I believed head shrinking belonged back in Victorian England when people were commonly felled by attacks of the vapors, or in modern Hollywood where stars overcome by exhaustion plowed their SUVs into parking meters at four o'clock in the morning. Level headed people like me, people who looked at things logically, could wend their way past emotionally crippling pit traps. But I was beat, I wasn't sleeping, and if spending some time lying on a couch talking about how much I loved my mother in a completely normal and healthy way with some guy wearing a tweed jacket and smoking a pipe would get my head and my pillow back to the collective bargaining table I was willing to give it a try.

"For you, I'll go talk to John."

"That's all I can ask. Now sit down, your waffle is ready."

Ten

The Dunboro fire department has no full time firefighters on staff. Even the role of Chief is filled by a volunteer. I was lucky enough to find John in his office at the fire station that morning catching up on paperwork before leaving for his real job.

John Pederson had been a volunteer firefighter in Dunboro for almost forty years. His real job over much of that time had been as a diesel mechanic for one of the big trucking companies over the border in Massachusetts. He had left both the department and his job at one point to voluntarily enlist and was deployed with a marine unit in Iraq as part of operation Desert Storm. There he had seen, as he puts it, 'a bunch of nasty shit.' He earned a purple heart and a twisted scar that ran from his wrist all the way up to his elbow from a piece of mortar shrapnel that had killed two marines next to him before coming to rest in his forearm. As a result, John Pederson considered himself to be just about the luckiest son of a bitch alive.

He had returned to Dunboro, the diesel work, and the fire department, and was later promoted to Chief of the department, a position he has held for more than fifteen years.

What little dark hair firefighting had left him with had been taken away by combat, his hair now pure white without as much as a single filament of grey. His body remained lean and hard, his skin toughened by sixty New England winters. He ached a little now and then, and the scar on cold wet days could throb and cramp up his whole arm. Firefighting, he was coming to realize, was a game for the young, and he thought with some regret it wouldn't be too many years before he would have to retire from the department which had been so much a part of his life for almost four decades.

He looked up from the stack of papers on his desk when I came in. "Jesus, Jack, you look like shit. Have a seat." He moved an air tank with a broken regulator from the second seat in his office and waved me into it.

"Thanks for the compliment. I'd hate to feel this awful and have it be my little secret."

"Still not sleeping?"

"Not much."

"You're a good firefighter, Jack, but you've got to develop a thicker skin. People are going to die. It's unavoidable. You do your best, you pick up, and you move on."

"That's easier said than done."

"I agree with you there. Say, have you tried. . ."

I held up my hands, "Please, no more homespun sleep aids. I've tried counting sheep. I've tried warm milk, or at least I've tried to try warm milk." I paused and shook my head. "Never mind."

"No, seriously," he continued, "this one is sure to work." He reached onto a shelf behind him and pulled out a book about twice the thickness of a phonebook. He dropped it down on top of the papers in front of him where it landed with a thud.

"What in the world?" I asked.

He spread his hands wide around the book like a spokes model, "The General Accounting Office Omnibus Spending Bill, Part One."

I could read the cover upside down but spun it around for a better look. It was exactly what he said it was, the Federal Government Spending Bill for 2002, or at least the first half of it. "And I'm supposed to beat myself unconscious with this?"

"No, you read it. Put you to sleep in an hour, guaranteed. I myself prefer the section on maintenance and upkeep of federal buildings. Check the marker."

I opened the book to the page where a small piece of yellow sticky note had been adhered and read the title. *Federal Buildings, Maintenance and Upkeep of, Subsection One: Federal Courthouses.* I didn't know what to say.

"Word of warning, though. Stay away from the sections on Social Security solvency and Medicare spending. Those will give you nightmares."

I looked up to see if he was kidding, but he looked completely serious. "I appreciate the offer, but I'm not quite sure this is what I had in mind."

"Fair enough. What can I do for you then?"

"I think I need to talk with someone."

He leaned back in his chair and folded his arms across his chest, "I'm someone. So talk."

"No, I – that's not what I meant."

He smiled, "I know. I'm just busting your balls." He sat forward again and dug into the center drawer of his desk. He pulled out a business card and held it out to me. "Here."

I took the card. It read, 'Beverly Dell, Counselor' with an address in Dunboro, just a little ways down Main Street from here.

"She any good?"

"She helped me out when I came back from Iraq. Then, and a couple of other times. Sometimes it helps just to talk with someone who is a good listener. Beverly is a very good listener."

I got up from my chair. "Thanks, John. I'll give her a call."

"It's already been done. She'll see you today at three."

"Huh?"

"Valerie called me yesterday and asked if there was someone you could see, so I set it all up last night. Oh, and the department will pick up the cost, at least for a half dozen sessions. We'll start with that and see how it goes. Good luck."

I laughed. Once again, Valerie was one step ahead of me.

On my way out of the station I stopped to swipe the digital camera from the glove compartment of Engine 2. I took it out to my truck where I connected it to my laptop, looking around furtively while I copied the contents of the memory card onto a blank CD. When it was done I returned the camera to the glove compartment and drove to a photo shop in Milford that could make prints of the pictures for me. What I was planning to do when I had them I tried not to ponder too deeply.

Eleven

Despite their slogan of *Photos in 60 minutes or less*, the photo shop was backed up and the prints would not be ready until that evening. My appointment with Beverly was still a couple of hours off. I considered going back to my shop to commune with the block of wood, but all I could think about was Michael Carston and the answers I had failed to get from him. Maybe I would have more success with Samantha, his wife.

Ordinarily I had the utmost confidence in my innate ability to travel an endless path of back roads and logging trails without losing my general sense of direction, but as I searched for the address of the Carston household I became disoriented by Amherst's many switchbacks and cul-de-sacs and began to have my doubts. Finally, when I found myself at the corner of Wheeler Lane and Wheeler Street, checking my notes for the fifth time to be certain I was in fact looking for Wheeler Court, I admitted I was lost. It brought to mind a time when I was in Atlanta, where it seemed every other street had the word "peach" incorporated into the name. I wondered briefly just who the heck the Wheelers were, and what they had done that merited so many roads named in their honor.

I checked the glove compartment for a map and found one for Southern California and another for, inexplicably, Utah. I'd never even been to Utah. I retreated to a gas station and purchased a thick map book for all of southern New Hampshire and northern Massachusetts.

With map in hand I returned to Wheeler Lane, where Wheeler Court split off as a narrow asphalt road passing between two enormous cypress pines, the street sign lost in the lower branches of the tree on the right hand side. I remembered distinctly passing it by on my first three trips around the loop, believing it to be a private driveway.

I turned down the narrow roadway, admiring the large, well-kept houses set far back from the road, many with elaborately landscaped yards. The house I was looking for was a biggish Tudor-style home reminiscent of English estates. Lilac bushes, just a profusion of spindly skeletal sticks in the fall, lined the front, while enormous oak trees ablaze in orange and gold sheltered it protectively from the left and right. Two children's bicycles, both pink with multicolored streamers hanging from the rubber caps on the ends of the handlebars, leaned against the central support pillar of the attached two-car garage.

I idled at the curb for some time, wondering what I should say to her. Had Michael already told her about the affair, or would I be the first? That was a position I didn't particularly want to be in. By what right was I here anyway? Who was I to be trampling around in these people's lives? Abruptly those thoughts were eliminated, replaced with the image of Patricia's hands. Finding her killer was all that mattered. I pulled the truck into the driveway, parked near the garage, and got out.

The front door was answered more than a minute after I had rang the bell, just moments before I considered pressing it again, by a thin woman, several inches taller than average, dressed in white slacks and brown V-neck sweater. She had large brown eyes, long dark brown hair with a just a slight wave to it, a narrow nose, thin cheeks, and a pair of lips that looked far too full for the rest of her face. The storm door remained closed between us.

"Mrs. Carston? Are you Samantha Carston?"

"Yes," she replied. With just that one word she revealed she had an English accent, a strong one.

"I'm Jack Fallon from the Dunboro Police Department. I'd like to ask you some questions about Patricia Woods."

Had I just said 'Police Department' or 'Fire Department?' I played it back through my head and wasn't sure one way or the other, but my mouth, with a certain pattering echo of a vibration in my lips, kind of felt like it had just said 'police.' First trespassing at a crime scene, and now maybe impersonating an officer. Both felonies, I believed. Way to go, Jack. As I was already standing there, the crime already committed, I couldn't see a reason to turn back now.

Mrs. Carston was looking at me blankly, as if she hadn't recognized the name.

"Patricia Woods?" I tried again.

Still nothing.

"Mrs. Carston?" I looked closely at her eyes. They were definitely focused on me. She had the appearance of someone you might see on the news after a disaster like a tornado or a devastating house fire, someone in shock, someone confronting the realization that their entire life has been destroyed.

"I guess we might as well do this," she sighed. She reached out and unlocked the storm door, then turned and walked back into the house without opening it.

I wiped my feet carefully on the doormat and went inside. The interior of the house felt as English as the outside did. The front hall was long and rectangular with dark wood flooring and white plaster walls and a serious crown molding wider than the rain gutters on my house. The ceiling was quite high, at least fifteen feet. A gold chandelier covered in dozens of teardrop shaped crystals hung down by a heavy chain. The living room was through a big rectangular archway to the right, all dark claw-footed furniture with rose colored upholstery. Three enormous still life paintings of dark bowls of fruit and bottles of wine hung on the left-hand wall over a large fireplace with an ornately carved walnut mantelpiece. A grandfather clock somewhere out of sight counted off seconds profoundly. A sweeping staircase went up to my left, and a second, smaller archway was ahead of me. I didn't know where Mrs. Carston had gone.

I was about to call for her when I heard the clink and rattle of ice cubes hitting a glass from the archway ahead, so I went that way. The passageway took a little jog to the right and opened into the kitchen. A mottled blue soapstone countertop with an elaborate hand-painted tile backsplash in a motif of glasses, grapes, and wine bottles lay underneath ranks of walnut cabinetry. Gleaming copper pots and pans hung from a black iron rack over a brushed stainless steel six-burner cook top.

Mrs. Carston returned to the counter after putting something back into a Viking refrigerator the size of a minivan. There was a tall glass in front of her filled with dark liquid and ice, likely iced coffee unless she was one hell of a drinker.

"Can I get you something?"

"No, thank you, I'm fine."

She lifted the glass, took a drink, and put it back down. I was about to ask a question when she said, "Do you like this house?"

"It's a very lovely ho-"

"I hate it. Ponderous fucking furniture, gloomy damned paintings. It was all his doing. He fancied himself some kind of English lord. He decorated his entire life to fit that image, right down to me," she pressed an index finger against her own chest and shifted into a cockney gutter accent, "went and got himself a proiper English woif, 'e did."

I had an urge to pick up her glass and give it a sniff. She sure sounded like Mary Poppins on a bender. "Mrs. Carston-"

"Please, call me Mrs. Tewkes. I may still be married to that bastard, but I'm certainly not going to go by Carston any longer than necessary, and believe me that shit stops here and now."

"OK, Mrs. Tewkes-"

She threw her head back and groaned, "Ugh! I hate that name too. Makes me sound like an English spinster. How old do I look, seriously?"

I wasn't going to go near that one with a thirty foot pole. "Please, Mrs. Tewkes-"

"Samantha. Would you please call me Samantha?"

"OK, Samantha-"

"I ask you, does this look like a home a Samantha would live in? Well I guess I'm going to own it after the divorce. Maybe I'll sell it. Or I could just burn it down."

"Please, Mrs. Tewkes," she gave me a severe look and I put my hands up like I was being held at gunpoint, "Samantha," I quickly corrected, "I need to ask you some questions about your husband and his relationship with Patricia Woods."

"You should ask him about that. I'm afraid I don't know anything at all."

"I've already spoken to him. Now I'd like to talk to you."

She continued on as if she hadn't heard me, "Comes home late for dinner last night. He does that a lot. He's a stock something, or maybe he's a bond something. Analyst? Trader? Maybe he does both stocks and bonds."

She paused to take a drink and I didn't interrupt. I was just trying to mentally catch my breath.

She continued, "The roast had gone cold. It's hard keeping a roast warm after it's been cut, but I had to feed the girls, don't you see? So I have this roast, and the choice is either let it turn cold or keep it in the oven and dry the living daylights out of it. So he comes home late, always tells me that it's his job and all, only that was a lie, wasn't it? It was never his job. It was always her. I've been seeing someone else, he says. It's not me, it's him, he says. Utter rubbish! Of course it's him! What did I ever do except keep the home and raise the girls? He's been seeing her a long time, hasn't he?"

"You don't know?"

"No, of course I didn't know. How would I know?"

"I thought in hindsight you might have noticed something."

"No, I haven't. I suppose that makes me seem a bit dense. I never had a clue." She shook her head, her eyes downcast, and uttered a single frustrated "Fuck," which, in her English accent, sounded strangely cultured. "Was there anyone else before her?"

"I don't know. Where is your husband now?"

"I threw him out of here last night and haven't seen or heard from him since, but I suppose he's at work. Then again I've often supposed he's been at work when he hasn't been. Have you tried her place?"

That stopped me cold. She didn't know Patricia was dead? Her comment was so casual and spontaneous; I couldn't imagine she was lying.

Samantha must have read something in my pause. "Is there something the matter?"

I didn't want to tell her about the murder just yet so I ignored her question and responded with one of my own. "Did you ever meet her?"

"Of course not, where would I have met her?"

"She was your husband's dental hygienist."

"Oh, then I suppose it is possible that I met her. We use the same dental practice, my husband and I. Still, it's a big one over in Nashua, three dentists and a lot of staff. It's also possible that I never saw her there."

"He didn't tell you about Patricia Woods?"

"No, what would he tell me?"

I heard the front door open and close. Two young girls, who according to my internet research were Mary, 10 and Alice, 8, came running into the kitchen. "Mommeee. Can we have a snack before dinner?" The two were dressed identically in pleated plaid skirts, starched white shirts, and polished black patent shoes with gleaming silver buckles. They both had their mother's hair and eyes, and as I looked at them, her general facial shape as well. It was as through Michael's genetics had contributed nothing to them.

"This is Mary and Alice. Girls, this is Mr. Fallon from the Dunboro Police Department."

Swell, so not only had I told her I was with the police, but she had remembered both that and my name.

"Hello Mr. Fallon," said Alice.

"Dunboro. That's where Shelly lives," Mary said.

"Yes, that's right. Now if you'll go change out of your school clothes I'll heat up some pizza pockets."

The two of them flew out of the room, the hard soles of their shoes clattering up the staircase in the main hall.

Samantha went to the Viking and opened the freezer drawer at the bottom. She took out a box, crossed the kitchen, and retrieved a cookie sheet from one of the low cabinets. She came back to the counter and put the sheet down, then began tearing open one end of the box.

"You have beautiful daughters."

"I do, don't I? Michael wanted boys. Though I suppose he's been a good enough father to them." She got the box open and dumped a dozen little dough puffs onto the sheet, which, if the box front was accurate, contained cheese, tomato sauce, and pepperoni. "I'm sorry for the interruption. Now, where were we?"

"I was asking you if your husband had told you anything about Patricia Woods."

She put the cookie sheet into the oven and spun the dial to the correct temperature setting. "And I asked you, what would he have told me about her?" She folded the box closed and put it back into the freezer.

I didn't know any way to tell her except the direct route. "Patricia Woods is dead. She died in a house fire on Tuesday night."

"Oh my!" She turned towards the oven, put her hand on the control dial and saw she had already set the temperature, and turned back. "Oh dear! It never occurred to me to wonder why you were here, but of course adultery isn't a crime, is it? At least not one the police investigate. Of course! I saw it on the news. The woman in Dunboro. Did, um, do you think Michael had something to do with it? Her death I mean."

"Do you?"

"Oh, Michael is a right bloody bastard, but why would he hurt her? He had the milk and the cow at home, or whatever the saying is." She took a sponge from a small basket by the sink and used it to wipe up some crumbs that had fallen out of the box. She rinsed the sponge and put it back, then dried her hands on a blue dishtowel pulled through one of the cabinet handles. She rested one hip against the counter. "Still, I'm probably the wrong person to ask. I thought he was a devoted husband and father, too, so it seems I knew almost nothing about him at all."

Twelve

Beverly Dell worked and presumably lived in a compact ranch house, white with black shutters, about half a mile down Main Street from the fire station. There was a long farmer's porch that stretched across the front and ran around the west side. The entire house had a sort of slumped look about it, a complete lack of any right angles or straight edges common among houses in excess of a hundred years old. A white picket fence, almost a toy fence standing only about eighteen inches high, surrounded a neatly kept postage stamp lawn with beds of mums planted for fall. A gravel driveway with sprigs of grass growing in between the wheel ruts ran up alongside. A burgundy Hyundai Sonata was parked there with a blue BMW Z4 convertible with Massachusetts plates behind it.

I parked my truck out on the street at five minutes of three.

Up on the front porch I found the doorbell covered with a green plastic sign with white lettering hanging from a thin chain that read 'enter,' and so I did.

The front hall was almost square, like a sitting room. Hallways led off to the left and ahead of me, while double solid-wood pocket doors were closed to my right. The hum of conversation could be heard through the doors.

I took a seat in a wingback chair covered in robin's egg blue coarse wool. Beside the chair was a vintage round teak coffee table with tiny spindly legs. Its surface was covered with magazines: *Us, Cosmopolitan, Redbook, Vogue.* All were current, but not my preferred reading material. I instead admired a mahogany table that stood across the front window covered in plants: mother-in-law's tongue, a Christmas cactus, an enormous jade, an avocado throwing tiny nascent leaves out of a pit half-buried in soil in a terra cotta pot. My mother had had a similar profusion of plants in our living room when I was growing up.

I got up and checked out the period moldings: crown, base, and chair rail. There were some interesting picture moldings around the hallway openings. The brick molding around the front door had a crack in it. All in all, most of the woodwork had held up well over the past one hundred years. I looked over the joinery in the teak table, but it was nothing special, just some run of the mill mortis and tenon work.

I sat down again and flipped through the magazines, picking up the *Cosmopolitan* just for the heck of it. Some starlet whose name escaped me at the moment was on the cover. She was wearing a yellow sundress with little white flowers on it, cinched in at her hourglass waist, breasts lifted high and air-brushed so that to the camera her skin seemed to have no texture at all. Her hair was piled up into countless ringlets and her makeup was immaculate, bedroom eyes and pouty lips.

I couldn't help but think Valerie would look about a million times better in it.

Inside an article promised to reveal to me twelve erogenous zones that will drive him wild. I've learned about four new ones I never knew I had and I'm only up to number six when the pocket doors opened.

"Mr. Fallon, I'm sorry to have kept you waiting. I'm Beverly Dell."

"That's quite all right. Thank you for seeing me on such short notice." I put the magazine aside and got to my feet, already feeling myself entering a sort of psychiatric self-assessment mode. What will she think of me reading the magazine? Did I stand up too fast?

She was of medium height, maybe a little on the heavy side. Her dark blonde hair, in a style I believe is called the Jennifer Aniston, framed her face, her cornflower blue eyes, and her button nose. She was wearing western jeans, extensively tooled western boots with low stacked wooden heels, and a maroon cashmere roll-neck sweater. She looked to be about fifteen years old, but was probably closer to thirty.

The doors squeaked and clattered on ancient bearing tracks as she pushed the two doors farther apart with both of her hands on one door and her rump against the other. She gestured for me to enter her office, shaking my hand as I went by. Too firm? Too limp? Her hands were slightly greasy from the recent application of hand crème, something that smelled like roses. I resisted the urge to wipe my hand on my pants. I worried what she would think of me if I did.

The doors closed behind me with a bang, a sound that seemed somehow very final.

She crossed the room and sat in one of two wingback chairs, these covered in maroon leather with brass studs. The color was such a close match to her sweater it was like a form of camouflage, a disembodied head and delicate hands with nails buffed and coated with clear nail polish were all that was visible. If she was planning to take notes, I didn't see how. Perhaps she was recording everything.

A brick front fireplace with slate hearth and white-painted wood mantle was centered in the wall opposite the chairs. There was an oak roll top desk in one corner. A second door across from the pocket doors must be how the previous patient left without passing through the waiting area. Shelving filled one wall, a small section of carefully aligned important-looking leather bound volumes, the rest stuffed with mass market paperbacks, their multicolored spines piled and tucked in at all angles.

"Would you like to take a seat?"

"Oh, of course." I took the other wingback.

"Nervous?"

"Nervous is probably the wrong word. I guess you could say I'm in unfamiliar territory."

"That's perfectly natural." She shifted in her chair, moving back and settling in. "John tells me you're not sleeping."

"No, I guess I'm not."

"How long since you had a good night's sleep?"

"Three days."

"Are you getting any sleep at all?"

"Some perhaps, but not much."

"Any dreams you can recall?"

"No." I leaned forward, my elbows resting on my knees. "I want to be perfectly clear up front, I'm not willing to take any medication. When I need to sleep, I'll sleep."

"Well, I think after three days you need to sleep, and you're not, but I'm not a doctor and I can't prescribe medications. I'm hoping if we just talk that we can come to understand why you're not sleeping and solve your problem without drugs. Insomnia is most often caused by stress. It could even be stress you yourself don't perceive. You haven't slept since the night of the fire, right? The fire in which a woman died?"

Wow, she goes right for the jugular. "Yes."

"Would you like to talk about that?"

I frowned and fidgeted uncomfortably.

The skin over her eyebrows crinkled up just a little bit. "You don't want to talk about it."

"No, I'm sorry."

"That's perfectly alright. Let's not push it. Tell me about something else instead."

"Like what?"

"Tell me a story. Firefighters have great stories."

I thought about going with the story about the guy hit by the logging truck, playing it for some shock value and rubbing her face in it. Then I realized my anger was unjustified, the product of an exhausted mind, and she was trying to help me. "How about my first fire?"

She leaned back in her chair, her eyes alight. She had a way of listening with her whole body, something about her that drew you into the conversation, made you want to talk to her. "That sounds perfect."

Thirteen

Like your first kiss, you never forget your first fire.

Ranks of heavy thunderstorms had been rolling across New Hampshire all day on their way to the Atlantic Ocean, on the weather map looking like waves of angry colors, mostly reds and yellows. I'd been on the fire department a grand total of perhaps two weeks, meeting about half of the firefighters but forgetting most of their names. I hoped there wouldn't be a test later. My first group of firefighting classes was scheduled for later in the month at the Firefighting Academy in Concord. I'd already spent a day at the hospital getting poked and prodded for my physical examination. The good news was, though I lacked any specific training useful in firefighting, I was at least physically fit enough to do so.

Valerie was off visiting an Aunt in Washington State. She had emailed me pictures of hikes she was taking almost daily. In the midst of a stretch of unseasonably warm and humid weather – we had clocked four days in the past seven over 100 – she had the gall to send me pictures of actual snow on the slopes of

Mount Rainier. Cruelty thy name is Valerie.

I was sitting at home, roughing it by eating cold leftover lo mein with Tonk. The electricity had been iffy all evening, the lights dimming and recovering as the storm rumbled outside. Tonk and I were snug in our house, all the beer, lo mein, and dog kibble we could eat while the storm raged impotently outside.

"Do your worst," I laughed as I angled the chopsticks to spear a prawn.

An enormous flash of heat lightening split the expanse of sky visible through the kitchen windows and left purple after images burned into my retinas. This was followed by an apocalyptic clash of thunder that rattled pots and dishes inside the cabinets and plunged the house into total darkness.

It was in that sudden stillness, the chopsticks halfway to my mouth, my ears ringing from the thunderclap and with the normal operational hum of the refrigerator silenced, that the pager went off.

I was glad to know I had recently passed a full physical. It meant that my heart, which was busily juddering in my chest like a mouse on a triple espresso, most likely would not fail on me.

I jammed the chopsticks into the takeout container and dropped it onto the kitchen counter. "Watch the house. Don't finish the lo mein," I told Tonk as I ran to the garage and jumped into my pickup truck.

The newly-installed red light bubble on the roof competed with flashes of lightening. The houses I passed were formless darkened hulks occasionally rendered in jagged relief like ultra-contrast photographs.

The fire station was fully lit, the emergency generator having kicked on automatically. The bay door for Engine 3 was open and empty, that vehicle with crew already on its way.

Engine 2 idled on the concrete apron backlit by the wash of light from the fire station. I grabbed my gear, mostly a patchwork of hand-me-downs from other firefighters past and present to tide me over until my own came in from the manufacturer. The bunker pants were too large and the boots slightly too small, but the jacket and helmet fit well. The gloves were brand new and the correct size, but not broken in and as stiff as one of Tonk's rawhide chews.

The back door of the truck was being held open and waiting for me. We took off as soon as I got inside and slammed it closed.

"What have we got?" I asked the firefighter in the seat next to me.

"Guy reported seeing a glow in the woods about a quarter of a mile away. Thinks it's near where his neighbor's house is."

Let me tell you, when someone a quarter of a mile away reports your house as a glow in the woods, that's not good.

"You're the new guy?" He asked. He flipped a switch on an overhead light fixture bathing the crew compartment in dim red light. It felt like we were onboard a submarine during wartime going to battle stations. He removed a facemask from a net bag clipped to his jacket and attached it to the regulator on the air pack already strapped to his back.

In the dim wash of red light I realized I was in luck – this was one of the guys whose name I had managed to remember, more or less. I was certain his name was either David Winston or Winston David. He was about my age, but had been fighting fires for more than fifteen years already, coming from a long line of firefighters stretching back at least three generations. Law of averages said his first name was most likely David. I could not, so far as I had been alive, recall anyone with the first name of Winston besides Winton Churchill.

I held out my gloved hand, "Jack Fallon. You're David."

He took my gloved hand in my own and shook it. Unable to close my fingers with the incredibly stiff gloves, he must have figured I had one of the weakest handshakes ever recorded. "Call me Winston."

Either he was being an unusual stickler for formality, or his parents had been big Winston Churchill fans.

"You certified on air packs yet?" he asked.

"No."

"Then you'll have to stay outside." He said this with real regret in his voice, like I would be missing some swell party taking place within the burning house.

The other firefighters in the rear cab with me, there were three of them, rode the sway and shudder of the maneuvering truck easily, like seasoned straphangers nonchalantly reading the New York Times during their morning commute. Each turn of the truck I had to grab the seatback or the door handle, once simply bracing myself between the ceiling and floor, to keep from tumbling into them.

The guy in the officer's seat leaned around to talk to us. "Patrol car on the scene reports a fully involved structure fire. I want you four in two teams on attack lines to back up the crew from Engine 3."

Winston spoke up, "We've got a new guy back here. He's not certified."

"OK. Winston, then you're with me on line one. Bill and Stevie, line two. Jeff?"

"Jack," I corrected him.

"OK, Jack, stay with Tom and the truck. Help him with whatever he needs."

"Can do."

We arrived at a scene I can only describe as a movie set at which no expense had been spared. Engine 3 was already there, shining red and clean and reflecting the firelight. Hoses thick and heavy with water ran from the truck into the house. A patrol car had taken up station on the street, the officer keeping back a fair sized crowd of extras, each looking like they had come directly from central casting. There was the guy with a dog, and the woman with two young children. There was even the obligatory old couple, her hair actually in rollers.

The house was burning perfectly. The pyrotechnic guys had outdone themselves. A simple two-story farmhouse with wrap-around porch showed picture-perfect flames curling from every visible window, the crisp white siding darkened with soot artistically above each one.

We stopped at the end of the driveway, a silver Subaru Forester blocking our path. As soon as the truck rolled to a halt the other guys popped open the doors, jumped out, and slammed the doors closed behind them. Tom and I were left alone in the idling vehicle.

"Go tell whoever that is to move their damn car! We've got to get a line to Engine 3."

"I'm on it."

I got out and ran over to the driver side window. An old guy with wispy white hair sat in the driver's seat, the light of the burning house mirrored in his eyes. He rolled down his window when I knocked on the glass.

"I'm going to need you to move your car."

"Go fuck yourself! That's my fucking house burning!" He yelled at me, flecks of spittle flying from his lips and spotting my face shield.

I turtled my head a little and turned away, stunned by his verbal assault.

Out the corner of my eye I saw a younger woman in the passenger seat put a hand on his arm and say, "Dad, please."

I stumbled back to the truck.

"What did he say? Is he going to move it?" Tom asked me.

"He told me to go fuck myself."

Tom shook his head in disbelief.

The backup lights on the Subaru came on and the car moved out of the driveway to park across the street. Tom maneuvered the big truck expertly between the mailbox on one side of the driveway and an ornamental shrub on the other and nosed his way to a stop about ten feet shy of Engine 3.

He came down out of the cab, opened one of the side compartments and pulled out a roll of four inch hose. I unrolled it and hooked one end to the intake on Engine 3 while he hooked up to the outlet on 2. He climbed onto the pump deck and activated the pumps, the hose between us and 3 filling up with water. I climbed up next to him and watched as he ran the panel, a dizzying array of levers, knobs, buttons, and gauges reading things like "tank to pump" and "idle speed preset." I hung my jacket on one of the deck grab bars and stood there sweating out my T-shirt.

The water flowed and the fire raged and I watched equally as slack-jawed as the people in their bathrobes across the street, only I had a better view of the action.

A tanker arrived from Hollis and connected to our Engine, feeding us its water. When it ran dry it pulled away and another tanker, this one from Brookline, arrived. Before it was empty the Hollis tanker had filled up at some watering hole somewhere and was back brimming with water and waiting in line.

The number of hoses multiplied, a dizzying collection of valves and splitters, gates and shunts.

A Red Cross van pulled up and three women set up a card table with bottles of water and bologna sandwiches which firefighters would eat one-handed while they held a hose or worked a tool with the other.

My carpenter's eye noticed a loss in the line of the roof ridge. It was just a small dip at first at one end and then became a noticeable sag across more than half of its length. The roof structure was starting to come apart.

The Chief must have seen what I did because just a moment later the horn on Engine 3 sounded to evacuate the building. Tom slammed his hand against the pump panel. "Dammit!" He jumped down from the deck and leaned through the driver's door to mash the steering wheel, adding Engine 2's horn to the call. Brookline and Hollis tankers joined in a moment later, a nearly tangible wall of sound which could probably be heard all the way up into the Merrimack valley.

The crews came out of the building hauling their hoses with them. Hasty attendances were taken and all were accounted for.

They renewed their fight from the outside, but everyone knew it was a lost cause. The roof line slid farther and farther out of true until it fell into the building, a cloud of embers like fireflies spiraling into the night. The walls went down a moment later.

Most of the house was in the basement now, no fewer than four hoses drowning every flame in sight until there was nothing left but wreckage, hot coals, and steam.

"Jack, get into the hole and help with overhaul." The Chief had appeared at the side of the truck.

I grabbed my jacket, strapped on my helmet, and walked to the remains of the house.

The wraparound porch was in good shape, though when the house had fallen the covering roof had been pulled off, leaving the roof supports standing crookedly connected to nothing at all. A ladder had been set down into the cellar, and two firefighters were climbing up, their faces streaming with sweat and blowing their breath like racehorses after the Kentucky Derby.

I climbed down once they were off the ladder, and it was like descending into a rainforest. It was ninety and humid outside the hole. It was probably a hundred and forty and twice as humid inside. The muck was almost knee deep, like ash soup served piping hot.

I slogged over to a battered and smoking three-drawer filing cabinet and opened the top drawer. The papers inside were burning. Someone handed me a hose nozzle and I ran water into that drawer and then the other two drawers in the cabinet as well. I then handed off the hose to someone else who had found hot coals in a pile of lumber that had probably once been the rear wall of the house.

My faced burned and my breath heaved, and I felt dizzy and nauseous, and I kept digging and moving shit around, trying to find any remnant of fire and put it out. All of the electrical wiring for the house, what seemed like miles of it, was down in the soup, and it wrapped around my ankles and tried to trip me at every turn. I climbed out as other firefighters climbed in to replace me, threw water on my face and ate a bologna sandwich, and then climbed back in again. I noticed on one of my trips out that the homeowners, the old man from the car and a woman roughly the same age, had moved up and were sitting in lawn chairs watching. Their daughter stood behind them. Like the world's saddest portrait.

As we got near the end I noticed one of the firefighters, a woman, I think from Hollis, digging through the debris with a purpose. She found a muffin tin, battered but still capable of turning out a muffin. She turned up a DVD copy of *Sleepless in Seattle*, waterlogged but which might still play. There was a cast iron frying pan in fairly good shape, a small porcelain doll, and a box of Christmas ornaments that had somehow survived unbroken. She carried these things and a few others up the ladder and presented them to the woman on the lawn chair. The woman accepted them with tears in her eyes and hugged them to her, filthy though they were, as if they were her last possessions on Earth, which they quite probably were.

We began to clean up. We just gathered up the hoses in bundles and threw them into the back of the Chief's pickup truck. The Red Cross ladies folded up their table and went on their way. The neighbors went back to their beds and their still-standing homes.

Several firefighters lined up and walked past the homeowners, saying they were sorry as they went by. Sorry for their loss. Sorry we couldn't save the house. I'm not sure which, perhaps both. I waited in line and said my "I'm sorry," but it seemed a small and empty thing to say.

We climbed aboard our trucks and headed back to the station.

We rode in silence for awhile, each with our own thoughts and the hum of the heavy-duty tires against the road.

"How do you feel?" Winston asked me.

"Sad," I replied, "and a little angry."

He nodded, "That's what it feels like to lose one."

Returning to the fire station our work was not yet done. Far from it. There were hoses to wash, air tanks to refill and masks to clean, and all the equipment taken off the trucks had to be inspected and replaced.

Winston and I ended up working together repacking hose on Engine 2.

He shook his head, "Can you imagine coming home from dinner and finding your house on fire?"

"Is that what happened?"

"Yeah. Early theory is a lightning strike started it."

I couldn't imagine what that would feel like, and didn't wish to find out within my lifetime.

"That's not all," another firefighter named Mike said as he came by carrying two more rolls of hose for us to pack, "twenty years ago almost to the day, that same couple came home from dinner out and found their home burning from a lightning strike. They lost that one too."

"No shit!" Winston whistled.

"The same couple on the same plot of land?" I asked.

"Twenty years ago," Mike confirmed.

While the scientist in me was certain there was probably some logical mitigating factor, like the possibility of a large localized iron deposit attracting lightening strikes to that particular piece of land, I nonetheless got a little chill up my spine. Those poor people must have felt like they were directly under the cursor when God hit the smite key.

"Could I have everyone's attention here?" The Chief's voice boomed from the rear of the station house.

We all made our way in that direction, gathering in a loose circle around him.

"I just want to tell everyone what a fine job you all did tonight."

There was some general low grumbling from the firefighters standing around me.

He continued with a little more force than before, "It was a hot one, it was a stubborn one, and when push came to shove we were just too late. I don't want anyone going out of here tonight," he paused to check his watch, "this morning thinking you didn't do a good job, because you all did. We may have lost the building, but no one was hurt, and that's the important thing."

There were nods and murmurs of agreement.

"And we saved the cellar hole," one of the firefighters said.

There was a small burst of laughter. That's a joke among firefighters so common I had already heard it before in my meager two weeks on the department.

The Chief smiled at him, "Yes we did, Stevie. We haven't lost one yet. Now I want everyone to finish up the trucks and let's try to all get home for a little shuteye before the sun comes up. OK?"

He wasn't Knute Rockne giving the 'Gipper' speech, and we didn't give him a 'Hip! Hip! Hurray!" as the group broke up and we went back to our various tasks, but he had sensed the low-level depression we all felt as a result of the loss. He had given us the boost we needed to get past it so we wouldn't be thinking about it the next time a call came.

Winston and I finished packing away the hose, and then assisted some other guys filling air bottles. By the time we got out of the station there was just the barest hint of pink visible on the horizon.

I was wasted. As I headed for my truck it almost seemed beyond me to put one foot in front of the other. Some of the other guys would go home, shower, pour several cups of coffee down their throats, and go to their day job like they hadn't just been up all night. I couldn't fathom how they did it.

Someone tapped me on the shoulder and I turned to see the Chief behind me.

"Welcome to firefighting, Jack"

Fourteen

Beverly frowned. "Sad story."

"Yeah," I breathed, "and no one died in that one."

"The woman in the fire."

I nodded.

"Do you want to talk about it now?"

"I'm not sure what there is to say."

"John says he believes you did everything you could that night. Do you agree with him?"

"I've had a lot of time to think about that, what with not sleeping and all, and I do."

"Is that what you think about at night?"

"Not specifically, no." I got up from the chair and walked to the wall of books. "Mind if I walk around a little bit?"

"Not at all."

I glanced at the paperback spines. There was a whole section of Greg Bear. She didn't look like a hardcore science fiction fan to me. I found it somehow easier to talk to the bookshelves instead of her. "Have you ever had trouble sleeping?"

"Everyone has trouble sleeping now and then."

"But like this, several days in a row?"

I saw her shake her head out of the corner of my eye.

"The nights are long. Incredibly long. And Valerie, that's my wife, and my dog are sound asleep. And I'm not tired. I know I should be, and physically I'm beat, but I'm not tired, not exactly. My mind keeps running. I lie in bed, and then I give up and wander around the house." I caught sight of copies of *The Demolished Man* and *Tiger! Tiger!* by Alfred Bester, both of them severely out of print. She was hardcore. "Nighttime television is awful. My wife calls it television of the damned."

I heard her laugh behind me.

Poul Anderson, Sam Delany, Larry Niven, a light smattering of Asimov.

"I'm getting more and more tense, less and less certain of my actions and decisions. I feel like I'm on edge all the time, and I've got this anger, this pent up rage." I turned around and went back and sat down, leaning forward again, elbows on knees. "Can you help me?"

She leaned forward as well, imitating me, putting her elbows on her knees, our heads only about a foot apart. "Mr.

Fallon, can I ask you a question?"

"Sure."

"You seem like a very level-headed person. Do you know why you're not sleeping?"

"I don't know. Maybe."

"Yes?"

"I feel as though I want to do something. For her."

"The woman who died in the fire?"

"Her name was Patricia Woods, and yes."

"Mr. Fallon, you yourself said you did everything you could to try and save her. What more can you do for her?"

"I want to find her killer."

As soon as I had said it I wanted to take it back, somehow suck the words back into my mouth. The frown on her face told me what she thought of that idea.

"Mr. Fallon-"

"Please, Mr. Fallon is my father. Call me Jack."

"Alright, Jack, that's not a good idea. I appreciate your sense of responsibility. It's almost chivalrous, really. But it's misplaced. It's misplaced, and it's unhealthy. You did your best to save her from the fire, and your responsibility ends there. There are other people who will catch whoever killed her."

She made a persuasive argument, but it wasn't working for me. Perhaps without cause or reason, I knew my obligation to Patricia was not so easily dismissed. I was also concerned that, despite Beverly's assertion, the Sheriff could not catch her killer. How had I gotten to Michael and Samantha Carston before the Sheriff did? Had Dawkins even talked to her coworkers yet? The thought of leaving Patricia's justice in his hands made me grind my teeth.

I didn't know if I could solve Patricia's murder; I had no illusions there, but felt that I had to do something.

"Do you understand what I'm saying to you, Jack?"

"Yeah. Yes I do."

"You need to let go. You need to distance yourself from her and that fire, for your own sake."

"I'll try."

"I don't mean to make light of this, and I don't expect you to simply change overnight. Your emotions are a part of you, and we're going to have to work together to help you achieve some balance in your life, to re-channel your energies into something else. When you relieve yourself of this burden, I suspect sleep will return to you naturally."

"OK"

She got up and went to the roll top desk, and flipped pages in a daybook. "I think given the urgency of your condition, I'd like to see you again tomorrow if you can make it."

"Her funeral is tomorrow. I'm planning to go."

"Do you think that's a good idea?"

"I think it will help me say good-bye. I think it will help me get closure." That last bit was sort of manipulative on my part. I knew counselor types loved the word closure. I was actually hoping to see who else was at the funeral and maybe ask a few questions while I was there.

Though I got the distinct feeling she saw right through me, she smiled, "OK." She flipped another page on the date book, and picked up a pencil poised to write. "I normally don't have hours on Sunday, but I'd be willing to see you on Sunday afternoon, say one o'clock, if that works for you."

"That will be fine."

She made a mark in the book, "I'll see you Sunday at one. It's been nice meeting you."

"Nice meeting you," I got up and touched hands with her, almost nothing like a handshake at all, and then hightailed it for the door in the far wall. I hadn't minded the therapy session, but at the same time felt like a kid who had just been let out for recess.

Fifteen

I sequestered myself in my workshop later that evening with my laptop and the envelope containing the prints of the photographs from the camera in Engine 2. With a work light clamped to the block of burled walnut, I carefully spread the pages out on the workbench surface, writing notes on the pictures as I looked at them, using the digital images on the laptop if I saw something I wanted to zoom in on.

They contained less information than I had hoped.

The shots of the living room established that it was the entertainment center that had caught fire from the rug. Though it had spread to the nearby wall, the damage to that area was superficial, or at least had been until the firefighters had chopped into it with axes looking for fire extension. The damage to the entertainment center was far more advanced and even, as I stared at it, seemed to have a curved shape to the charring that matched the arc of the rug.

There was likely evidence of the accelerant used still

contained within its fibers. I contemplated another felony, going back into the house to get a sample. I decided against it, not for any fear of committing another crime – I was well and truly down that road already – but because I didn't know what I would do with the sample if I had it. I'm not a chemist, I don't have a lab, and in any case I expected the accelerant to be something plentiful, readily available, and anonymous, like home heating oil. Not exactly the sort of clue that would lead me to the killer's doorstep.

The picture of her clothing, neatly folded in a pile on the bathroom floor, I somehow found terribly depressing. They were well-treated, what looked like a sweater, jeans, underwear, and socks. She was a person who had taken care of her things. I found myself wondering if there might be something in the pockets, and again thought about returning to the scene of the crime. I then realized collecting the clothing might have been one of the things the Sheriff had been doing the night he had nearly caught me at the house. It seemed like a long shot anything of significance would be her pockets anyway. Sure, detectives on television solved crimes by finding matchbooks with a phone number scrawled on the cover, but I held no such illusions things were that easy in real life. I tossed that picture aside.

The next one I considered was of the chain and padlock.

The chain looked like any other to me, without any markings that I could see in the photo. A little research online informed me that manufacturers did stamp some kind of emblem on the steel to identify it as theirs along with some model data so that the properties, strength and whatever, could be looked up. However, the stamped letters were not on every single link but only periodically along the length of the chain, and they were small, which would be difficult to see in good light and impossible covered in soot in a photograph with much of the contrast destroyed by the camera flash.

As uninteresting as the chain was, I found the picture of the lock fascinating. It was the style of padlock that used a key. Where was the key? Had it been located in the bedroom? Did the killer still have it? Furthermore the lock was a very peculiar color, something like a dayglo orange visible even through the coating of soot. The word 'Locktight' was very clearly visible in white on the padlock body.

A little poking around on the computer convinced me there was not now and as near as I could tell had never been either a company named Locktight selling padlocks, or a lock sold under the Locktight name. I didn't know what to make of that. The killer certainly had not made his own lock. Maybe that meant it came from a mass manufacturing house in China or Thailand. Some company that bashed out a few million low quality locks without bothering to trademark the name because the locks were junk and the name wasn't worth protecting. Where would one buy such a lock? Flea markets? Maybe they could be had at salvage and odd lot stores. Would it be possible to build a list of places that sold such a lock and go through them? Even in New Hampshire that process could be daunting, and of course I had no way of knowing for certain the lock had been purchased in the state.

It was the closest thing I had found to a clue thus far, but I had no idea what to do with it.

The door to the shop opened and Valerie came in wrapped in her terrycloth robe, Tonk at her heels. "What are you doing out here? Come to bed."

"I won't be able to sleep."

"You won't if you don't try."

She had me there. Still, on top of all the previous stuff my mind had been grinding over the last three nights, allowing sleep to elude me, I had inadvertently added two more things. One, I was becoming increasingly worried the Sheriff might have seen me that night in the house, and I was just waiting for him to show up here and arrest me. Secondly, and this was a biggy in my mind, I agonized over what the Sheriff would do when he talked to Michael and Samantha Carston and they mentioned already having talked to me, Samantha especially as I had told her I was with the police. Why that shoe hadn't dropped already was something of a mystery itself.

"What are you working on?" Valerie asked as she moved to the workbench and began shuffling through the pictures. A look of horror dawned on her face. "Are these from that fire? The one where the woman was killed?"

"Yes." I had thought for just a moment about denying it, but there seemed little point. The woman's clothing, the chain, the occasional back or helmet of a firefighter caught in the frame; there was nothing else they could be.

"What are you doing with these? They're evidence in a murder investigation." she said, her voice rising.

"They were taken with a fire department camera. Why shouldn't I have them?" I replied lamely.

"Jack, can't you see? That doesn't even make sense. You're not thinking clearly."

"I'm fine," I replied, over emphasizing the f, sounding like a petulant teenager.

"You're not fine. You're going out at night, getting injured, doing God only knows what. Is there something about this murder you're not telling me?"

"Like what?"

"I don't know like what." She paused and licked her lips, ducking her head a little and lowering her voice, "Are you involved?"

I wanted to laugh, harsh and bitter, at the thought of my wife suspecting me of murder. "No, I'm not involved. I'm trying to solve it."

She pressed the knuckles of one fist against her mouth, mumbling slightly as she spoke around it, "Oh my god, Jack, when you said that this morning I thought you were kidding, but you're serious."

I said nothing, shuffling the pictures around on the tabletop, willing myself to see something new in them, something significant so I could lessen my growing sense of impotence.

"You can't," she began, then stopped, letting her hand down. She began again, speaking in a very slow and even voice, as though talking to a child. "There are people who solve murders, Jack. Those people are called the police."

"I know that," I snapped.

"Then would you care to tell me what the fuck are you doing," she said in the same reasonable tone of voice, but now laced with cloying sarcasm.

"I've got to-" I started, but then somehow lost that train of thought before I could complete it. "That is, I want-" I tried again, but missed that train as well. Frustration ballooned inside me.

Her brows drew down, her voice softened, a look of concern on her face, "You're not sleeping and you're behaving irrationally, Honey. I'm worried about you. I want you to come inside and we'll call Beverly Dell in the morning."

I felt like my whole life was a car careening out of control, my emotions running completely unchecked. I could no more contain myself than I could stop the rotation of the Earth, and I exploded.

"I need to do this! Just leave me alone!" I shouted.

Tonk yipped and ran from where he had been lying at our feet, taking refuge behind the drill press in the corner, peeking at us past its bulk. Valerie looked hurt at first, but then her face hardened with steely anger, her lips thinned over gritted teeth. She stalked across the workroom and opened the exterior door. Tonk took the opportunity to dart past her and out into the night. She looked back at me for just a moment; she took a breath as if she might say something, but then didn't. She stepped outside and slammed the door hard enough to shake the entire structure, the fluorescent light banks overhead swaying on their chains.

I stood, unsteady in the shifting light, my hands clutching the edge of the workbench.

Sixteen

I discovered that the Evergreen Cemetery in Rutland, Vermont was something of a misnomer. Treed primarily with sugar maples, their leaves of red, orange, and yellow when struck by the high autumn sunlight appeared to be on fire. A classical New England church dominated the scene, white siding, black shutters, and white steeple reaching skyward. It looked to me like a replica and not original construction. Either that or it had seen exceptional care and maintenance across the decades. All the lines were true, there wasn't a sagged sash or cracked board anywhere I could see. Was it old or new? Had I gone inside I could have answered the question easily by examining the quality and style of the joinery, but I wasn't in the mood.

My business was outside, next door to the church in front of a rectangular mausoleum made of blocks of some brown stone with a broad arch over the main entrance. A small white popup tent had been erected in front, one of those mechanical units that can be set up by just a couple of people in seconds. Whoever held the patent for the design must have made a fortune, and nobody had been killed, writhing in biochemical agony, to make it. In front of the tent stood rows of white plastic folding chairs, most filled already with mourners when I arrived just a few minutes before three on Saturday.

A short plinth made of white plaster at the rear of the gathering held funeral scripts. I took one and found a seat in the last row in the rightmost chair, out of sight and, I hoped, out of mind.

The script was a single sheet of paper printed on both sides and folded in half to make a one-page booklet. The front cover showed a picture of Patricia, the edges blurred with Photoshop and melted into a background of clouds and sky. Beneath read: *Patricia Ann Woods*, the dates of her birth and death making her twenty-four years, six months, and a handful of days old. The inside cover held more pictures, cropped into a collage of Patricia during her life. I couldn't bring myself to look at them closely.

The opposite page held a poem of sorts. I read it through a couple of times, but couldn't place it.

A ship is about to set sail
You stand on the deck
We stand on the shore
Calling your name
A bell rings
The ship moves away
Further and further away
Until we can no longer see it
And we cry
But at the moment we cry
At the moment we lose sight
On a distant shore
A cheer goes up
The ship is coming
The ship is coming home

On the back of the booklet was a simple map, drawn by hand. The church was a box with a steeple on top and a cross inside it. An amorphous blob was labeled Meeney's Pond, the body of water I had passed just up the road on the way here. In the lower right hand corner of the map was a box with a triangle on top, a square on the triangle, a swirl of the pen above. It was a child's drawing of a house with roof, chimney, and smoke. *The Woods Residence, 162 Hillside Avenue.* Beneath that was written: "*For those wishing to express their condolences after the service, there will be a gathering at the Woods residence. Family and friends are welcome to celebrate Patricia's life and the time we were blessed to share with her.*"

Family and friends. I wasn't sure I qualified. I didn't see firefighters on that list.

I put the sheet on the ground at my feet.

Patricia's family, her parents and her younger sister, sat on similar folding chairs underneath the tent near the rear. A priest sat with them, their heads together, their lips moving but the words too soft to hear.

A podium stood at the side of the tent nearest the mourners, beside it a pedestal, a bronze urn on top. I could see shirring of the urn surface, but couldn't read the letters from here. That was OK. I had a pretty good idea what it read.

My neck felt stiff and I tipped my head back, my eyes closed. Dappled sunlight filtering through the branches of a maple tree high above me turned my vision red, pulsing with the beating of my heart.

Seventeen

Sitting there underneath the spread red wings of that maple tree, part of Patricia's funeral and yet apart from it, I was transported back to one of the first funerals I had attended as a firefighter, that one for the son of Russell Burtran.

Joining a fire department is, in a lot of ways, like instantly multiplying your family by a factor of one hundred or more. You go to picnics, attend football, baseball, and hockey games. You become part of an enormous networking system, helping sons, daughters, nieces, and nephews find jobs or get recommendations for college. You're invited to Christmas and Thanksgiving dinners. You attend baptisms, weddings, anniversary and birthday parties, graduations, and, yes, funerals.

When you first join, it is the funerals that are the most awkward.

It might be the funeral for an old-timer; someone who retired from the department decades ago. It might be for a relative of another firefighter. You're new to the department and you hardly even know the guy standing next to you, you probably don't know the deceased at all, had in fact never met them while they were alive.

Still, you go.

You go out of respect for the firefighters who came before you. You go to support those men and women who stand beside you on the line. I saw a Discovery Channel documentary on firefighters shortly after 9/11 that had called us the brotherhood of the flame. Not a firefighter myself at the time, the appellation seemed gallant and heroic. Now that I'm a firefighter the name makes me cringe, a nickname perhaps more fitting for a competitive barbecue team, but the sentiment is right.

The funeral for Russell's son began with us gathering at the fire department. All the other firefighters wore their Class A uniforms: dark blue slacks and jackets with brass buttons gleaming, light blue dress shirt, dark blue wool tie, patent shoes polished to a mirror finish, Maltese cross pinned over the bill of their caps. The officers even have gold braid epaulets. My Class A was on backorder with the uniform store, so I was wearing a dark grey suit. I've gotten a lot of miles out of that suit, having purchased it for my interview for graduate school. Back then I had worn it with a white broadcloth shirt, a black tie with little gold chevrons, and a silver Daffy Duck tie clasp in acquiescence to my image as a closet rebel. For this occasion I paired it with a blue dress shirt, solid dark blue tie, and left the Daffy Duck tie tack at home, going instead with one that was just a simple gold bar with a cubic zirconium embedded in it.

In the crowd of the other firefighters I felt like the world's worst version of *Where's Waldo*.

Russell's car was parked outside, freshly washed and waxed and decorated with black bunting courtesy of the other firefighters. He rode in the car alone. His wife dead of ovarian cancer something like eleven months ago, the death of his son had left him without family. There were rumors circulating that he had a brother somewhere, but if so he was not in attendance that day. We were all he had.

The small processional, half a dozen cars, made their way to the town cemetery, which, if you opened the Encyclopedia Brittanica, or I suppose today that would be Wikipedia, to the entry on the small-town cemeteries, was exactly what you would expect to find: an irregular trapezoid at one end of town surrounded by white picket fencing in good repair, painted often courtesy of the local Boy Scout troop.

The town cemetery has long been completely full, forcing people to be buried out of town at the newer Walmart-equivalent cemeteries in Nashua or Manchester, offering a wide range of burial options all at low, low prices for your interment convenience with all the warmth of an automotive assembly line. The exception to this is the old families, those who can trace their origins back to the pilgrims. They somehow shuffle, stack, reorganize, and otherwise squeeze ever more people into their ancient ancestral burial plots.

The Burtrans were one such family, occupying a section in the northeast corner surrounded by its own ring of weathered river rocks. The headstones in their area went way back. Starting with the freshly chiseled markers of Russell's wife and his son, their edges so clean it looked like you could cut yourself on them, they regressed through older and more weather-rounded stones like some sort of time lapse aging photography, ending in a lump of stone so worn it would require some type of advanced *CSI* technique to get any information off of it at all. Such a stone if found, say, alongside a trail in the woods or on the beach would be taken as just a random stone. It was only its proximity to other headstones that gave its purpose away.

I stood near the rear of the small group while first the priest and then Russell said a few words. I could neither see nor hear either of them because of the other firefighters in the way, but by looking to the right I could see the new headstone perfectly. It was a piece of solid New Hampshire granite rough cut into the classic tombstone shape like all the others around it, with the front face simply sawn off smooth and engraved with the words "Daniel Sullivan Burtran" and "Beloved Son" on the line beneath that. The dates appeared at the bottom, a little quick math placing them just eighteen years and two months apart. The end result of an implacable and immutable equation of physics that has claimed many lives; he had run his car into a tree.

I realized Russell, without family around him, was the end of the Burtran line. He was the last Passenger Pigeon, the final Dodo bird. A family that had been a part of Dunboro for a time so long its earliest headstones could not even impart to me how long that had been, was going to come to a close. I could not help but wonder about the Fallon line, Valerie and I without children and with only sort of loose hazy plans to have them in the indefinite future. My father has a brother. He has a son. Perhaps I'd leave that responsibility up to him, which, standing there in the cemetery at that time seemed important and immense.

The pile of black earth covered by a sheet of Astroturf carpeting was nearby. The coffin, massive in shining bronze that looked like it could survive a mortar hit, hung over the hole suspended by canvas straps, ready to be winched down at a moment's notice. Three guys in stained jeans and T-shirts leaned on shovels and smoked cigarettes while they waited just outside the line of the picket fence. Even the old timey cemeteries seemed pretty impatient those days.

To one side I noticed a pack of teenagers all identically dressed in dark slacks, white shirts, and varsity letterman jackets. Their jackets identified them as members of the Dunboro High School track team, but even without that I would have thought them runners, thin and long legged, shuffling nervously like a pack of gazelles which smell lion in the air.

It was easy for me to put myself in their place. When I had been about their age a friend of mine was killed on the way home from the prom. He was in the front passenger seat of a car when the driver, a little buzzed on spiked punch, rear ended a cement mixer. It was a closed casket ceremony by necessity. I had stood at that funeral shaken by my dawning understanding that as a teenager I was tough to injure and quick to heal, yet somehow perplexingly those factors didn't add up to immortality.

A shuffling of the crowd around me brought me back from the funeral of the past to the funeral of the present. The young woman who I had believed to be Patricia's younger sister Rachael had taken the podium. Slim with very pale skin, she had hair of such a vibrant shade of red it competed with the fall colors of the sugar Maples around the cemetery. She had moved her sister's urn from the pedestal onto a corner of the podium. It looked awkwardly like she was preparing to give away an unusually-shaped Oscar. She was so young up there, not necessarily so much younger than her twenty years, but far too young to be put through this.

She swallowed, pressed her lips into a thin line, swallowed again. "My sister was a beautiful person. I'm sure all of you here today know that, and I thank you for coming." She paused. "She was a great sister and a great friend, and just such a nice person." I could see a subtle shifting of the muscles of her face as though through a telescopic sight, the first cracks in the dam of her emotions. "I miss her." She stopped. "I miss her," she repeated. She tipped her head back, eyes looking towards the sky. If there were answers to be found up there she couldn't see them; tears were running freely down her cheeks. "How could someone do that to her?" she wailed, then put her head into her hands, her elbows resting on the podium.

My failure to save Patricia from the fire, my fault or not, felt like an open wound.

Her parents went to her. The three of them hugged together, just barely holding each other up. The priest joined them. "Thank you all for coming," he said quickly, and then turned them gently away from the audience, putting his body between them and us, shielding them in their grief.

Several people rose from their seats and then stood around, uncertain if there was something else they could or should be doing. Then by singles and twos, and then in increasing numbers, they made their way silently to their cars.

I bent over and picked up the script from the grass at my feet. Twisted by a feeling of failure I can't overcome, ever the glutton for punishment, I plan to attend the reception. Beverly, were she here, would tell me not to go. She would tell me my actions are misdirected, that I have to separate myself from the event I knew was tearing me apart. Within my head, even in her voice, those warnings held no power. I felt scraped raw, turned inside out, and fully deserving of a hearty dose of self-flagellation.

I made my way along the paths back to where my truck was parked. I was almost there when I heard from behind me, from clear across the cemetery, Rachael sob "I mu-mu-miss her so mu-mu-much!" This hit me like a physical blow and I actually stumbled, my brain for a moment consumed by her grief and forgetting how to perform the simple act of putting one foot in front of the other. I placed my hand against the door of my truck to steady myself and then rested my forehead against the window glass, cool and smooth against my skin.

I was not surprised to find myself crying.

Eighteen

After the funeral for Russell's son several firefighters, Russell included, reconvened in the Wayfarer Pub, a bar in a converted farmhouse in Milford. The owners have fought for many years to get the bar included in the registry of historic places, claiming it has hosted such noteworthy patrons as George Washington and Thomas Jefferson. Regardless of whatever storied history the place may possess, things have gone steadily downhill since then. The Wayfarer Pub was not what you would call a happy pub. People don't go there to hook up or hang out, and the echoes of Karaoke have never been heard within its walls. People go there to drink, and if the rumors are true about it being open since colonial times, more sorrows have been drowned there than souls onboard the Titanic.

Despite a large number of windows, the place was dark. All the woodwork had been coated with lacquer, what to my eye looked like it could easily be a hundred years worth, which had darkened with age to the color of a cup of strong coffee. It sucked the light right out of the air.

I stood at the bar drinking a kamikaze, a drink I had developed a tolerance for back in college. A healthy dose of vodka is masked by a shot of triple sec with just enough lime juice to fool yourself into thinking you're having a good time. Russell was alone at a table in the far corner drinking scotch neat from a short, heavy glass bigger than a shot glass. At around the third or fourth refill someone decided to just leave him the bottle; it perched on the table near one edge.

I watched for the better part of an hour as a firefighter or sometimes two went up to his table and said a few quiet words. If Russell listened to them he gave no sign, and after a few minutes they would wander off and leave him drinking in solitude. I wanted to offer some words of condolence, but I hadn't been on the department long and didn't know Russell well. If people who had known him for more than thirty years could give him no solace, what could I do?

Winston David came up to the bar next to me, put his empty beer mug down, and signaled the bartender for a refill. He noticed the direction I was looking, towards Russell's table, and glanced that way too for a moment before shifting his gaze down to the surface of the bar.

"He'll be all right," he said to himself as much as to me.

"You think so?" I asked.

He gave a tired shrug. "I don't know. Losing his wife to cancer and then his kid commits suicide."

"Suicide?"

He looked left and right down the length of the bar. Apparently comfortable with our distance from other people he leaned in and lowered his voice. "Carl was the first guy on the scene," he said, referring to Carl Pittman, one of the officers on the DPD. "When he got there the kid was still alive."

"Wait a second," I interrupted, "I thought he died in the accident."

"He did, but not right away. He was conscious when Carl got there, but he was bleeding out from a chest wound. He asked Carl to hear his confession."

"His confession?"

He took a drink from the mug the bartender had refilled and wiped the forearm of his uniform jacket sleeve across his mouth. "Have you ever been to a fatal?"

"A fatal car accident?" I shook my head. At that time I hadn't.

"People that are dying sometimes seem to know that they're dying."

He must have seen in my face some of the doubt I was feeling because he insisted. "It's true. Don't ask me to explain it." He scratched at the growth of stubble on his neck, and then smoothed the ends of his moustache with his thumb and forefinger before continuing. "A few years back there was a motorcycle accident on Route 13. Guy got thrown off his bike when he lost control on an ice patch. He ended up so far into the woods we had to go looking for him. I found him impaled on a tree branch about twenty yards out. I went to check him for a pulse, though it seemed like a waste of time, but he was actually still alive. Not only was he alive, but he was looking at me. 'Hang on. I'm going to get help' I told him, but when I turned to go he grabbed me by the collar of my coat. There were two quarts of blood soaking into the dirt and leaves at the base of the tree and a branch through his chest the thickness of your arm, and his grip was like iron. 'I've been having an affair' he said to me."

Dave stopped and took a drink from his beer. I waited for him to continue but he didn't.

"And?" I prompted.

"And nothing. He died right then. Didn't let go, though. I called on my radio and John came over. It took the two of us to get me loose."

"I don't get it. Did he want you to tell his wife?"

"I sure hope not because I never did." He pivoted at the bar so that he was facing directly at me. "I think when someone is dying like that, cut off short, that they want to try and lighten their burden. They don't want to drag their lies and all the rest of the shit of their lives along with them wherever they're headed. They want to just let it all go."

I took a swallow of my kamikaze and grimaced. Because my hand had been wrapped around the glass this entire time the ice had melted away and the drink was warm and watery.

"So Daniel tells Carl that he drove his car into the tree on purpose," Winston said almost casually.

"What?" I sputtered, choking on my drink. It took me a moment to remember how this conversation had started. "Why?"

He shook his head. "Teenagers. Every problem is insurmountable and every pain is earth-shattering."

I leaned a little to the side to look at Russell just as he downed a scotch, then reached unsteadily for the bottle and poured another inch into his glass.

"Does Russell know?"

"I don't think Carl would have just told him, but if Russell asked him flat out, maybe." He reconsidered this. "Probably."

"How do you get past something like that?"

111

"Fuck if I know." Dave rotated the mug on the bar, watching the overlapping rings of moisture obliterate each other. "Maybe you don't."

Nineteen

I sat in the truck for a long time after Patricia's funeral collecting myself. I watched as Sheriff Dawkins approached the family and questioned them, awkwardly, and then stood tapping a small black notebook against his thigh as they walked away from him to the limousine provided by the funeral home.

The reception afterwards was held at the Woods home, a beautifully preserved turn-of-the-century cape on a hill overlooking downtown Rutland. The exterior woodwork was immaculate though painted an unfortunate shade of avocado. I guess the paint makers wouldn't mix it if no one bought it.

Lurking in the corner of the living room I felt like an interloper, watching as her parents mingled and made small talk and put up a brave front with their friends and neighbors. I began circling the living room aimlessly, nodding to people I passed, looking at the art, mostly oil paintings of desolate seascapes. I then examined the pattern and weave of the enormous Oriental rug that covered the floor. In front of a baby grand piano I stopped to look at the photographs arrayed across its top. There were very few pictures of the parents; this was a family that was all about their children. Pictures of the two girls, Patricia and Rachael, at work, play, asleep, candid, posed, silly, serious, graduating, bike riding, softball playing, sunbathing, cooking, and on and on. I recognized many of them from the collage in the funeral script.

The pictures were in rough chronological clumps; young on the left, old on the right. On the left, a square wooden frame stained blue held a picture of Patricia and Rachael, both in pigtails, dressed as ballerinas, paper bags with twine handles clutched in their hands decorated with pumpkins indicating it was Halloween. Near the middle of the pack there was a picture in an oval maple frame of Patricia as a teenager, astride a blue Schwinn in jeans ragged at the knees and a Pink Floyd *Dark Side of the Moon* T-shirt. Next to it a picture in a narrow crystal frame shot through with silver filaments showed Patricia, lithe and dripping wet, in a blue and yellow racer's swimsuit as she stood on a dock in front of some unidentified body of water. Far to the right, a picture in a metallic gold frame was of Patricia dressed smartly in a black skirt and blouse with white collar and cuffs, proudly holding open a diploma in its binder.

Photographically speaking, this was as old as she would get, forever encased in glass at age twenty or twenty one.

I turned away from the pictures and crossed to the buffet. A table had been pushed against the wall and loaded down with deviled eggs, a cold cut platter, a veggie plate, five kinds of cheeses and seven types of crackers, a tower of little triangular tuna sandwiches with the crusts cut off, and a coffee service. I took a Styrofoam cup from a stack and filled it from the urn, mixed in a couple of sugars with a red plastic stirring stick and carried it outside.

The view from the front porch was glorious, all the way down the length of the valley vibrant in hundreds of fall hues. The steeple of the church next to the cemetery where the funeral had been held was visible, a flawless spire of white, sticking well above the trees that surrounded it. I moved down the length of the porch and sat on a bench swing supported by chains anchored in the porch roof. Sitting there, I tried to think of some way to figure out who had killed Patricia and why. It always seemed as easy as doing a connect-the-dots picture on the cop shows on television. Every person you talked to led you naturally to some other person, and the picture gradually emerged. In real life it didn't seem to work quite like that.

I was so engaged in my own thoughts that it was probably several minutes before I noticed a woman had sat down beside me on the bench. She was Patricia's sister, Rachael. I recognized her instantly from the funeral and the pictures on the piano. She wore a long black skirt and black sweater with mother-of-pearl buttons. Her pale complexion looked bleached against the dark background of her clothes, with the exception of circles the color of bruises under her eyes.

She stared at me intently, as if she expected me to tell her something, though I had no idea what that might be.

"Hello," I said.

"Hello," she replied and continued staring.

"I'm very sorry for your loss," seemed like a safe thing to say, and so I did.

"Here's the thing," she began; my expression of sympathy tossed aside, "I was reading a *Cosmo* a couple of months ago. You know, *Cosmopolitan* magazine?"

Her delivery was fast and clipped, almost manic. It was understandable given the stress she was under, but a little unnerving all the same.

"My wife reads it from time to time."

She nodded, but it was more like she was keeping internal time to some hectic beat than acknowledging my answer. "They were talking about wedding crashing, tips and techniques for sneaking into the weddings of people you don't know. Free food, free drinks, a party, you know?"

This was kind of a new fad that was beyond me. Though Valerie and I enjoy weddings I couldn't imagine how awkward it would be to be at a gathering where you didn't know anyone. Oh, wait, I could. I was at one now! I nodded encouragingly to her anyway, having no idea where she was going with this, and took a sip of the coffee. It was terrible. It had probably been brewing in the urn for hours. I put the cup carefully down on the porch at my feet, all the while maintaining eye contact with her, like I was trapped in a small room with a wild, unpredictable animal.

"They had interviews with these supposedly hip urban professionals, people who told stories about actual weddings they had crashed. Real zany stuff, like talking to a friend of the bride about how you had met the bride at college, only *she* had met the bride at college and never met you, and you couldn't come up with the name of the college when she pressed you for it."

She stopped and stared at me. I was not sure she had blinked yet. Did she even have eyelids? I was kind of sorry I had put the cup down, because as bad as the coffee had been, holding the cup would have given me something to do with my hands, which had an almost overwhelming urge to white-knuckle the bench armrest like I was in a car going way too fast.

"Yes?" I asked. If there was a logical progression here, I couldn't see it.

She sighed, exasperated. Did she have to spell everything out?

"One of the people they interviewed said that wedding

crashing was so passé. Been there, done that, got the T-shirt. What the cool people were doing was funeral crashing. Not so much for the party now, but to mingle with people you don't know and reminisce about times you never spent together. Like the ultimate inside joke because you're the only one on the inside."

It sounded to me like one more piece of evidence the human race was completely losing it.

"And here we are, and I've seen Aunt Susan and Uncle Theodore and most of the neighbors are here and our cousin Scott from Pennsylvania who used to yank on my underwear and give me wedgies when we were little, and I saw that cop at the cemetery, and I don't have the slightest fucking idea who you are."

The speed with which she had delivered this zinger left my brain treading rough conversational waters while it tried to formulate an answer. "Me?" I said.

"Yes you." She leaned in close, checking behind her to see that the doorway to the house was empty of witnesses, and dialing her volume down several notches. "So help me, if you're here to play some stupid private fucking joke because this is how you get your jollies, or worse yet, a reporter, I swear I'll go get a knife from the cheddar cheese block and stab you in the heart."

"No, Rachael I . . ."

At the sound of her name from the mouth of a stranger she recoiled as through from a venomous snake.

"No no no no no no no." I said, a machinegun staccato of denial, turned sideways on the bench to face her with my hands held up in front of me in surrender. "I'm a firefighter. I found your sister in the house."

She sat next to me with her face frozen, whatever she was

thinking a complete mystery to me. Then her eyes welled up and tears spilled down her cheeks in a rush. "Oh, shit!" she said, and got up and ran back into the house.

I was stunned beyond words. What the hell had just happened here?

I sat straight on the bench again and contemplated the view once more. The multicolored photons of fall smashed into my retinas at light speed, performing their chemical magic upon the cones that resided there, but leaving no impression upon my mind. Numb. I felt numb. I had no desire to give this family any more pain regardless of my desires to fulfill some debt of honor I felt I owed to Patricia while playing *Magnum PI* sans Ferrari. Staying here any longer would be stupid and insensitive.

I stood up and dumped the cup of coffee into a rhododendron at the edge of the porch and went down the front steps, but before I reached the street I heard Rachael call to me.

"Wait, please."

She stood at the top of the steps, a ball of Kleenex clutched in her right hand that she used to dab at her nose. She sniffed loudly. "I'm not – that is to say that I didn't mean – I'm sorry I was so rude earlier. I want to thank you for trying to help my sister."

"No apologies necessary. I'm sorry I couldn't save her."

She came down the steps, stopping one shy of the bottom, and even then was still three inches shorter than I was. "What was it like, the fire?"

I didn't want to get into that with her. Beyond the desire to save her from the more graphic details, there was the very real problem that I had no idea what the Sheriff had told her, what he had revealed and what he was playing close to the vest. Most of all, whatever final image she had in her mind of her sister, I didn't want the one I carried to replace it.

She either saw my discomfort in my face or read it in my silence. "I'm sorry. That's not a fair question. Did you know my sister, um," she paused, "before?"

"No, I had never met her."

"She was very special."

"I'm sure she was."

A collection of emotions played across her face while she alternately crumpled up the tissue in her hands, then smoothed it out and folded it up neatly into a square, then crumpled it up again. "I'm sorry; I don't know your name."

"Jack. Jack Fallon."

"Jack, do you have a car here?"

"A pickup truck, just down the road."

"Can you give me a ride somewhere? It's not far. Mine's trapped in the garage."

She nodded towards the garage that stood at the end of the driveway alongside the house. Six or seven cars were parked down its length blocking her car in.

"Sure."

"I'll be back in just a minute."

She turned and went back into the house. I wondered where she wanted to go while her parents were inside holding the reception for her sister's funeral.

When she came back out she had changed out of the dress

into blue jeans with hiking boots and a red and black checked flannel shirt under an orange down vest. She was carrying a small off-white cardboard box about six inches on a side. Interior decorators would probably have called its color ivory or perhaps bone.

"Do your parents know you're leaving? I wouldn't want them to worry."

"Yeah, it's OK."

I led her down the street to my truck and then unlocked it so she could climb inside. She sat on the seat with the box perched carefully in her lap.

"Where to?"

"Down to the end of the block, and take a left."

I started the truck, checked my mirrors, and pulled away from the curb.

She looked at the dashboard, noticing the modifications I had made to mount the toggle switches that ran the lights and siren. "It must be exciting being a firefighter.'

"It's not like the movies if that's what you're thinking." I signaled and turned left. "It's a lot of standing around pointing a hose at burning buildings eating bologna sandwiches. It's a lot of hanging out in the rain and the snow directing traffic around car accidents. It's a lot of early mornings and late nights. Very little of it is exciting or dangerous. Most of it is just work."

"Oh." She was silent for awhile, and then said, "Take a right at the stop sign."

I did. "Can I ask you a question?"

"I guess so."

"Do you have any idea why someone would want to hurt your sister?"

She looked at me carefully. Though I didn't take my eyes from the road I could feel her staring at me.

"Jack, what were you doing at my sister's funeral?"

"I'm the firefighter who found her."

That answer, admittedly evasive on my part, didn't fool her for a moment.

"I'm sure there were other firefighters there that night, but you are the only one here."

I drummed my thumbs on the steering wheel. "Would you believe I don't know?"

"No," she replied simply. "Turn left at the light."

I turned left and the road went up a long hill that must have been a real joy in the winter when it was icy. "I can't help feeling like I failed that night, like I'm somehow responsible. It's like I'm trying to figure out how to make up for that now. Somehow," I repeated.

"I don't understand."

"Honestly neither do I exactly, but I'm here, asking questions, trying to help. Trying to help Patricia. Trying to help myself. I don't know." I shook my head in frustration. Between Beverly, Valerie, and now Rachael, I had given variants of this speech three times. I was glad to see it was becoming absolutely no better or less awkward with each telling, perhaps even a little bit worse.

Instead of commenting on my little monologue she pointed, "Turn in there, on the left, beyond the sign."

I pulled off the pavement past the sign that read 'Juniper Trailhead' and into a small parking area of compacted dirt. She unbuckled her seatbelt and opened her door as soon as I turned off the engine.

"Where are you going? Should I wait for you?"

"No, it's not far. I can walk home." She closed the door and headed for a trailhead that opened off the near side of the lot. I lost sight of her among the trees just a little ways up the trail.

I sat in the car listening to the ticking of the cooling engine and the croaking of frogs in some nearby bog. The last light of the afternoon slanted down through the trees fading from gold to pink. I became concerned she would be injured in the dark on her way up or even later back down in nearly complete darkness. I took the flashlight out of the center console of my truck and followed the trail she had taken.

Almost immediately I could see why she had changed into hiking boots. The trail was a jumble of small and large stones, some better described as boulders. The hard soles of my dress shoes made the going fairly treacherous and they were taking a real beating, but I managed to keep from breaking an ankle.

After about half an hour I had not come across Rachael and it was a good deal darker. Tall trees loomed above me on either side. I turned on the flashlight. The trail had become a little easier, more steeply inclined but now mostly dirt covered in pine needles. Here my hard soles tended to slip, but it was an improvement nonetheless.

Twenty minutes after that, I climbed over a ridgeline and was headed back downhill. I was worried I had missed a fork in the trail somewhere. Would she have come this far in nearly pitch darkness?

I was just thinking about turning back when the trail opened up into a stony clearing glowing preternaturally in moonlight.

There was a pool of water in the middle in a shallow basin fed from a small waterfall at one end. Rachael knelt on a flat granite slab near the water's edge hunched over something with her back to me. She must have caught a reflection of the flashlight beam because she suddenly stood and spun around shielding her eyes. Streaks of tears lined her cheeks.

I held the flashlight down at my feet so it wouldn't blind her. "I'm sorry. I didn't mean to intrude on anything. I was afraid you might get hurt out here in the dark."

"Do you have a knife?"

I noticed the box was open at her feet and she was holding a clear plastic bag in her hands. The neck of the bag was held closed with a loop to tape. She had managed to stretch the tape out like taffy but not break it. Inside the bag were ashes, about one human being's worth.

"Patricia?" I asked.

She nodded.

"Do your parents know?"

"No, but I know this is what she wanted. She loved it up here. It's not like they're going to open the urn to check."

I didn't know about that. I thought maybe someday they would check, but didn't feel like contradicting her at that moment. I know I had opened the urn of my maternal grandmother to have a peek. There was some irresistible morbid curiosity to see what the ashes of a person looked like. I can't imagine I'm unique in that regard.

I handed her my pocketknife and she cut the tape and then handed it back to me. I turned off the flashlight and retreated to the edge of the clearing to give her some privacy. She went to the pool, the bag hugged to her chest, then knelt down and poured the ashes in with a swirling motion.

When she was finished she folded up the plastic bag and put it back into the box, then picked up the box and rejoined me. "We can go now."

I turned on the flashlight and led the way back, losing my footing and sliding down the steep portion on the seat of my pants. What the hell, it was time to buy a new suit anyway.

Rachael didn't seem to feel much like talking and I was willing to let her have her space. It wasn't until we were in the truck headed back to her parents' house that she spoke the first word since the clearing. "No."

"No what?"

"No, I have no idea why someone would want to hurt Patricia," she answered, as if there had not been a two hour gap in our conversation.

I was disappointed, but not particularly surprised by her answer. What had I expected her to say? If she had known of someone who wanted Patricia dead, she would have told the Sheriff and all this would be over by now. Still, I wondered where that left me.

"Did she owe anyone money?"

"I don't know. I don't think so."

"Any problems at work?"

"She was a dental hygienist. Do you think someone killed her over a bad cleaning?"

I had to admit, she had me there. "A bad relationship? A jealous boyfriend?"

Rachael was silent as I pulled the truck to the curb in front of the house. She was probably tired of my amateur attempts at sleuthing. Just as well – I had more or less run through everything I had learned from six seasons of *The Rockford Files*.

"She was seeing a guy named Mike. He lives somewhere in Amherst."

Michael Carston. I already knew about that, but was curious to hear her take on it. "Any idea if there were any problems there?"

"He was married," she said plainly. "That didn't seem to be a problem for her. She told me she was very happy. That it was going great."

I was surprised at the candidness with which she had revealed her sister's involvement with a married man, but I could see her determination in the hard set of her jaw. She had loved her sister and was fully prepared for herself and her family to suffer whatever humiliation was necessary to see her sister's murderer caught.

"His wife didn't mind?" I asked.

"She never said anything about that, but I'll tell you speaking as a woman, though I'm not married, if I find out my husband is cheating I'll kill him, not her."

I thought about that. Surely if Valerie found out I was having an affair, I would be the one to face the brunt of her wrath, but that didn't mean all women felt that way.

Rachael looked at me expectantly. Perhaps she thought I was just starting to get into the swing of this digging for clues thing, but I was going to disappoint her. I was completely out of productive questions. "It's getting late. Your parents are probably worried about you. If you think of anything else would you call me?"

"I don't have your number."

I dug a business card out of my wallet and handed it to her. It read 'Jack Fallon, Physicist. Lectures for all occasions: Wedding, Bar Mitzvah, Briss' with my phone number at the bottom. I had had 500 of them printed when I got my PhD and still had several hundred of them lying around. I had crossed out the old Manhattan number with a blue pen and written in my local one.

She moved her lips while reading the card to herself, then looked up at me and raised one eyebrow.

"Inside joke," I said in response to her unasked question. "Call me?"

"I will. Thanks for the lift."

"You're welcome."

She got out of the truck and went up the walk to the front door. The door opened, and I saw her stand in profile, backlit by the lights from inside. She stood there watching me until I put the truck into gear and drove away.

Twenty

Another day, another sleepless night.

I had spent it in the workshop, slowly and carefully cutting the burled walnut block into panels, which I lined up on the surface of my workbench. The envelope with the pictures was next to them, but it had remained unopened. I had spent so much time staring at the photos that I could visualize them perfectly just by closing my eyes. They had joined with the images of Patricia's hands in my mind like some ghastly slideshow.

Valerie had not come out to ask me to come to bed, and I had not gone in to kiss her goodnight, and there we were. I very likely would have been sleeping on the couch had I been sleeping.

By morning I was stir crazy with the desire to get out of the shop, away from the pictures and my laptop, though lacked any greater plan than that. Norma's seem to me to be as good a destination as any.

Norma's was a restaurant not far from what most people sort of jokingly referred to as bustling downtown Dunboro, a three hundred yard stretch of Route 13 in which clustered Norma's, a Dunkin Donuts, a bank, a gas station, and a perpetually empty store which had last held a bike shop. Norma's was housed in a converted two-story barn originally constructed in 1889 with light blue trim and shake cedar siding that had turned a dull silver over the years. The inside of the first floor had been hollowed out when it was converted to a restaurant, strategically-placed rustic hand hewn oak posts taking the place of removed load bearing walls. The stalls for the animals had been taken out as well making one big room for seating. The original tack room had become the restaurant's kitchen after the renovation. I had no idea what was upstairs in the hay loft; I had never been there.

There was an average crowd for a Sunday morning, which meant most of the tables were occupied. Norma's had been in the Michelin guide to New England for an outstanding Sunday brunch several years earlier and getting a table on a Sunday morning had been difficult ever since.

I waited by the front door until Norma noticed me on her rounds of filling up coffee mugs and water glasses from carafes which she held in each hand.

She came over, put the carafes down on the hostess podium, and pulled me into a big hug. Norma is a hugger. She is what would euphemistically be called a woman of size. Her skeleton is well padded, all the corners rounded and softened. That, and her fondness for paisley-print dresses, made a hug from Norma feel like being enveloped in a small sofa. "Jack, it's so good to see you!"

Norma knew just about all of the firefighters by name. She had gone out of her way to do so after we had stopped her kitchen fire dead in its tracks. The damage had been so well contained that she had managed to reopen the restaurant in only two days.

"You too, Norma."

"I haven't seen you in here in awhile. Can I get you some breakfast?"

"Just coffee, thanks, decaf." My insomnia seemed to be affecting my appetite. I had only managed one meal yesterday, breakfast, yet felt little or no hunger this morning.

She released me and turned away. "You can't live on coffee, you know," she said over her shoulder as she grabbed the carafes and headed for the kitchen door.

In minutes Norma was back with a small brown paper bag that she handed to me. "I put a breakfast sandwich in there with the coffee. I'll put it on your tab."

There was no tab, and it embarrassed me to take food for free I was perfectly capable of paying for, but she refused every offer to pay. I wasn't willing to make a scene about it.

I thanked her and took the bag out to my truck. No sooner had I closed the door than the smell of bacon and eggs filled the vehicle with their warm salty goodness. My stomach rumbled, and I opened the bag and unwrapped the tinfoil package inside. The sandwich, Norma's version of an Egg McMuffin only on a homemade biscuit instead of a processed English muffin, disappeared in six bites. I then took the coffee from the bag, broke out the little plastic tab in the lid, and took a sip. I actually groaned in pleasure at how good the food in my belly felt.

I felt re-energized and had a sudden inspiration as to what I should do next. I started the truck and drove out of the parking area.

Patricia had lived at number three Laurell Court, about half a mile down from Yancey Lane on the right. Laurell Court runs between Yancey Lane and an overgrown dirt road called Beeker's Way, though you would unable to find Beeker's Way on anything other than a few old logging maps and some of the better drawn maps of local snowmobile trails. Laurell Court itself swerves suddenly left and right, with two slight rises along the way. Both the turns and the rises have caught many an inexperienced driver on dark winter nights, and the trees on both sides of the road showed the scars from hard fought battles with the bumpers and grills of numerous cars and trucks which the trees always won.

There were only six houses on the entire road; each set back on generous wooded lots, the smallest of which was almost four acres. I parked my truck in the driveway of the home for rent again. The two lines in the gravel where I had spun my tires were still raw and visible on the ground.

I got out and walked up the driveway and down the street, stopping at the end of Patricia's driveway to look at the house. It looked much the same, though the windows had been boarded over. The police tape across the front porch posts was broken and flapped in the breeze.

I continued down the road to the neighboring house, a term that at best loosely applied as the nearest neighboring house was over a quarter of a mile away through dense woods as the crow flies.

Number one was a Swiss-style chalet, the eves and front porch overburdened with gingerbread trim painted hot pink against the house siding which was pale green. Wow, was that hard on the eyes. The woman who answered the doorbell was grandmotherly, her hair white, her face pouchy and wrinkled. She had a mole on one cheek, like a Wicked Witch of the West thing, blue-black with three long distinct dark hairs growing out of it. I tried really hard not to stare at it, so hard in fact it was probably awkward how much I *wasn't* staring at it. The entire situation was more uncomfortable still because the woman who answered the door clearly knew me and I, even though I have a pretty good memory for faces, didn't have the slightest idea who she was.

"Jack Fallon! So good to see you! How is your wife?"

"She's fine."

"That's good. I suppose you're here about the fire next door."

"Yes, did you see anything that night?"

"No, I was asleep until your fire engines woke me up. That house is so far away, and Kevin's humidifier makes so much noise at night."

I wracked my brains for who Kevin might be other than presumably her husband, drawing a complete blank. Maybe Valerie would remember. "Did you know the woman who lived there?"

"She was young, pretty, red-brown hair. I'd see her jogging along the road sometimes, but I never spoke with her. Can you believe that awful thing happening here in Dunboro?"

"Sad," I agreed. "I'm asking around to see if anyone may have seen anything."

"Have you talked to the other houses on the block?"

"You're the first."

"Well, number five has been empty for awhile. Mr. Pernicky took a job in Indianapolis and the house is up for rent. Mrs. Gruber in number six has been visiting her sister in Maryland and wasn't here the night of the fire. I'm collecting her mail for her."

"I'm glad I came here first. Anything else you can tell me?"

She scrunched up her face, looking a little like a shrunken

head in the process. "You might want to try Dennis and Marlene in two. They just had a new child, and from the way that child hollers I can hear it with my hearing aid turned off. I bet they're awake at night. Oh, and although I don't know her name, I've seen the woman in four also jogging. Maybe they've gone jogging together."

"Did you ever see them together?"

"No, but I just figured, you know, joggers." The way she said it was like they were all part of some club, like Rotarians.

I smiled at her, "That covers everyone on the block."

"That does, doesn't it?"

"You've been a big help."

"Be sure and tell your wife I said hi?"

"I will," just as soon as I figure out who you are, I added silently to myself.

She closed the door and I went back out to the street, considering my options from there. Occasional long-shot jogging partner or sleepy new parents? They were both so tempting I pulled out a coin, assigned heads, and gave it a flip. I caught the coin in my right hand and slapped it onto the back of my left. I lifted my hand. New parents it was.

Number two was a small ranch house, yellow vinyl siding with brown trim. A garden surrounded by a peeling white picket fence out front was completely overgrown, tomatoes rotting on the vine, pea plants run wild and then dried brown. Up two wobbly steps to the front porch, I could hear the cries of an infant through the closed door.

I rang the doorbell, waited, waited some more, and was about to ring the bell again when the door was opened by a male zombie, a verified member of the walking dead. Deep circles ringed his bloodshot brown eyes. Tired brown hair, uncombed, fringed his skull at the ear line, the top mostly bald. He wore jeans and a rumpled denim work shirt rolled to the elbows with stains on both shoulders. And people thought I looked bad. With the door open, the wailing of the child was a whole lot louder.

"Dennis?"

"Yeah?" Dennis' eyes widened just a little bit at the sound of his own name, like he was just waking up. "Something I can do for you?"

"I'm with the Dunboro Fire Department. I'm going down the block talking to neighbors about the fire last week. I was wondering if you saw or heard anything that night."

"Honey, who's there?" I heard a voice call tiredly from somewhere in the house.

Dennis raised his voice and called back, "Some guy from the fire department. He's asking about the fire down the block last week." He shrugged apologetically, "It's kind of crazy here."

"Is it a boy or a girl?"

The man smiled tiredly, "A boy. My little man."

"He'll be sleeping through the night before you know it." Having no children I had no idea if it was true, but it seemed like an encouraging thing to say. Tonk had slept through the very first night we brought him home from the pound, and pretty much every night since.

"That's what my mom keeps telling me. Of course, she went home to her house in Newton last weekend and hasn't been back since."

"So, did you see anything? Hear anything?"

"Hear anything about what?"

"The fire."

"Oh, no, I'm sorry. I didn't even hear the fire trucks."

"Did you know the woman who lived there?"

He shook his head, "No, I'm sorry, I didn't."

"Your wife?"

"I don't think so. You want to ask her?"

I sighed, "No, I don't think that's necessary. Thank you for your time."

Dennis shrugged again, turning away, his eyes already glazing over. The door closed softly.

I looked at my watch. Was it even worth talking to the jogger? Why not, as long as I was in the neighborhood? The alternatives of the workshop and the pictures were too depressing to contemplate.

I went back up the block. In the driveway of number four was a woman facing away from me. She was wearing white sneakers and shiny black spandex running tights with a stripe of yellow winding several times around her right leg climbing up to her waist. She had her left leg up on the bumper of a green Subaru Forester and was bending forward, stretching out her calf and thigh.

I cleared my throat.

She stood up and spun, her hand coming to her throat. "You startled me."

Now that she was standing I could see she was wearing a white T-shirt with a Hard Rock Café logo on it and a black jog bra underneath that showed through the thin material of the shirt. The white earplugs to an iPod were in her ears, the iPod itself clipped to the waistband on her tights.

"I'm sorry, Mrs . . . ?"

She fumbled with the iPod and hit pause. "Mrs. Long. Stephanie Long." She held out her hand.

I took it and gave it a light quick handshake. "Jack Fallon. I'm with the Dunboro Fire Department. I'm sorry again. I'm going down the block asking about the fire last week. Did you see anything that night?"

"No, I'm sorry. I didn't know anything was going on until the fire trucks showed up. Poor Patricia!"

"You knew her?"

"Oh, not well, no. We'd go running together sometimes in Mine Falls Park. Do you know it?"

I nodded. Mine Falls was a pretty good-sized green space in Nashua. An area of trees and paths, some paved, some dirt, a river meandering through it to a pond at one end. In summer it was filled with low impact day hikers, runners, and mountain bikers. In the winter you'd see cross country skiers and even the occasion snowshoe enthusiast depending on the snow cover.

"Well, we ran on sort of similar schedules, and sometimes we'd see each other down there – just coincidence, we never planned it – and we'd run together. I knew her by name, she knew me, but that's about it."

"You wouldn't talk during the run?"

"I'm pretty serious about my running, not a lot of talking,

you know." She tapped the iPod with her fingernail.

I was already tuning her out. Talking to neighbors had been a complete bust. It seemed Patricia and her neighbors had spent little time or effort getting to know each other. That was more of a societal statement than a reflection on Patricia or Dunboro. Did anyone know their neighbors anymore? If I was going to find out about Patricia's life and the people in it, I was going to have to do it from another angle.

Stephanie had kept talking, "Sometimes we'd just run together for a little while, and then we'd come to a place where the path split and we'd take different turns. Sometimes I'd see her running with some kid and I'd just say hi and go my own way."

"Some kid? A child?"

"Not like a child, but he was young, maybe a teenager, maybe just a little older."

"Could you describe him?"

"Shaggy dark hair, thin, gangly. I don't know. A teenager."

"And it was the same one every time?"

"Usually she'd run alone, but when I saw her with someone else other than me it was always him."

"When was this?"

"Oh," she leaned against the car, palms on the bumper, "it's been awhile. Sometime last year? Maybe even a little bit before that."

"You didn't happen to catch a name, did you?"

"No, I'm sorry. Is it important?"

Given the time frame, he must have been Patricia's boyfriend before Michael. So what? Did he have anything do to with her murder? "To be honest," I said, "I have no idea."

Twenty-One

"What happened at her funeral, Jack?"

"I wish you would call her Patricia."

It was one thirty on Sunday and I was back in Beverly
Dell's office, pacing out the bookshelves, sixteen feet of them
along one wall, eight feet high. The bookshelves had been added
recently, sloppy work, all filler and thick white paint where the
pieces didn't quite fit together.

She wore a pleated navy blue skirt that hung to mid-calf, a
white silk shirt with pearl buttons, dark stockings, and black
leather pumps with surprisingly high, pointy heels. Not stilettos,
but close. She looked like she was planning to go out
somewhere dressy later. Was she dating someone? Was she
married? I discretely checked her hands and didn't see a ring.
She did have a thin gold chain around her right ankle.

"I appreciate your need to humanize her, Jack, but as a
firefighter you're going to need to keep perspective. You can't

carry a list of every person you don't save around in your head. No one can live like that."

There was a shelf devoted to Ray Bradbury, one of my personal favorites. Still, I've never been a guy who keeps books he's read, with the exception of some technical books I've kept for reference, and wondered a little bit about people who do. Did they plan to read them again someday, or did they just like having them around?

"That's hard to do. It's doesn't seem right."

"I know, but that's the way it has to be. The alternative is too self-destructive."

Now on my fifth day without sleep, I could see her point. Still, I knew my sister, an oncologist on Long Island, lost patients. It was inevitable. What had she told me? Each doctor keeps a private cemetery they walk through alone. Doctors lost patients, firefighters lost, what did we call them? Victims? Clients? I went over to the chair and sat down. "Let me ask you a question. Have you ever had a patient, someone you've been counseling, commit suicide?"

"Yes, I have," she said quietly.

"You have to get to know them to treat them, right? You can't treat patients without humanizing them."

"Of course."

"So how do you do it?"

"I try and do the best I can, and understand that's all I can do. There will be more people I can help in the future, but I can't do that if I can't get over the ones I couldn't help in the past."

I nodded, but more to myself than to her. She left me alone, let me assimilate that at my own pace.

Then, "What happened at Patricia's funeral?"

"I saw her sister and her parents there. I spoke with her sister at the reception."

"About what?"

"Why would a woman date a married man?"

"Patricia's sister is dating a married man?"

"No, Patricia was."

She leaned back in her chair, carefully folded one leg underneath her, smoothing her skirt down over her knees. "There could me many reasons. Without having known her I would have no way of knowing what her motivation might have been."

"Can you give me some educated guesses?"

"Some women do it for the thrill. Sampling the forbidden fruit and all that. Sometimes a woman will date a married man to demonstrate her power, her independence, or as a way of avoiding commitment. If a woman believes all men are liars or cheaters, dating a married man reinforces her belief of the men in the world around her. A woman with low self-esteem might date a married man because she doesn't believe she deserves more. There could be other reasons as well which I haven't covered. Does that answer your question?"

"I notice you didn't mention love. Couldn't there be love between them?"

"Without going into how often lust is mistaken for love, the woman has to know a relationship with a married man is fundamentally limited. He won't leave his wife, or if he does then she would have to live with the understanding she destroyed another marriage, another family, whatever he might have told her about how unhappy he was. And beyond that, if she becomes his wife, she would always have to wonder about him, the old saying about a man who cheats with you will someday cheat on you."

"You make it sound like such fun."

"Oh, I'm sure there's an element to it that is fun, or at least exciting, or no one would do it, but it's in no way a healthy relationship. Does it have anything to do with her murder?"

"I don't know." I didn't know. I was trying to put together a puzzle and I almost certainly didn't have all the pieces. I didn't even know what picture I was trying to make. And I got the feeling some joker had run into the room and turned off the lights on me. "I'm going to talk to some of her coworkers tomorrow morning, see if they know anything about her personal life that might lead me somewhere."

"Getting yourself more involved is not going to help your insomnia."

"I know, but I need to try. Can you understand that?"

"No, Jack, I honestly can't understand that. Do you think you can catch her killer? Do you think you can do something the police can't?"

I didn't have an answer to that, and so kept quiet.

"You need to start thinking about yourself. There can be serious side effects to long-term insomnia." She said this forcefully, and then more softly, "I think we should have another session tomorrow." She got up from her chair and went to the appointment book on her desk.

"I said I'm going to talk to her coworkers tomorrow."

She sighed, "You said tomorrow morning. How about after that? Two o'clock?"

"You're going to help me in spite of myself, aren't you?"

"I'm certainly going to try." She made a mark in the appointment book, then returned to her seat. "Your wife called me," she said as she sat down.

She waited to see if I had any comment so I threw her a sort of noncommittal grunt.

"She's very worried about you."

Her concerns were starting to feel as though they were smothering me, and that internal anger, that tension, created a twisting sensation in my guts. I clenched my jaw and bit down on the inside of my lip, tasting blood.

"I'm worried about you too, Jack," she added.

I gave her a grim smile, devoid of humor, "Aren't we all."

Twenty-Two

There's something about the dentist office that is at once futuristic and medieval. The gleaming stainless steel instruments, the X-ray machine looking like a cross between a robotic assistant and a Buck Rogers death ray as it hangs from its articulated arm over the patient, the fingernails-on-a-blackboard scream of the drills and the moaning of the condemned. You can tell you've walked into a dentist office even blindfolded, assailed at the door by the commingled odors of disinfectant and burning teeth. There's also the distinctive glassy rattle of the little window sliding open on its bearings in front of the receptionist. I've never seen those windows at any location other than a dentist office.

The receptionist slid open her little window shortly after I walked in the door, announced by a wooden wind chime mounted on a bracket which the door whacked every time it opened. "Mr. Fallon? If you'll take a seat, we'll call on you when we're ready."

I sat down in one of the wooden chairs with blue leatherette

cushions in the waiting area. The only other people there were a
mother with her child, a thin boy with a shaggy mop of brown
hair who sat Indian-style at her feet, looking at a *Highlights*
magazine on the floor in front of him. He was bent over so far,
his elbows resting on the floor, that it seemed like some
advanced yoga position, something that made my hip sockets
ache just watching him.

It was sort of a blast from the past seeing a *Highlights*
magazine again. I recalled reading them myself as a child about
the same age as this one was now on the floor of Dr. Marquette's
office in Colebrook. Almost thirty years later kids are still
looking for the shape of a spoon hidden in the grain of a tree
trunk.

On a table at my side were *Soap Opera Digest*, *Modern
Bride*, *Popular Mechanics*, and *Knit Simple* magazines.
Seriously, a magazine devoted entirely to knitting?

"Mr. Fallon, if you'll come with me please?" The name on
the tag pinned to her scrub top read "C.J.", and she wore white
sneakers and surgical scrub green ensemble, the top of which
was patterned with many big disembodied teeth floating over the
green background. She had brown curly hair, a small face, and
pale eyes, a color which depending on the light could have been
either grey or very light blue.

I followed her up a flight of stairs to the second floor, which
was subdivided with a number of high cubical walls reaching
most of the way to the acoustic tile ceiling. Somewhere off to
my right I could hear the sucking sound of the saliva vacuum.
She led me off to the left.

The cube she took me to was, I imagine, much like all the
other spaces on the floor. There was a large dentist's chair, all
steel and green vinyl, which probably would have looked right at
home next to an iron maiden or a rack. A white-enameled steel
desk unit stood against one wall. On top was a tray holding an
array of instruments, a trial-sized toothpaste, a toothbrush, and

several spools of dental floss. A white plastic clipboard with papers on it and a plant in a hammered copper pot were next to the instrument tray. On the wall hung a particularly graphic poster displaying the horrors of gum disease; a smile of big, yellow, misaligned tombstones jammed haphazardly into bleeding and weeping sockets. Lovely.

She hung a little bib around my neck on a chain. As I leaned back in the chair I could feel my shirt stick to the sweat on my back.

Did I mention I don't like going to the dentist? It was probably the result of having seen *Marathon Man* too many times as a teenager.

She hooked a little stool on wheels out from under the desk unit with her foot and pulled it underneath her as she sat down and picked up the clipboard. "Mr. Fallon, I see you're a new patient here. Are you new to the area?"

"No, my wife and I have been living in Dunboro about three years now."

"Where did you live before?"

"New York City."

"So the last time you saw a dentist would have been back in New York?"

I shook my head. "I went for a cleaning during the summer, around July, at a dentist in Milford."

She made a few marks on the papers on the clipboard. "OK." She put the clipboard aside and flipped on a light mounted on a double-jointed arm which she adjusted so it shined on my face. Next she picked up a small dental mirror and a wickedly sharp-looking pick from the tray. Hadn't there been a slasher flick where the killer had used one of those? "What seems to be the problem today?"

"I don't have a problem."

"Are you looking for a new dentist?"

"Not particularly."

"So what can I do for you?"

"I'd like to talk with someone here who knew Patricia Woods."

She put the instruments back onto the tray, carefully aligning them with the other instruments already there. "I don't understand. You made an appointment. Are you a police officer?"

"I made an appointment because it seemed like the easiest way to reserve a block of time without interrupting other patients, and I'm not a police officer, I'm a firefighter. I'm the one who found Patricia in the house."

"I knew her," she said carefully, continuing to minutely adjust the instruments, "we all did, but I don't understand what it is you want."

"I want to know more about her. I need to know what happened and why."

She was silent for so long that I thought I was losing her so I pleaded my case, "Since the night I found her in the fire, I haven't been able to sleep. Please, I need to understand."

I was pretty sure she wasn't going to answer me, and then she said, "I'll tell you what. The other hygienists and I are going to lunch together at the Chinese place at the end of the block at one. Could we talk then?"

I wasn't sure I wanted to do some type of mass interview; I would have far preferred to talk to them separately where their individual memories were less likely to contaminate each other. I also realized I was unlikely to get a better opportunity. A quick glance at my watch showed me I must be the last appointment before her lunch break. "OK. I'll see you there." I started to undo the clip holding the bib on.

"As long as you're here, do you want a cleaning?"

"Well..."

"*Marathon Man?*"

"What's that?"

"The movie, *Marathon Man.* Whenever you think of dentists you think of that movie, right?"

"How did you-?"

"I could see it in your face the minute you sat down. That movie ruined dentistry for an entire generation. If I asked you to describe your feelings towards dentistry in one word, what would that word be?"

I thought about it, quickly narrowing it down to two choices, but unable to get it easily down to one. "Can I use two words?"

"Sure."

"Fear and trepidation."

She laughed, a full throaty sound. "That's original. You do realize with modern techniques that dentistry is nearly painless."

I finished undoing the bib clip and handed it to her, "It's the nearly part I have trouble getting around. One o'clock at the

Chinese place?"

"Yeah."

"I'll see you there."

I left her and found my way out of the dental cube farm.
When I got to the sidewalk outside, I began to go towards the
truck, but then had no idea where I would drive to for twenty
minutes. Instead I walked to the Chinese restaurant, a little hole
in the wall with some Chinese characters stencilled on the big
front plate glass window with the words "Happy Garden"
underneath them in red. Inside it was just a half-dozen brown
Formica tables with tubular aluminum chairs around them, the
cushions covered in some gold fabric. A long counter at one end
of the room separated the kitchen and dining areas, steam rising
from several woks over burners.

"Table for one?" A man in black Dockers and a starched
white shirt asked.

"My, ah, friends will be along soon. I'll need a table for-"
How many? C.J. had used the word hygienists I was certain,
plural, which meant there were at least two others besides her. I
tried to figure out how many hygienists an office of that size
might need and realized I didn't have even an educated guess.
"Five. A table for five, please."

He grabbed five menus and led me to a table for six by the
window. "Can I bring you anything before your friends get
here?"

"Some tea would be nice."

"Right away." He left, then returned moments later with
white ceramic pot of tea and five little white cups. I poured a
cup, tasted it and found it very bitter, and added two packets of
sugar.

I sat there quietly stirring my tea and thinking of what questions I wanted to ask, until C.J. came into the restaurant with two other women.

She spotted me at the table and the three of them came over. "Mr. Fallon, this is Kathy" she indicated the woman on her left, "and Teresa," she indicated the woman on her right.

Kathy was the oldest, with her brown hair shot through with some grey. She was thin almost to the point of emaciation, with pinched features and a mouth bent into a permanent frown. Teresa was young, dirty blonde, with a round cherubic face which almost looked like she still had baby fat. She was probably very close to Patricia's age, and I pegged her for the person at the office who would have known her the best. She also struck me as the gossipy sort, and I thought that if I could figure out how to get her rolling she would talk easily.

"Thank you for coming to speak with me. Take a seat. I'm buying lunch."

Teresa and C.J. took seats. Kathy remained standing. "We talked about it on the way over. We're not sure we should talk to you before we've talked to the police."

The police hadn't talked to them yet? It had been, what? I counted it out silently to myself. It had been seven days since Patricia had been murdered, and for me six sleepless nights. I wondered from what angle the Sheriff was working on the case, because he should have been down here talking to her coworkers first thing. What the heck had he been doing all this time?

"How about I ask some questions, and you answer the ones you want and don't the ones you don't. Either way, lunch is on me. Fair?"

"That seems fair," Teresa said, "Doesn't that seem fair, Kathy?"

She sounded almost like she was pleading with Kathy, who grudgingly took a seat at the table. If I had a problem here, Kathy was it.

The man came and took our orders and left. I stuck to small talk, asking how they had become dental hygienists, telling a few of my funny firefighter stories. Even Kathy loosened up a little bit, her mouth changing from a frown to indifference. Nine-eleven was definitely helping me here; since that date people have been giving firefighters a lot more courtesy and respect. If not for a sort of misplaced hero worship it was possible that they wouldn't even be talking to me.

I measured time, waiting until the food arrived before asking my first question. "Was Patricia at work that day?"

Kathy snapped back on her frown. You can't win them all. Teresa answered quickly, "Yeah, she was there a full day. Seven to four-thirty."

"Did any of you notice anything? Did she behave strangely?"

Teresa shook her head. "I didn't notice anything? C.J.?"

"No."

Kathy just keep frowning, took a sip of tea, and her frown deepened. To be fair, that was probably the bitter tea and not my fault at all.

"Did any of you know anything about a man she was dating?"

Kathy and C.J. looked blank, but Teresa looked uncomfortable, so I decided to follow it. "Her sister told me about him. She said his name is Mike and that he's married."

Teresa relaxed a little, relieved she wouldn't have to reveal that which I already knew. "There's not much more to say about it that I know." She toyed with her chicken with cashew nuts without eating much.

"Were there any problems in the relationship? Do you know if his wife knew?" I dug into lunch special number six: beef with broccoli, fried rice, and an egg roll. The fried rice was a smidge too salty, but otherwise it was quite good. The egg roll had just the right amount of crispiness and chewiness to it. The broccoli was perfect with just a little crunch left instead of being cooked into mush as so often happens. I'd have to come back to this place again with Valerie.

"She seemed happy about it. She would talk about their dates, and once showed me a bracelet he bought her. I have no idea what his wife knew, or what she thought about it if she did."

"Did you ever see them together?"

C.J. answered this one between mouthfuls of vegetable chop suey. "He was her patient, so we all saw them together many times. But Patricia was always completely professional at work. You would not even have known they were dating to look at them together in the office."

I wasn't getting anywhere with Mike from Amherst. Patricia had told her sister and coworker that they were happy together, that she knew he was married and accepted it. From my talk with Samantha Carston she certainly seemed upset about the affair, but I didn't think she knew anything about it until after Patricia's murder, though no one else had confirmed that yet.

Kathy ate steadily, I think spicy shredded pork, without speaking. I was kind of amazed at her metabolism given how thin she was.

"Have you talked to her last boyfriend?" Teresa asked.

"Did you know him?"

"Not really. Not any more than I knew about Michael. I just remember her telling me she broke up with him when she started seeing Michael, like a year ago, that he wasn't happy about it."

C.J. and Kathy were rapt. This was entirely news to them. Me too.

"Did she say anything specific? Was she afraid of him?"

Teresa started, suddenly embarrassed to be the center of attention. "No, I didn't mean anything like that at all. He was just some kid."

"What do you mean, some kid?"

"She told me he was young. I got the feeling she meant that he was in college, or maybe even high school."

So, Patricia dated young guys, maybe high school guys, and married guys, and maybe this was the same person her neighbor had seen Patricia running with from time to time. Or maybe not. A whole lot of maybes.

"Did she ever tell you his name?"

"Dan."

"That's it?"

"That's all I can remember her telling me."

Wow. Next stop, some guy named Dan, who was in college, or maybe high school, and was maybe a runner, and was maybe local, or maybe not. I wished myself luck; I'd need it.

Twenty-Three

"I feel like I don't know what I'm doing anymore."

I was back in Beverly Dell's office, contemplating an entire shelf of Frank Herbert books. She was apparently something of a Frank Herbert Dune purist, sticking only to books Herbert actually wrote in his lifetime, not those written by his kids in the series after his death.

"That's to be expected. It's been six nights since you've had any real sleep, right?" Beverly spoke to me from a perch on the edge of her roll top desk. She was in full western mode; blue jeans, dark green blouse with white stitching, tooled leather boots with low wooden heels. She had hooked the heels of her boots on one of the drawer pulls and rested her elbows on her knees.

"Yes." A personal record for me. I had once before stayed up one hundred and four hours in a row as a graduate student to finish a lab report. I was at – it disturbed me at the amount of time it took me to do the simple math – one hundred sixty hours and counting. I think I was nearing a world's record, though the Guinness Book had stopped accepting record attempts which jeopardized someone's health years ago.

"Have you had any hallucinations? Movement in the corner of your eye that turns out to be nothing when you look at it? Auditory hallucinations of any kind?"

"No, nothing like that. Is that what I have to look forward to?"

"Perhaps. I'm far from an expert on the science of sleep. Some articles I've read recently indicate that hallucinations are fairly common."

"Uh-huh." I tried reading some of the spines of the books in front of me, but had trouble focusing, then had trouble making sense of the letters when I managed to focus on them, almost as if they were written in a foreign language. "I spoke to Patricia's coworkers earlier today."

"I remember you saying you were planning to talk with them. What did they tell you?"

"Patricia was dating some young kid before the married man."

"How young?"

"They didn't know. Maybe he was in college, maybe high school."

"She was just a few years out of college herself, wasn't she?"

"She didn't go to college, but she was about that age, yes."

Beverly shifted her seat on the edge of the desk, unhooking the heel of one boot from the drawer pull and letting that leg dangle free. She leaned back with her palms on the desktop, "Young adults out on their own for the first time will experiment with many different types of relationships, trying to find the most compatible fit. There's nothing unusual about that."

"One of them said the kid was upset when she dumped him for the married man."

"Upset enough to kill her?"

I shrugged and turned away from examining what I hoped was her foreign language science fiction collection. Either that or I was in serious trouble. I went over and flopped into one of the two wingback chairs rubbing my palms on the knees of my jeans. "I don't know."

"What do you know about him?"

"I've pretty much told you everything. Oh, except his name is Dan."

"Dan? That's it?"

"That's all I have. I don't know how I'm going to find him."

She got off the desk and came and sat down in the other chair. "I think I should refer you to a doctor in Concord, a sleep specialist who can give you more directed care into your insomnia."

"I'm not sure what a doctor can do for me that you can't. I'm not going to get doped up on medication."

"Jack, you know what's keeping you awake," she said firmly but not unkindly, "your inability or your unwillingness to let Patricia's death go. You're a firefighter, Jack. You did the best you could, and, through no fault of yours, she died. You need to at least be looking for a way to accept that. I'm beginning to think you may need to be hospitalized." The way she dangled that last part out felt a little like a threat.

"What can I do?"

"Go home. Let the police do their job. Someone is going to solve Patricia's murder, but that someone doesn't have to be you. I need you to at least try to help yourself or I can't help you."

I leaned my head against the chair back and closed my eyes. I had been a problem solver my whole life. I had chosen it as a career. That's what a PhD in physics meant to me. I would look at the big fundamental questions: Where did the universe come from? Where was it going to? What did it all mean? I would look at these questions, I would develop equations, and I would find the answers.

Except people didn't come down to math. There was no theorem I could apply, no formula I could develop, that would tell me who had killed Patricia or why. There was no filter that I could use to separate the signal of the guilty from the overwhelming background noise of the innocent. I was going to have to understand that. I was going to have to internalize it. And I was going to have to get some sleep.

"I'll try, and I'd like to keep trying with you."

"Promise?" she asked emphatically, but she smiled when she said it.

"I promise."

She got up from the chair and went over to the appointment book on the desk. "Is tomorrow morning or afternoon better for you?"

"My schedule is wide open."

"Tomorrow at four?"

"Four it is."

I left through the side door, passing a white Toyota Camry parked behind Beverly's Hyundai in the driveway on my way to my truck parked on the street. My phone rang just as I was opening the door, so I closed it again and pulled my phone out while leaning against the side. The caller ID showed me an unfamiliar number.

"Hello?"

"Mr. Fallon? This is Rachael. We met at my sister's funeral and you gave me your card."

"I remember, Rachael. What's up?"

"I found some letters written to me by my sister. I thought you might like to see them."

I took a deep breath and let it out. Was this any way to separate myself from Patricia's murder like I had promised Beverly that I would?

But I had a single question I needed to know the answer to. I would ask it, get my answer, and then let it go. "Did you read them over?"

"Yes."

"Was there any mention of her last boyfriend? A boy named Dan?"

From her sharp intake of breath I knew there was something there. "What, Rachael? What did she write?"

"Well, it isn't so much what she wrote, but reading over the letters jogged my memory. In the letters she just talks about how

157

he was some high school kid she dated, and then she broke up with him to start dating Michael last year."

This wasn't exactly news. "OK."

"She told me later on the phone he was upset about it. She was worried about how upset he was."

"What are you saying? Do you think he killed her?"

She said the next so quietly that I almost thought for a moment the call had been dropped. "He committed suicide."

"What?"

"He killed himself, Jack, and my sister blamed herself for it."

Christ.

Twenty-Four

If you had asked me exactly what had changed, I probably couldn't have told you. Maybe talking with Beverly Dell was actually helping me in some vague, hard-to-define way. Maybe I was finally recovering from some unrealized trauma at seeing Patricia dead. Or maybe my subconscious had simply decided to stop torturing me at night. I had a dead ex-boyfriend, a live married boyfriend, and no idea who had killed Patricia or why. I had tried my best and was getting nowhere, and it was long past time to let it go.

Valerie and I sat down for dinner. We had roasted pork loin with a mushroom wine sauce and the last of the season's sugar snap peas from our garden steamed to perfection. I felt, as I sliced the pork into hearty three-quarter-inch thick planks which trailed a succulent steam into my face, like a gyroscope spinning out the final fragments of its angular momentum.

The sky outside faded from blue to indigo to black as we ate, and I talked about Beverly and things that had been said in her office. I apologized for my behavior, and said I was working to try and let Patricia and her murder slide into the past. At least that's what I said, but as I said it, it somehow felt like something less than the truth and more like something I desperately wanted to be true.

Afterwards we took Tonk out for a last chance to do his business before bedtime. He snuffed in the high grass at the edge of the woods while we walked. I reached out hesitantly and found Valerie's hand and our fingers entwined as we passed the old rock wall that borders the Southern edge of our property.

Rock walls like it crisscross the state by the hundreds if not thousands, thrown there by pioneer farmers who had no doubt cursed every time their plow blades threw up another geological remnant. Such things today have taken on the aura of some kind of rural kitsch and are sometimes stolen, stone by stone, to be reassembled as part of the elaborate landscaping on the grounds of a multimillion dollar estate in Connecticut or New York. A similar wall two streets over had been removed quietly over the span of a weekend last summer, though the people who lived there were undergoing an ugly divorce and maybe the wall had been taken as part of a custody battle – we never did get the whole story. I was happy to report that our wall appeared intact in the meager light cast by the razor's edge of the waxing crescent moon.

I called Tonk in from the rough and the three of us headed indoors and upstairs. Tonk headed directly to his pillow in the corner of our bedroom while I brushed my teeth and Valerie took her face off, a process requiring roughly the same chemicals used to strip varnish from an antique desk. The price of modern beauty.

The sheets were crisp and smooth as I slid between them, the pillow soft behind my head. Without a word Valerie kissed me on the eyelids and molded herself to me, her body warm and supple, beautiful and naked, next to mine.

Sleep, effortless sleep, was a wide placid pool yawning

beneath me. I could feel myself already slipping into the cool water, drifting with the gentle eddy currents where ever they would take me.

And then my pager went off.

Twenty-Five

Viewed from high above, as seen, for example, by someone casually looking out the window of a passing jumbo jet as they Hoover up a small foil packet of honey roasted peanuts, Dunboro looks like a rumpled bed sheet dyed in shades of green and grey. Narrow ridges of granite and iron shelter shallow valleys of oak, pine, and maple from the worst Nor'easter gales and, more germane at the moment, radio signals. The voice pager on the passenger seat hissed and crackled but did little else. I listened anyway – you never know when you'll get a lucky reflection off an iron deposit or a skip off the atmosphere, the sound coming in as clear as if the dispatcher were broadcasting from the pickup bed – trying to get some idea of what I was headed into. A five-alarm blaze? A cat stuck in a storm drain? I regulated my adrenaline level like Sherlock Holmes titering opium, listening to every pop and click as if it might contain information of great import. By the time I reached the station house however I had not gotten lucky. I had only managed to filter the single word "fire" from the ether, and I was not even certain if it was used as a noun or an adjective.

Engine 3 was idling on the apron when I arrived. I grabbed my gear, jumped in the back, and away we went.

"Engine three responding with a crew of three." I heard Russell Burtran radio in, which dispatch acknowledged a moment later.

"Mr. Fallon, so good of you to join us," Bruce Jonet said from the seat next to me.

His twin brother Robert leaned forward in his seat so he could see me past Bruce. "Hey Jack, how's it hanging?"

I put my arms into the sleeves and shrugged on my jacket, "I could complain, but who would listen? Any idea what the call is?"

Robert and Bruce both shook their heads, but Russell filled in the details by yelling at us over his left shoulder from the officer's seat. "Gentlemen, there's a car burning in front of a residence which the good citizens of Dunboro would like us to extinguish. Brothers Jonet, you're on the hose line. Fallon, I'd like you to check on the home owner."

Our assignments given, the brothers strapped on their air tanks and attached their facemasks to the regulators while I ran the clasps on my jacket and put on my helmet. When the truck rolled to a stop I popped the door open on my side and jumped to the ground.

There, I froze.

The turn of the century compact ranch house, the wide farmer's porch, the black shutters, the white siding now painted orange by the firelight of the Hyundai Sonata burning in the driveway, the color of which was a little difficult to determine now but which I was certain had been burgundy until quite recently.

We were at Beverly Dell's house.

A feeling of undeniable dread grew within me.

Bruce was stuck in the doorway behind me, waiting for me to move. "Fallon! Get out of the way! Gawkers behind the police line!"

I took half a step forward and he and his brother shouldered past me causing me to stumble. When I regained my balance I looked out into the street where Bobby Dawkins had parked his cruiser partially blocking the road. He stood beside it keeping crane-necked neighbors in winter coats and fuzzy slippers, like some peculiar species of bird, away from the fire. Everyone loves a good show.

I shook off my paralysis and jumped the short picket fence surrounding the yard, leaping up the four steps onto the farmer's porch in a single bound and coming to the front door. In training class they had flung the mnemonic 'try before you pry' at us, hoping we would take an extra second to attempt to open a door normally first without destroying it, just in case it was unlocked. How they expected me to do that when my heart was running a hundred and forty beats per minute was beyond me.

I completely ignored the doorknob, letting my shoulder do the work. Ancient brick molding and jam splintering as the door burst open and bounced hard against the wall. Fragments of wood scattered across the carpeting.

"Beverly?" I called, an unmistakable edge of panic in my voice.

The house was silent except for the sound of my own rasping breath.

The light bars on the police and fire vehicles lit the room stroboscopically as though dozens of people were just outside taking hundreds of pictures, flash frying the shadows of the plants alongside the windows into stark relief against the far wall.

With no knowledge of where the light switches were, I opted to turn on the flashlight clipped to my jacket and moved quickly down the hallway to my left. It only ran for a short distance, just two bedrooms and a bathroom, and I searched them all and found them empty. I came back into the front hall again and then did the living room and kitchen. Beyond the kitchen I found a master bedroom suite addition, something tacked onto the back of the house in the late 70's or early 80's which didn't fit in with the architectural style of the rest of the house. I searched it: the bed was unmade but empty. I checked the office last. Standing on the same spot where I had stood for the first time less than five days earlier, I listened to the thrum of engine 3's heavy pumps and the snap, crackle, and pop of the radios outside.

She wasn't here.

My heart was pounding in my throat as I went back through the front hall, my boots crunching on the pieces of wood, and onto the porch. The Brothers Jonet had knocked the fire down. The car was just a smoldering shell, though small puffs of thick black smoke escaped past the weather stripping around the trunk.

Robert came from behind the fire truck twirling a pry bar in his hand like a parade grand marshal. "I think the spare is still burning," he told his brother who was standing nearby holding the hose nozzle, "I'm going to open the trunk."

He drove the business end of the bar into the crack between the bumper and the trunk lid and leaned on it. The heat-stressed metal creaked and then the trunk popped open. The lid hinged up allowing a plume of dark smoke to escape. As it cleared, Bruce and Robert looked inside.

The pry bar slid from Robert's grip and fell to the pavement where it rang very loudly and distinctly even against all of the background noise.

"Holeeeey fuck." He said.

His brother dropped the nozzle he was holding and turned away. He took several stumbling steps and fell to his knees, tearing the respirator mask from his face and vomiting into the grassy strip next to the driveway.

I moved down the four steps off the porch on feet that felt like they were not my own, slowly past the fence line to the car. As I walked up the side of the car towards the trunk I got a view of a trapezoidal slice of the trunk interior that grew wider the farther I moved.

A pair of western boots came into view first, tooling marks still visible in the darkened leather, and a single glowing ember, like an eye, looking at me from the depths of one charred low-stacked wooden heel. A heavy plastic strap, some kind of zip tie, remained holding the ankles together. Clad in denim jeans, the legs had been folded accordion style at the knees and hips so the body could be fit into the trunk. The blouse of indeterminate color had become untucked at the back, the exposed strip of skin blackened, blistered, and oozing viscous gravy. I thought of the pork roast I had carved earlier that evening and had to swallow hard. The hands were drawn behind the back, whatever was binding them, probably another zip tie, had embedded deeply in the flesh of the wrists leaving an ugly red channel.

The head and face, exposed to the fire, had taken the worst of the damage. The hair had burned and curled up into a short, stiff brillo. As soon as I noticed it I became aware of the reek of burned hair, and then it was like I couldn't smell anything else. The ear on the side of the head that I could see and most of the nose was gone. Several strips of clear tape, like packing tape, had been placed over the mouth, the lips and skin behind it remarkably well protected by just those few layers. The eyelids had burned off and the vitreous humor had boiled away, leaving the eyes themselves shrunken up like raisins deep in their sockets.

Though burned almost beyond recognition, I knew this was what was left of Beverly Dell.

I turned away from the trunk, trying to look at or think about anything other than what was inside. Bruce, who had stopped vomiting, was sitting heavily on the bumper of the fire truck next to Russell and his brother. The neighbors were all on tiptoes trying desperately to see. I had an urge to grab them by their lapels and rip them right out of their fuzzy slippers to drag them over, one by one, and show them what they were missing. Bobby Dawkins and I locked eyes for a moment, and then he snagged a teenager with a cell phone camera trying to slip by him. Could CNN be far behind?

It was all crazy. Was there some thread connecting Patricia and Beverly? Or was it possible that two murders in a town the size of Dunboro both involving fire less than a week apart could be *not* connected? In the past week the quiet town of Dunboro was starting to look like a sequel to *The Hills Have Eyes*. I couldn't make any sense of it.

There was one thing I did know, though. My good night's sleep was shot to hell.

Twenty-Six

The trucks and equipment were cleaned and repacked without any of the usual banter. For a department that hadn't had a death at a fire scene in so long tales of it were handed down almost like some kind of oral tradition, two murders in a week were weighing heavily. When the work was completed the guys just kind of drifted off, feet shuffling against the concrete floor, the door on the west side of the station house swinging closed on its hinges with a bang, the sounds of their cars driving away.

I was sitting on the rear step deck of Engine 2 debating what I should do with myself when John came around turning off the lights and found me there.

"Shit, Jack, come on back to my office."

We went up the stairs at the rear of the station house into his office. He left the overhead fluorescent lights off and instead turned on a green-shaded banker's lamp with a brass stand. It looked oddly incongruous on a desk littered with pieces of

firefighting equipment; an ax which needed sharpening, a tank
regulator with the back taken off, a flashlight with a cracked
case. He sat down in the leather desk chair heavily, the springs
squawking like angry birds. I took a seat in the other office
chair, a straight-backed oak job with a green leather cushion. I
flashed on my interview with the Sheriff in this room that felt as
though it had taken place a lifetime ago.

We sat in silence in the muted glow of the lamp.

He leaned forward and pulled open the lower right hand
drawer in his desk. Digging way into the back he came out with
a dusty bottle of Jack Daniels.

"Care for a snort?" He held it up in the light, the amber
liquid sloshing inside.

"Whiskey? It's not my drink."

"Not mine either." He spun the cap off of the bottle and sat
there for a moment resting it against his knee. "To Beverly Dell.
May the son of a bitch who killed her rot in the hottest corner of
hell." He drank from the bottle and held it out to me.

I took the bottle from him by the neck. "To Beverly Dell,"
I agreed, and drank. It tasted to me almost exactly like
turpentine smelled. I handed the bottle back to him.

"I've known Beverly since the day she was born. Knew her
older brother, too."

"I didn't know she had a brother."

"Jacob was killed, oh, ten years ago in a car accident down
in Mass. Beverly was fifteen or so at the time." He took a drink.
"God, why does there have to be so much fucking tragedy in the
world?"

The way he said it sounded almost like a prayer.

"Can you think of anyone who would have had a reason to hurt her?"

"Not a soul."

He held the bottle out to me and I raised my hand in refusal, then figured what the hell and took the bottle and drank. The second taste was less chemically than the first, holding hints of wood and warmth.

"I know her mother, Loretta, too. She lives in Phoenix now. My wife writes to her regularly, and we still get a Christmas card from her every year. She helped me through the Ridge fire. Helped a bunch of us through it. Christ, I'm going to have to call her and tell her about Beverly," he said this last piece to himself.

He reached out and took the bottle from me and drank quickly, the burden of having to make that phone call nearly punching through his composure.

"Loretta did the counseling thing also?"

"Like mother, like daughter." He held the bottle out to me. "You want more?"

"No, I'm good."

He screwed the cap on and secreted the bottle back into the depths of his desk, closing the drawer with his foot before leaning back in his chair. "You heard about the Ridge fire?"

"Just bits and pieces. I know a kid died."

"Two kids died. The Lowerey's had like thirteen of them at the time. Don't hold me to that, I might be off by one or two. I'm not even sure they knew how many kids they had." He gave a weak smile. "They lived in a house up on Ridge Road, only it was closer to a big pile of lumber than a house. Every time they had another kid, they'd cut a hole in a wall and stick on a room. No plan, no structural work, just room after room. If a hurricane came through here it would have torn that house to pieces, but no hurricane came, and they just kept adding and adding." He stopped there staring off into space.

"The fire?" I prompted him.

"It wasn't much of a fucking fire, I'll tell you that," he picked up the lost thread. "Started in a wood stove vent, mostly contained to the living room, but it filled the whole structure with smoke. We arrived and there were kids everywhere. We'd be trying to get a head count, and one of them would be like 'Where's Jimmy?' and two of them would run back into the house. Guys would keep going in to drag the kids out, and they'd keep running back in again. It was fucking nuts." He eyed the drawer like he was thinking about getting the bottle out again, but then decided against it. He crossed his arms over his chest and leaned back deeper in the chair, which squealed in protest. "The fire got into the walls, and that was all she wrote. There were no fire stops, no doors we could close or roof points we could vent to contain the fire. It was like trying to stop a pile of burning leaves. We just threw water on it and crossed our fingers that all the kids were out."

"But they weren't"

"Nope. Not when all was said and done. Two kids. Their youngest and their oldest, the first and the last. I'm pretty sure I had seen Bill, that was their oldest, outside when we got there, so I think he went back in after the little one."

"When was that?"

He looked up at the calendar hanging over his desk. It was three years old, turned to March, and showed a picture of a broken split rail fence and a field beyond it covered in snow and ice. "Twenty-seven years ago, April third." He pulled up that date faster than he could have the date of his wedding anniversary. "Beyond some car accident deaths, and those are a whole different thing to a firefighter, that's how long it's been since the fire department has had a death in Dunboro. What's happening in my town, Jack?"

As bad as it was for me, I was starting to understand the depths to which the town of Dunboro was being shaken by the murders. The sudden loss of innocence was bringing Dunboro at supersonic speeds into the 21st Century, where murders had become so commonplace it was impossible to turn on the evening news without hearing about one.

"I wish I knew. You going to be OK? Should I call your wife?"

"No, I'm fine. Let her sleep. Tomorrow is going to be a bad one for her. She and Loretta are like sisters."

I left him there in the office and drove back to my home through the darkened streets of Dunboro, dawn still a couple of hours away. I went straight to the workshop, pulled out sheets of sandpaper in gradually increasing grit grades, and got to work sanding and then polishing the panels to a near mirror finish. The ache that set up residence in my wrists and shoulders was exactly the sort of mindless work I hoped would give me some respite from the image of Beverly burned in the trunk of her car.

It didn't work.

Instead I fell into a sort of trance where my mind ran unfettered by the rules of physics or logic. I became convinced that somehow I was at the crux of it all, that I had led the killer from Patricia to Beverly, that I was even responsible for the death of Patricia. I was afraid for Valerie. I was afraid for every person with whom I crossed paths. Would the next fire call be to the fire station itself? Would we be pulling John's body from the smoldering wreckage?

I nearly jumped out of my skin when I heard the door open

behind me.

Valerie came into the shop wrapped in her yellow terrycloth robe with Tonk at her heels, "I heard the truck engine but you didn't come inside. Is something the matter?"

I wiped my hands on a dust rag, and then noticed my sweatshirt was covered in sawdust and brushed at it ineffectively. "Beverly Dell is dead. Someone murdered her."

I watched her face crumple. "What, Jack? How?"

"Someone stuffed her into the trunk of her car and set it on fire."

"Oh my God, Jack!" She came into my arms, sawdust getting all over her robe. "What's going on? Is it related to Patricia's death?"

"I don't know."

"What are you going to do?"

"I'm going to talk to the Sheriff tomorrow. I don't know much, but maybe what I know will help him somehow."

"I'd rather have that conversation now, if it's all the same to you." Bobby Dawkins said from the doorway.

Valerie and I jumped apart like teenagers caught fooling around behind the woodshed. I wondered idly if there was some maximum number of jolts the human heart could take – if at some point it would just seize up like a bad engine or blow out like an old tire. Valerie stood with her hand pressed over her heart.

"I'm sorry, ma'am. I didn't mean to startle you."

The way he said ma'am sounded so Old West that I halfway

expected to hear spurs jingling on his boot heels as he crossed the shop to introduce himself. "I'm Sheriff Bobby Dawkins."

"Nice to meet you Sheriff, considering the circumstances. I'm Valerie." She took his offered hand and gave it a brief squeeze.

The introduction completed he turned to me, "If you know something about what's going on in my town I'd like to hear it."

That was the second time that night I'd heard someone refer to Dunboro as their town. The first time I had heard that phrase used had been from the mouth of Rudy Giuliani after 9/11. It had sounded like a cheap preplanned sound bite then, but coming from the mouths of these men, the Fire Chief and the Sheriff, it felt genuine. These were men who would lay down their lives to protect their town and the people who lived there.

"Would you mind if we did this inside?" Valerie asked as she bundled her robe around her. "I'm going to freeze to death unless Jack wants to turn the heat on in here."

"This doesn't involve you, Mrs. Fallon. And given the circumstances I'd rather talk to your husband down at the police station." His voice held an edge to it, just a bit of menace.

"Jack?" Valerie asked me uncertainly.

"It's OK," I assured her, though I had no idea how much trouble I was in. Perhaps, I realized, it could be quite a lot. I met the Sheriff's eyes. "Let's go."

Twenty-Seven

I had been uncertain if the Sheriff would allow me to drive my own truck down to the police station or if he would handcuff me and cram me into the back of his patrol car. I decided to force the issue, walking away from him after we exited my workshop and heading towards the garage. He hadn't told me to stop, so perhaps I was in less trouble than I thought. I pulled in at a Dunkin Donuts on the way and bought a medium decaf coffee black, and though he had waited while I did so, idling in his car in the parking lot, he didn't follow me inside to nab me if I tried to make a break for it out the back.

The front door of the police department opened into a short stretch of cinderblock hallway painted pale yellow, scarred wooden benches placed on either side of the entranceway. Beyond that was an open area to the left that contained four desks, a number of plain wooden desk chairs, and several unlabelled doorways with no indication of where they might go. Bathrooms, closets, holding cells; there was no way to tell. The room was empty except for the two of us.

The Sheriff pointed me to one of the chairs, "Sit."

I sat. Wiseass that I am, and sleep deprived to boot, I considered barking and lolling out my tongue but didn't. I put the coffee cup in the corner of the desk in front of me.

Somehow up to this point in my life I had never been in a police department before. I was not disappointed to find it as depressing and flatly functional as any other government office I had ever been in. The slice of drizzly grey sky visible through the windows didn't help any. It was rapidly turning into one of those miserable, dank New England fall days which never make it into the tourist brochures. The day was brightened somewhat by the camera lights being set up outside by news crews, the second gristly murder in Dunboro in less than a week making regional headlines. It was only seven in the morning and Beverly's car was probably still too hot to touch. Man, those guys moved fast.

He went around and sat down on the other side of the desk, wasting no time getting down to brass tacks. "What are you doing here, Mr. Fallon?"

"You tell me. You're the one who told me to come down here."

"That's not what I meant and you know it. First you find Patricia at the fire, and then I see you at her funeral. Now I see you at the fire that killed Beverly Dell. Care to comment?"

"I'm a firefighter, so I find it hardly surprising that I would be at fires in town, do you?"

"And the funeral?"

"Paying my respects."

"Then you knew her?" He pulled the black notebook from his hip pocket, flipped back the cover, and uncapped a pen.

"Not before the fire, no."

"So you've attended the funerals of everyone who died at a fire you responded to."

"She was my first. If I continue the trend in the future I'll be sure to let you know."

I was laying it on a little thick, and Bobby let me see his disproval with a solid frown. "How are you connected to the murders of Patricia Woods and Beverly Dell?"

"I'm not." I insisted, "What makes you think they're even connected to each other?"

"Do you have any idea how many murders have been committed in Dunboro in the town's history?"

"None."

He looked surprised that I knew that, and a little upset, like a guy who has just had a really great joke ruined by someone else who spit out the punch line first. He closed his notebook and placed his pen on top, then leaned back in his chair and folded his arms across his chest, "So tell me, how am I supposed to believe that the one person who has shown up at every crime scene is not involved?"

I didn't have an answer for him, and the quickie waking nightmare I had had in my shop, that I was somehow the link between the two murders, was starting to feel a lot less ludicrous. "What about her boyfriend?" I heard myself say, somewhat lamely.

"Michael Carston? I don't think he has a link to Beverly Dell, do you?"

He paused, but I didn't have an answer for him.

"Come on, don't be shy," he said, his voice full of sarcasm, "I want to know what you think," then the sarcasm dropped away and the menace was back, "because he told me you questioned him about their relationship the day after Patricia was murdered."

I opened my mouth but nothing came out.

"Oh, and here's something odd. His wife, Samantha. She says someone identifying himself as a Dunboro police officer spoke with her also."

"I didn't . . ."

"Identify yourself as a police officer? Boy, I sure hope not, because you would be in a heck of a lot of trouble if you did." He stood up and came around the desk to lean over me. I felt myself involuntarily shrinking back in my seat, like a mouse trying to make itself look smaller when the shadow of a bird of prey passes overhead. "When you went to the house fire in which Patricia died you wrote in your witness statement that the front door was locked, that you had to break it open. Is that correct?"

The question threw me and my mind tried to look at it from every angle to see if there was some hidden meaning in it. I couldn't find one and my delay in answering him was becoming obvious, so I went with the truth. "Yes."

"What about the back door?" He said quickly.

It was then that I saw the jaws of the trap looming in front of me. I was coming to realize that regardless of what some people thought about him, Bobby Dawkins wasn't stupid. "I didn't check it."

"I did. It was locked with a floor cleat. Only I went back the night after the fire and it wasn't locked. What do you think about that?"

He knew! Somehow he knew! He had seen me? Or my truck? I shook my head slowly.

He opened his mouth, and while I couldn't imagine what he was going to say next, I was sure I wasn't going to like it, that it was very possibly going to end with the phrase 'you're under arrest.'

But before he could say whatever it was, he was interrupted by the appearance of a man at the office entrance. "Sheriff Dawkins?" the man asked.

The Sheriff stood up and I instantly found myself breathing easier, as though I had been under some great atmospheric pressure which had just eased. "Yes?"

The man came forward, presenting his business card with the flourish of a magician pulling a bouquet of flowers from a hidden tube in his sleeve. "G. Franklin Tolland. You called my office earlier concerning a patient list for Beverly Dell."

As the business card changed hands I caught a glimpse of raised black and silver script, the words 'Attorney at Law' against the ivory of heavy high-quality card stock. Snazzy.

G. Franklin Tolland reminded me more than anything else of the government legal eagle that had swooped into the lab of a naïve twenty-six year old graduate student and bludgeoned all his plans for making the world a better place with a thick stack of legal documents and governmental edicts. The recollection ignited an instant dislike for him within me.

The G-man was dressed in full legal formal wear with a dark blue perfectly tailored suit, crisp white dress shirt, and red power tie. The reading glasses perched on his nose were a surprisingly cheap plastic pair, like something you would buy off the disposable rack at Rite Aid. His chiseled features, ice blue eyes, and perfect hair must have been a problem for him at any trial with women on the jury, as I'm certain they had to stop the

179

proceedings every time one of them swooned. I wondered if his friends addressed him as G., Franklin, or Mr. Tolland.

The Sheriff seemed torn between dealing with the lawyer and finishing with me. He took several moments to decide. "Yes, of course. Thank you for coming down." The Sheriff turned back to me and uttered a single word, "Out."

My desire to launch out of the seat and dash for freedom as though shot out of a cannon was tempered by my need to hear about Beverly Dell's patient list. It seemed so clear to me that the murderer would be one of her patients. Whoever it was had killed Patricia, and then later, perhaps because they had confessed to her, killed Beverly. That was the connection.

I picked up my coffee cup and walked out of the office area as casually as I could, so casually in fact that I probably presented some peculiar air of exaggerated casualness, walking stiffly and prominently upright like a poorly-mechanized robot. Down the hallway I opened the exterior door, but then instead of leaving I stepped back quickly and let it sigh closed on its hydraulic arm. I tiptoed back and took a seat silently on the bench on the left hand side, placing the cup on the floor at my feet. Leaning back with my head against the partition wall I closed my eyes and opened my ears.

There was the scrape of chairs being pulled back, a slight creak from the one the Sheriff sat down in.

"When you contacted me early this morning I had my associates compile a list of Mrs. Dell's clients including everyone she had seen in the past year, though the request is highly irregular." Tolland's voice boomed, like he was addressing an entire amphitheater. It positively echoed off the hard surfaces of the office. "I'd like you to note that clients she had not seen in the past year will not appear on this list."

I found it interesting that he thought of 4AM or so, which is certainly when Bobby must have contacted him, as early this morning. I wondered what he would consider the middle of the goddamned night. Maybe the next time I had insomnia I would call him and we could take in a movie together. Maybe not.

"I appreciate you responding so quickly given the irregularity of my request," the Sheriff said, "but I believe the name of someone who has murdered two people in Dunboro is on that list, so if I could see it?"

"I'm afraid I'm not going to be able to simply let you peruse this list at your leisure, Sheriff. There are certain client confidentialities that need to be preserved."

"But Beverly Dell wasn't a doctor."

"Doctor or not, her clients had an expectation of privacy in the things they revealed to her, even to the fact that they were seeing her at all."

"And is dead." The Sheriff added flatly, which I gave him points for.

"Mrs. Dell's death does not alter the state of her clients' right to privacy." Tolland answered smoothly with an oily and practiced lawyerly ease.

"OK, I understand that. So what can you do to help me?"

"I would be willing, in the spirit of limited disclosure, to confirm or deny whether or not specific people appear on this list."

There was a long pause and I thought maybe Bobby was wondering if he could do better with a court order or if it were worth pushing Tolland more right now. He must have decided no to both, because I heard him ask, "Patricia Woods?"

There was the sound of papers being flipped, "No," Tolland replied.

"Michael Carston." Bobby spelled the last name for him.

"No."

"Samantha Carston."

"No."

As far as I was concerned Bobby was doing a pretty good job; off the top of my head I couldn't think of anyone else to ask about. But I was worried that the killer was someone whose name we didn't even know yet, and couldn't see as this was the way to get it.

"Rachael Woods."

Bobby was just shooting in the dark now. Rachael lived in Vermont. Why would she come to Dunboro to see a counselor? And what possible reason could she have had to kill her sister? He got another 'No' for his troubles.

This stupid lawyer game was infuriating. It may have satisfied some twisted ethical boundary, but it felt a lot like that kid's game where you take turns guessing positions on a grid to try and find the opposing player's navy. B-2. You sunk my battleship! That was it. We were playing a game of *Battleship* over people's lives. The name of the killer was on that list. I was certain of it. Why did lawyers have to be such pricks all the time?

I got up and stepped past the end of the wall. "What about me? Jack Fallon."

Bobby's head quickly swiveled and his eyes shot darts at me.

The lawyer turned around in his chair and looked confused. "What about you?"

"Am I on that list?"

The question shocked Bobby. It clearly showed on his face. If I ever held a poker night, he was on the invite list.

Tolland adjusted his glasses on his face and leaned back in the chair, the folder holding the list open on his lap. He flipped some pages, his lips forming the word, "Fallon, Fallon," over and over again silently. Finally he looked up. "Yes," he said, "you are."

Twenty-Eight

"You're," Bobby paused, agitated, his hands grasping at nothing but air, at a complete loss for words, finally settling on "unbelievable," as he pacing back in forth in front of his desk. "What were you thinking?"

I was seated behind that desk, feeling something like a school kid being lectured to in the principal's office. That feeling was reinforced by the fact that I was seated in an unpadded oak office chair very similar to those that had been used in public offices everywhere back when I had been in school. Now everything was probably ergonomic this and Swedish that. Incidentally, it had seemed pretty comfortable when I had first sat down but now was seriously putting my ass to sleep.

A thick and lengthy silence had followed the revelation of my involvement with Beverly Dell. Bobby had looked at me like I had suddenly sprouted a second head, and not some run of the mill second head either but something like the head of a griffin or Pauly Shore. G. Franklin Tolland had squared up the papers in the folder and left the building without another word, surely convinced the Dunboro Police Department was being run by inmates recently sprung from the state asylum in Concord.

"I was beginning to wonder if he had a real list at all, and wasn't just looking at his grocery list. Did you think of asking him to check it for eggs and milk?"

He stopped pacing and leaned over the desk, his hands in fists on the desktop, his shoulders hunched. I had a momentary belief that he was going to slug me, and like a cartoon character I would fly back through the wall leaving a Jack-shaped hole.

"How long had you been seeing Beverly Dell?"

I practically choked on my first answer, that I had been seeing her since Patricia's death, as if just uttering the connection aloud would somehow solidify my role as the link between them. It just wasn't true in any case; I had waited several days before seeing Beverly for the first time.

"Well?" Bobby demanded.

Normally proud of the speed of my mind, I was foundering in conversational quicksand. "Since Friday."

"And you didn't know Patricia Woods before the fire?" He leaned over farther, a presence that blotting out the sky.

"No. Absolutely not. No way." I thought I doth protest too much and bit down on my tongue.

Bobby stood hulking over the desk for another moment, breathing heavily through his nose like a bull about to charge. "Shit!" He pushed himself off and spun away, crossing the office to stare at a poster on the wall showing the procedure for the Heimlich maneuver. Had I been at that moment choking, I suspect he would not have bothered to apply it.

I got up from the chair and went to the window, not so much because I was interested in the view outside but to put as much distance between Bobby and me in a room which seemed suddenly far too small. It also allowed some blood to flow back to my ass, which I was halfway concerned would need to be amputated if I spent another moment sitting in that chair.

"What would you say if I told you I thought you were the connection between Patricia and Beverly?" Bobby asked from right behind me.

I let out an involuntary grunt of surprise. I hadn't heard a sound as he had come back across the room, not so much as a scuff against the linoleum floor. Did the Dunboro Sheriff have ninja training?

I spoke to him without turning from the window. I was focusing completely inward, nearly unaware of whatever I was seeing. The Hindenburg could have been burning out there and I would have missed it. I felt like a pool player trying to work out the tricky geometry between Patricia, Beverly, myself, and some fourth person about which I knew absolutely nothing. Was there even a shot there? "How could I be? It doesn't make any sense. It's got to be what you decided this morning when you called Tolland: one of her patients." Of course I was one of her patients, the fact of which I had helpfully just made Bobby aware. "One of her *other* patients," I emphasized.

"Who?" He demanded.

"Someone from Patricia's past who wanted her dead. Somebody we don't know about yet."

"We?" He said acidly.

"What I meant-"

He grabbed me by the shoulder and turned me, using his strength, his thumb digging into the mass of muscles and nerves in the joint. I felt my knees go soft. "I don't know what you think you're doing here, but there is no we, and whatever it is, it stops now. Are you hearing me?"

"Yes," I answered, but I must have sounded insufficiently contrite, because he increased the pressure until white spots flashed behind my eyes and I sagged, his hand the only thing holding me upright. I thought with a small change in his grip he could have snapped my collarbone if he wished.

"I want you out of my investigation and out of my office," he said threateningly, lips stretched tight over his teeth. He held on for a moment longer, allowing me to experience the whole spectrum of pain, a subtle pallet with thousands of colors, and then he released me suddenly. I felt lightheaded and grabbed the edge of the windowsill to keep from falling.

When my knees were up to it I stumbled out of the office and pinballed down the short hallway. On the way past the bench I kicked over my coffee cup and spilled the little bit left in it on the floor, then actually missed the door, colliding drunkenly with the left side of the door jam. Managing somehow to get the door open I went out to my truck and leaned against the bumper, blinking my eyes in the bright sunlight, my forehead covered in greasy sweat.

There was a parking ticket on the windshield; a two hundred and fifty dollar fine for parking in a space reserved for a police car. A moveable 'No Parking' sign embedded in a concrete block had been placed in front of my truck sometime while I was in the office. How the hell had he managed that?

Twenty-Nine

I hooked the cup of tea on the counter in front of me with my left thumb and turned the mug ninety degrees clockwise, the tip of my right index finger sliding along the curve of the rim as a guide. I then hooked it with my right thumb and turned it ninety degrees back.

The tea was cold. It had been cold something like four hours ago when Valerie asked me if I was coming to bed, which I assured her I would in just a few minutes. Lies, all lies.

When I had been at Columbia University a number of students had gone on a hunger strike to protest the University's investment in companies which in their view supported apartheid in South Africa. A friend of mine, one of the hunger strikers, later told me the first week or so without food was hard, that thoughts of food and hunger pangs constantly dogged him. However somewhere in the second week, he claimed, his desire for food had just kind of faded away. His body, having realized no food was forthcoming, had resorted to some new biochemistry, likely something that involved self-cannibalism of whatever muscles or organs the body deemed of lower importance.

In a similar way, now passing into my eighth sleepless day, I felt as though I no longer needed to sleep. My body somehow had been altered to encompass this new sleepless reality, though I was concerned at what form my self-cannibalism might take. What parts of me would be devoured as a replacement for sleep? I wondered if it might turn out to be my sanity.

On the kitchen windowsill sat an old-style radio scanner, a chase of red LEDs on the face illuminating as it swept a pre-programmed block of frequencies. I had set them for the fire departments across the Souhegan Valley: Milford and Brookline, Amherst and Bedford, Mason, Wilton, Hollis, and of course Dunboro. The region was for the most part quiet, the LEDs running freely, pausing only for moments at anomalous signal packets, off-frequency bits of electromagnetic communications ricocheting off the troposphere from hundreds of miles away, ghostly echoes of other emergencies, other tragedies, taking place in Vermont or western Massachusetts or southern Maine.

I splayed the fingers of my left hand, resting the tips along the rim of the mug like the perching of some nimble, exotic spider, and turned the mug one hundred and eighty degrees clockwise, then adjusted it fifteen degrees back.

I envisioned it as a gear, a part of some large, complex machine; one that wrecked families and destroyed lives for some horrible unknown purpose. The individual gears represented Patricia and her sister Rachael, the boyfriend past whom I knew only as Dan, Michael and Samantha Carston, myself and Beverly Dell, and other gears not yet named. They appeared to spin freely, their teeth unmeshed, but that was just an illusion, a consequence of my lack of understanding of the mechanics that drove them. They were all somehow connected, they must be, and if I could only get the mug into the correct orientation these linkages would appear and all the other gears would fall into alignment around it, and the purpose, the awful reason of that machine, would become clear to me.

The scanner locked up on Brookline's frequency for a single motor vehicle accident, no PI or entrapment. The PI was short for Personal Injury. Why they abbreviated personal injury but then always said entrapment instead of simply saying something like 'no PI or E' was a mystery to me. Brookline Fire units signed on a few minutes later responding to the call.

I trapped the sides of the mug with the flattened palms of both hands and rolled it between them, seesawing it forward and back, twenty degrees each way, feeling the minute grate and scrap of the bottom edge against the surface of the countertop as it moved.

One of the largest gears held the face of Bobby Dawkins, who was probably a heartbeat away from chopping a hole in the floor of the police department and burying me under it. I had to admit that through my meddling I had been a distraction for him, and was forced to consider the possibility that the investigation would fail because of me. That thought was sudden and jagged, and freighted me with a new, fresh burden of guilt I didn't know how to bear. A whole new facet I could have explored with Beverly Dell were she not dead.

A fire alarm activation woke the fire department in Milford, and moments later a sleepy Milford deputy Chief came on the radio saying he would look into it, which was then acknowledged by the dispatch center. The scanner continued on its merry way.

I grasped the mug by the handle, tilted it, lifted it from the counter, and then put it back down forty-five degrees counterclockwise from where it had started.

Beverly Dell. She was the gear connected to both Patricia and the killer. I was certain of that much, but as far I could see that didn't give me any good ideas of who it could be nor, as long as the fortress of G. Franklin Tolland held that list of patients, how to figure it out. A crafty detective on a television show would know this was one of those times to blur the lines between right and wrong, picking the locks to Beverly Dell's home and office with a penlight clamped between their teeth to get a look at her files. Though I knew how to pick locks from a brief period in my college years when lock picking was a common pastime for a budding scientist, with the threat of Bobby Dawkins hanging over my head I was hesitant to blur anything.

The dispatch center came on for a radio check, announcing it was oh-four hundred hours, time for the shift change. I pictured the guy at the console releasing the transmit button and standing up from a worn, wheeled office chair, his back cracking audibly as he gathered the coffee cups, the power bar wrappers, the Post It notes the operator had stuck around the console display to track active calls and the units involved. The next shift dispatcher would take the chair, settle into it like a hen on a nest, rolling the squeaking wheels back and forth to get the proper distance from the console. They would put down their own first cup of coffee, maybe a paperback novel or a crossword puzzle next to it, two working pens next to that.

It was a ritual repeated every eight hours a day, three hundred and sixty five days a year.

The biggest gear, the one turning all the others, was the one with no name on it. I pictured it as cast from iron, rust pocked, with teeth that slanted outwards sharply from the body and ended in viciously pointed tips. The label I had stuck on it read 'murderer,' written in a black marker on a worn piece of duct tape, the silver dulled to pewter, the edges threaded and ratty.

I stared into the mug as I turned it around and around, the liquid inside rippling darkly with the motion like a tiny, disturbed pond.

The scanner stopped on the light corresponding to the frequency for Amherst, and the first inrush of air as the dispatcher prepared to speak was shallow and quick, infused with the high-pitched hum of an adrenaline rush.

There was a fire at the Carston house, a big one.

Thirty

I hunched over the wheel as I drove at velocities far beyond the margin of safety, siren wailing at a fever pitch. The first Amherst units on the scene had reported a structure fire, firefighter speak for an actively burning building. The call currently stood at a single alarm, but I dreaded that at any moment it would be elevated to multiple alarms, an indication the fire was out of control, the entire home ablaze, prompting calls for assistance from adjacent towns of men and equipment.

When I arrived I found two Amherst trucks were there, one parked in the street in front of the house feeding water to a second engine parked in the driveway. A minivan of some indeterminate dark color was idling in the driveway behind it. Two hose lines manned by four firefighters were doing a good job of keeping the fire contained to the right side of the house while several guys on ladders were venting the roof. The fire Chief in a white turnout jacket and helmet directed all the action from a vantage point in the middle of the front lawn like an orchestra conductor. It looked like most of the house was going to be saved, though the smoke and water damage would be extensive.

I pulled past the driveway and parked up the street, then got out and jogged back to the minivan.

Samantha Carston powered down the window when I knocked on the driver's side glass. Under circumstances that I had seen reduce many people, man, woman, young and old, to tears, sitting on the front lawn watching everything they own in the world go up in flames, Samantha Carston exuded an inner strength. Her brown eyes were clear and her cheeks were dry. Her brown hair, mussed from sleep, was thrown back over her shoulders. A linen fold had pressed a line into her face which began at her jaw and ran up into the hairline by her right ear.

"Anyone hurt?" I asked.

"No, we're all OK here," she said so softly I had to lean forward to hear her over the rumble of the fire truck pumps.

I cupped my hands against the rear window glass and peered into the back seat where I could see the two girls dressed in big puffy fleece pajamas, asleep intertwined like kittens.

I looked away at the sound of an approaching siren and saw the Dunboro police cruiser pull in. Dawkins had made good time given that he probably hadn't been listening to the fire department frequencies, and must have heard it relayed later through the Amherst PD dispatch. He parked in the street a good distance behind the fire truck, to leave room for it to back up if needed, and crossed the uneven lawn at a stumbling run to a minivan.

"Can you tell me anything about what happened?" he asked when he arrived at the minivan window.

"We were all in bed when the fire alarm went off. I grabbed the girls and came down the stairs. The living room was on fire, but we made it past the archway and out the front door. I got in the car and pulled it out into the street so the fire truck could pull in when it got here."

"Did you call the fire department?"

She said, "Onstar," and pointed to the Onstar button on the dash.

A red Mitsubishi angled to the curb with a squeal of rubber just in front of Bobby's cruiser. Michael Carston got out and, leaving the door open, ran down the street and up the driveway. He stopped next to Bobby at the open window.

"Oh my god! Sam, are you and girls alright?" He tried to look past her at the girls in the back seat.

"We're fine," she responded in a tone so cold Michael shied back.

"Sam?" he asked uncertainly.

"Don't you 'Sam' me. This is your fault!"

"My fault?"

"That bitch dies in a house fire in Dunboro and now this happens!" Her voice rose. Bobby, embarrassed, turned away and studied the crowd of neighbors gathered across the street, feigning great interest. I noticed the operator on the fire truck pump deck in the driveway crane his neck to see past the end of the truck at what all the shouting was about.

"What?"

"Whoever killed her wants to kill you! Tried to kill us! And you aren't even fucking," she took a quick glance over her shoulder at the girls still sleeping in the back seat and instantly lowered her voice to a whisper, "you aren't even fucking living here."

Michael leaned in close to the window and dropped his volume as well, "That's crazy. No one wants to kill anyone. You're overreacting. Did you call me here just to yell at me?"

"I called you out of simple human decency, something I'm sure you've completely forgotten about, so you wouldn't see it on the news first and worry. I didn't call you to come here. That was your choice. I'd prefer you weren't here at all."

Michael stood up from the window and gaped. Without another word he turned and stalked across the lawn towards his car, pulling his cell phone from his pocket and dialing as he went.

Bobby continued the thread of the conversation as if Michael had never arrived.

"Did you see anyone when you came out of the house?"

"No, I'm sorry. I didn't. I was carrying the two girls and trying to get my car keys out of my purse."

"Maybe a car driving away?" I offered.

"No. I didn't see anything."

"Did you-" Bobby began but was interrupted by the explosion of Michael Carston's car. An enormous sphere of flame spiraled into the air as fire and smoke rolled out of all of the windows. I thought through the windshield I could see a figure writhing in the driver's seat.

I ran out to the street and dragged the lower speedlay hose line off of the Amherst truck.

"Give me pressure on lower speedlay!" I yelled at the guy at the pump panel, his jaw hanging open as he looked back at the burning car.

"Who are you?"

"I'm the guy who's going to put that car out!"

He must have decided I knew what I was doing as I spread the hose out on the lawn to keep it from kinking as it pressurized and grabbed the nozzle, because the next thing I knew the line was firm and heavy in my hands. I pulled the valve control and water shot out almost throwing me onto my back, the pump delivering water at a pressure far too high for an ordinary hand line, probably the same pressure he had been using to feed the other truck. Clamping the nozzle in my armpit and gritting my teeth, I set my heels into the soft sod of the lawn and directed the water into the front seat of the car. As I pushed the fire back I could definitely see a body in the front seat and I concentrated my efforts on keeping the flames away, though I knew it was a futile effort.

Michael Carston was dead.

I was doing a pretty good job of forcing the fire into the back seat of the car when the gas tank exploded, spreading fire back into the front seat and completely engulfing Bobby's car behind it in flames. I ducked down as the expanding ball of fire rolled over my head.

"Crap." I heard Bobby say from somewhere behind me.

The neighbors across the street said "Oooh," as one, as if they were watching a fireworks display.

I think I smelled the hair on my head singe.

One of the crews from the house came over and threw water into Bobby's car.

The Chief called a second alarm and requested trucks and manpower from Bedford as well as Amherst police and ambulance. He came over and put his helmet on my head and draped his jacket on my shoulders. "Try not to get yourself killed, son."

Working the car fire without breathing gear was brutal. Shifting winds would throw a choking smoke cloud into my face forcing me to fight the fire from a much greater distance than preferable. The second crew stepped forward and pressed the attack, and we were just getting both cars under control as the first Bedford crews arrived.

I gladly let them take over for me. My arms were weak and quivery from the effort of fighting the high-pressure hose.

I gave the Chief back his jacket and helmet which I noticed were not all that white anymore and went over to the ambulance where I sat on the stretcher. One the EMTs handed me a damp washcloth. Without a mirror to work with, I just rubbed the cloth over my face more or less at random, and was only a little surprised to find it mostly stained black when I was finished.

The EMT had me tip my head back and he put drops in my eyes that burned like hell at first and then felt much better. He examined my right forearm and pronounced that I had a first degree burn, which I hadn't even realized, but as I looked at it noticed it was red and all the hair had burned off. He put a cold compress on the arm and wrapped it all up with clean, white bandages.

Bobby came over. "Why am I not surprised to find you here?" he said angrily.

"Can we get into that later? You've got a real opportunity here."

"How so?" He folded his arms across his chest.

I didn't need Beverly Dell to tell me he was adopting a posture of resistance. My approach had to be enticing enough to spur his interest.

"This fire wasn't meant to kill anyone," I said.

"What do you mean? Michael's in the car and the car goes up in flames. Sounds like murder to me."

"I'm talking about the house fire."

"I don't understand."

The EMT was leaning over me shining a penlight in my eyes. "Just a second." I gently pushed him aside. He shrugged and put the buds of a stethoscope in his ears, lifted my shirt, and put the diaphragm against my back. "The killer wants Michael, but since Michael moved out after his wife found out about the affair the killer doesn't know where to find him."

"Couldn't he just follow him from work?"

The EMT told me to take several deep breaths, which I did.

"Probably, if he knew where Michael worked, if Michael is even going to work. Instead he decided to set a fire at his house. The fire started way off in one corner of the house, and it didn't block the stairs from the second floor. If that same fire starts at the bottom of those stairs the mother is stuck on the second floor with two young girls, trying to decide between dying of smoke inhalation and jumping out of a second story window into the ornamental rock garden in the back yard with her children in tow. This way, the family gets out, Michael shows up, and the killer's problem is solved."

"But the killer took a big risk killing Michael here. There are like a hundred witnesses." He gestured with his arm taking in all the fire personnel and the crowd of onlookers.

"I agree it would have made more sense to follow Michael from here to wherever he was staying and kill him there, but he didn't, and maybe you'll solve this thing here and now. Talk to the people on the street. With luck, someone saw the killer near

Michael's car while he was over talking to us, or maybe just before it exploded."

I watched as the internal debate went on behind his eyes. On the one hand, I'm sure he dearly wanted to ream me a new one, but on the other I clearly wasn't involved; I had been standing right next to him when the car exploded. In the end there was only one right choice and thankfully he made it. "Don't go anywhere."

"I've got nowhere else to be."

"Wrong," the EMT said. "You're going to the hospital."

"The hospital?" I asked.

"Unless, that is, you'd like to refuse transport, but I think that would be a very bad decision. You've got a burn on your arm, your eyes look like crap, and I'm not thrilled with how your lungs sound."

I took a deep breath and felt alright, but then hawked and spat a gob of grey phlegm, very dark grey phlegm, into the gutter. I wondered if, by firefighting, I was signing myself up for a really vicious case of lung cancer somewhere down the road.

"Apparently I'm going to be at the hospital," I told the Sheriff, "That OK with you?"

"OK," he started to trot off towards the crowd.

"Sorry about your car," I called after him.

"Tell me about it." He pulled the notepad from his hip pocket and headed across the street.

"Lie back, please." The EMT pushed me back onto the stretcher.

He rolled it into the ambulance and latched it to the floor, then closed the rear doors behind him as he climbed in. The ambulance pulled away from the curb and did a hard U-turn, which the EMT absorbed with his knees and ankles with the skill of a surfer running a pipeline. He put a blood pressure cuff on my arm.

I affected a bad Dudley Moore impersonation. "Drive through the park, Bitterman." I called to the driver, "You know how I love the park."

"Everybody's a comedian." He replied over his shoulder.

Thirty-One

My own cell phone lying forgotten at home on the kitchen counter, I borrowed one from a bored looking guy with a roofing staple driven through the palm of his right hand who was sitting in the emergency room waiting area next to me. He was so casual about it; you would have thought he had a two and a half inch long staple through his hand all the time. He asked me if I thought he should just pull it out and go home.

"That's a roofing staple," I said, pointing out the obvious.

"Yeah, so?"

"So it's five o'clock in the morning. Were you roofing at night?"

"Naw. I drove it through my hand yesterday afternoon. It wasn't really bleeding, and it didn't hurt too much. Damned if I was going to miss a Sox game over a little thing like this."

"I'd wait for a doctor."

He nodded like I had just imparted the wisdom of the Pharaohs and let me make my phone call.

I tried to keep it as light as possible, opening with "Hey! Guess where I'm calling from," but I could tell right away Valerie wasn't having any of it, and frankly I couldn't blame her.

"You woke me up when the truck sped away more than an hour ago and you call me now like it's no big deal? Where the hell are you?"

"I'm at the, uh, hospital."

"The hospital? What happened? Are you alright?"

"I'm OK, a small burn on my arm-"

"You're burned? Where are you? St. Joes? I'll be there in twenty minutes."

"It's nothing more than a sunburn, really," I insisted, "There's no reason for you to come down. I just wanted to let you know where I am and that I'm fine, and I'll call you to come pick me up as soon as I've seen a doctor."

"Pick you up? Where's your truck?"

I grimaced at the one question I had hoped she wouldn't ask, and I gave myself a mental head slap for having led her there. In the ensuing silence I tried on a number of different responses and found none of them fit, they all just led to more questions, which led to more questions still.

"Jack," Valerie said uncertainly.

I thought for a moment of pretending the call had been dropped and hanging up, but worried once I went down that road I wouldn't stop, and at the end of it was a person I didn't want to be. And Valerie deserved better.

So I took the time and laid it all out; the photographs, returning to the house the night after the fire, the funeral, and meeting with Michael and Samantha Carston and Patricia's coworkers. Valerie listened without comment, and it felt to me a little what I thought Catholics experienced in the confessional; the opportunity to unburden one's mind and soul without judgment or reprisal.

"I love you," she said to me softly when I had finished, all the cell towers aligning to make her sound so clear it was as though she was standing right beside me. "You're crazy and you're risking your life which I hate, but I love you." I could hear her smile, picture it lighting up her entire face.

"I love you too. I'll call you after I've seen a doctor."

"OK."

I hung up the phone and felt renewed, and yet at the same time experienced a peace I had not known since the night Patricia had died. I thought about finding an empty bed somewhere, certain I would sleep, but then noticed that at some time while I had been on the phone Bobby Dawkins had shown up.

I returned the phone to the man I had borrowed it from. He reached out to take it with the hand that had the staple through it and the phone clattered against the staple with a brittle, insectile sound that sent a shiver up my spine. Had he not been sitting in an emergency room I would have said, 'Seriously, dude, see a doctor.' Instead I thanked him for the use of his phone and went over and slouched in a chair by the window, my feet up on the baseboard heater cover, and waited for the coming dawn. Without a word the Sheriff came over and sat down next to me.

We sat like that, side by side, in the waiting area of the Southern New Hampshire Medical Center for several more hours. The place wasn't super busy, but a steady stream of patients kept arriving with injuries which moved them ahead of me in the queue. The time just kind of melted away as we watched a parade of knife wounds and alcohol poisonings and unspecified head injuries drag themselves by. Fun and hijinks on a Nashua Tuesday night.

The waiting room had recently been renovated and the old uncomfortable molded plastic seats had been replaced with well-padded chairs clustered in little privacy nooks buffered by real plants in big ceramic pots. The walls had been painted soothing beiges and blues. Skylights overhead had initially shown us simple squares of blackness, but in the past twenty minutes or so were definitely starting to leak a pallid grey light of dawn. It was a great place to sit and think; try and connect the dots between Patricia Woods and Beverly Dell and Michael Carston.

I caught a glimpse out of the corner of my eye of the television hung from the ceiling where CNN showed ten seconds of what had to be cell phone video of the fire at the Carston house. I could see myself leaning forward as if into a stiff wind, fighting the high pressure hose as I attacked the fire in Michael Carston's car, the image doing a jitterbug in the shaking hands of whoever had made the video.

Somehow CNN had connected this fire to the other two murders, and the story was really starting to pick up steam. They had been running it every half hour since I had arrived.

Bobby Dawkins likely wanted to take me somewhere and commence another round of grilling, which I suppose he felt he couldn't do while I was injured, even mildly so, and sitting in a hospital. I was again confronted by the fact that, had the Sheriff been not so focused on me, maybe he would have figured out who had killed Beverly Dell, and Michael Carston wouldn't be dead. Perhaps I even bore some responsibility for the death of Beverly Dell. All my poking around had accomplished nothing more than muddying the waters.

Maybe I had come into it almost like it was a game, I had to admit to myself, an intellectual exercise in higher mathematics and murder, but that had been stupid of me. Egotistical and stupid. I wanted to apologize to him, but didn't know how to begin except the straightforward route.

"I'm sorry," I said.

"Sorry for what?"

"For screwing up your investigation."

"Yeah, well," he muttered, as if he was too exhausted to say anything more. Perhaps he was getting as little sleep as I.

"Any luck with the crowd?"

He shook his head, but whether that meant he hadn't had any luck or he wasn't willing to discuss it with me I wasn't sure. Given that he didn't follow that up with anything I assumed it was the latter.

I saw past his shoulder that a small group of two nurses and two doctors had gathered by the double doors leading to the ambulance arrival ramp. One of the nurses was looking out through the doors, her hands cupped against the glass to cut down the reflection of the room lights. One of the doctors was very young, and he danced from foot to foot nervously like a JV quarterback about to start his first game. The other doctor and nurse were talking closely, the doctor counting off something on his extended fingers.

When the staff in an ER clumps together, something bad is coming.

I unwound the bandages from my arm and stuffed them into the pot of the plant next to me, and let the chemical cold pack which had gone warm long ago fall to the floor by my chair.

"What are you doing?" Dawkins asked.

"Something's coming in. They might need our help." I got up from the chair and crossed the room.

"What's coming in? Help who?" He got up quickly and followed.

I passed by the young doctor, who was rolling his neck around like a bobblehead and slightly jogging in place, and went directly to the other doctor just as he was finishing his discussion with the nurse. She nodded once and took off at a run deeper into the hospital.

When he saw me step up he asked, "Something I can help you with?" in a tone which clearly implied he was in little position to help me with anything. The doctor was of average height, trim, with a thoughtful face and compassionate eyes. He definitely looked the part of the doctor you would want leaning over you when you ended up on a stretcher in an emergency room. The nameplate on his white lab coat read "Dr. Talbot."

"I'm Jack Fallon and I'm a firefighter," I said, "and this is Sheriff Dawkins from Dunboro. We're both trained in emergency first aid and triage." I realized as I said it maybe the Sheriff of Dunboro wasn't so trained, but he had to have at least CPR training, and so I plowed ahead, "I'm wondering if we can help you. What's coming in?"

"A bus full of leaf peepers just rolled over on Route 3."

"Where's your staff?"

"You're looking at it. I've got a nurse out on maternity leave and a doctor who went home sick earlier. They're sending half of the patients to St. Joes, but even so I'm not sure we can handle half here. The rollover was at high speed and nobody was wearing seat belts. The EMTs on the scene say it's bad. Very bad."

"Well, you've just found two more bodies, however you'd

like to use us."

Ordinarily he probably would have dismissed the offer because he had no way of knowing who the hell I was, but Bobby Dawkins standing next to me in full uniform gave us credibility. "I'm glad for the help." He shook both our hands. Get on a pair of sterile gloves from the box at the nurse's station and help the EMTs as they come in any way you can. Some of those ambulances are going to be making a couple of round trips, so we have to get the victims stable and get them unloaded ASAP."

"We're on it."

I went and put on a pair of surgical gloves, then pulled two more pairs from the box and shoved one each into my back pockets."Take extras. You'll want to change gloves between patients."

"OK." He tugged on the gloves which, though sized extra-large, were tight on his hands.

We went through the double doors and stood underneath the portcullis outside. One of the nurses joined us.

"I'm, uh, not actually CPR certified," he whispered to me, a little nervously. "I let it lapse a few years ago."

"Don't worry about it. Just do whatever the EMTs tell you." I looked over at him, and his breathing seemed a little rushed and shallow to me. "You good?"

"Good," he replied, which he punctuated with a little nod, more of a rapid up and down snap of his head, which made it look to me like he was anything other than good. I just had to hope he wouldn't hyperventilate and pass out, become a problem himself.

From where we stood we could see a long way up West

Hollis Street. The first two ambulances, their emergency lights popping and flashing appeared at the farthest end of our vision. Their sirens carried to us, the sound distorted by the distance.

Less than a minute later they arrived almost simultaneously and had three patients between them. Prepared for the worst, I was surprised to find the injuries far from life threatening. There was a cleanly broken ankle, a dislocated shoulder, and a head wound that looked to me to be bleeding a lot but nothing more. The two doctors and nurses swarmed and the patients were brought inside. I stepped forward to take one corner of a stretcher but a hospital orderly got there before I did, and Bobby and I were left standing there blinking in the deeply slanting light of the newly risen sun as the two ambulances drove away.

"No big deal," Bobby said, looking a little relieved.

"Huh, guess not," I replied.

It all went to hell after that.

Thirty-Two

Another ambulance arrived moments later. The driver screeched to a halt and came around to open the rear doors. He helped out a woman who cradled her right arm painfully in her left. Both bones of her forearm were broken, the ends misaligned. The muscles had pulled the arm shorter, the skin sagging and bunching at the break, the unsupported muscles and tendons writhing underneath like snakes.

I helped get her into a wheelchair that had been brought out by an orderly.

"Why wasn't she in one of the first ambulances?" Bobby asked.

"The first one took the people we could load quickly," the driver responded, "She was pinned in the wreckage and it took time to get her out. There's worse yet to come. Half the bus is twisted up and crushed. We don't even know how many people are trapped in there. Four fatals at the scene already."

The driver left with the wheelchair and Bobby came over to stand beside me. He was almost panting through his open mouth and his color sucked.

"Take it one patient at a time. Try to stay calm and keep breathing."

He closed his mouth and took several deep breaths through his nose. A little color returned.

"Better?"

"Just super," he replied.

"Little help?" Came a panicked call from the back of the ambulance.

I looked in to see the EMT, a stocky blonde woman, struggling with a guy who was almost as huge as Bobby. The guy lying on the stretcher had a badly broken femur, the white jagged end of bone poking through the leg of his jeans which was damp with blood.

A massive compound fracture, probably halfway to shock, and not only was the guy wrestling with the EMT but he was winning.

I jumped into the back of the ambulance and took one of the guy's arms and pinned it down. With my help, she got the other arm pinned as well.

"Where are your restraints?" I asked the EMT.

"He broke them," she replied tersely.

The man lifted his good leg and drove it down, using the momentum to sit up. He got both arms loose and slammed me back against the wall, not injuring me but rattling whatever was stored inside the compartments behind me. Bobby stood just outside the ambulance looking in.

"Get in here and hold down his legs," I shouted.

Bobby climbed reluctantly in and stared down at the exposed bone in undisguised horror. "I don't want to hurt him."

"You won't hurt him any worse than he's hurting himself!" the EMT hollered.

Bobby looked at the patient a moment longer, like a person standing on the edge of a dock thinking about jumping into a lake but worried the water might be frigid, and then threw himself diagonally across the man's legs and lower body. He took one of the man's free arms and trapped it beneath his shoulder in the process.

I managed get the other arm under control and held it down against the stretcher, both hands on the wrist, my knee pressed into the crook of the elbow. The man growled and strained, his head thrashing from side to side.

The EMT stripped the sterile wrapper from a hypodermic needle with her teeth. She bit the protective cap over the needle off and spit it over her shoulder towards the driver's seat, then pulled out a vial from one of the drawers mounted on the wall and started filling the hypo. "Just hold him. A few seconds more..." She tapped the side and depressed the plunger slightly to evacuate the bubbles, then drove the needle into the man's shoulder and ran it all the way home. Immediately the man's struggles lessened.

We were lit suddenly by the headlights of another ambulance pulling in behind us.

"You good here?" I asked.

"Yeah, thanks," the EMT nodded as she unrolled a blood pressure cuff.

I handed off the arm I was holding to Bobby who trapped it with his own, but whatever the EMT had pumped in was working because the guy was well on his way to la la land.

Jumping down from the ambulance, I ran around the back of the other one, stripping off the pair of gloves I was wearing and shoving them into my pocket as I pulled on a new pair. I had trouble with one of the gloves, the fingers twisted and tangled, and I was only sort of half paying attention as I opened the rear doors. When I finally got the glove straightened out and looked in it was as though time had slowed.

On the stretcher inside was a young girl, somewhere just shy of a teenager, who looked as though someone had tried to fillet her. Her shirt had been cut open revealing the prepubescent buds of her breasts, her chest crisscrossed by deep cuts, a twisted piece of aluminum sticking out of one of the cuts several inches. I had learned in emergency first aid class about the criteria used to determine if a foreign object should be left in the body until the victim got to the hospital or taken out at the scene, but had never actually come across a case where it was left in. The girl literally fountained blood from the wounds in three or four fine sprays in conjunction with the beating of her heart. I could see them clearly, the red wetness of each arc as it shot upwards, then pattered down on her chest, the nearby wall, the floor by the edge of the stretcher. A big square of bandage lay loose on her stomach.

The EMT had a stethoscope in his ears, blood smeared on one lens of his glasses, and he was fiddling with an IV bag. "Get in here and lean on this bandage," he called to me. "She's not going to make it to an operating table if we don't keep some blood in her."

I got into the ambulance and placed the bandage over her chest, covering the wounds while avoiding the piece of aluminum as best I could. I leaned down on the bandage which squelched sickeningly as I did so.

"Good. Good," the EMT breathed.

There was already an IV in the girl's left arm, and he inserted another one into her right and squeezed the bag, forcing fluid into her body. Two orderlies showed up at the doors.

"Lift her out, but go easy," he told them. "Keep the pressure on," he said to me.

It was awkward climbing down next to the stretcher. The wheels and legs unfolded and banged me in the shin, right on my bruise. We rolled slowly in a pack towards the emergency room doors which opened automatically ahead of us.

Just inside the doors we were joined by the older doctor who noticed my hands on her chest. "You got her?"

"Yeah, I think so."

After that time sped up again and everything became a blur. There were more doctors, and more nurses. We ended up in a surgical suite, bright lights and blue tile walls, and at some point someone gently removed my hands and lifted the edge of the bandage. Blood fountained again immediately, and the surgeon reached into the wounds with his gloved hands, one finger disappearing all the way to the second knuckle, to press off the bleeders.

I stepped away until my back came up against a wall and I watched for a time as instruments were handed around and bloody gauze pads hit the floor, and then I turned and made it out into the hallway.

Away from the girl my head cleared and I stripped off the bloody gloves, depositing them and the other pair I had worn in a biohazard bag behind the nurses' station. Then I put on a new pair and got back to work.

I saw Bobby twice more, but then had no idea where he

went. There were more ambulances and more patients. More broken bones, cuts and bruises, and internal injuries. One man had had his forearm amputated a little south of the elbow. At some point I found myself keeping a twelve-year-old boy company in the waiting room while they sewed a few quick stitches into his mother's cheek. I lifted and I carried and I lost count.

Three hours later as the ER was finally winding down I decided to heck with it. I'd had been there half the night and most of the morning and had yet to see a doctor, but that was alright. It was no big deal compared to the human carnage I had seen. I called Valerie to come and get me.

Thirty-Three

"You look OK." Valerie said, checking me out with little sideways glances as she drove.

"I'm fine, hardly worth the trip to the hospital."

"What did the doctor say?"

"I never got around to seeing one, but a twelve year old boy in the waiting room thought I looked cool."

"That's our HMO for you."

I laughed and hugged her against me.

She pushed me away, "Ewww. You smell like smoke."

It was late-morning when we got back home. In the driveway we found Bobby leaning against the fender of his pickup truck, an ancient Dodge the original color of which had been something light like white or yellow but was now mostly rust. I had no idea when he had left the hospital or how he had gotten home.

He had changed out of his uniform and was wearing a pair of jeans and a blue sweatshirt with 'Ski Sunapee' on it in white lettering. Tonk was sitting at his feet.

As we got out of Valerie's car he said "That was," he paused and shook his head, "something." He reached down and scratched Tonk behind one ear, which Tonk leaned into while flapping his foot against the ground.

Of the original thirty nine people onboard the bus there had been nine dead and twenty-four injured, twelve seriously. I wasn't sure something covered it adequately, but let it go.

"I'm starving. Have you had breakfast yet?" I asked him.

"No. How's your burn?"

"I'm fine, just a little singed. Come on inside." Valerie, Tonk and I led him into the house where he took a seat at the dining room table.

I had made the rectangular table out of planks of Brazilian cherry, splined together and worked with fine grit rouge until it glowed, then routed it with a bull nose edge. The legs of the table were simple cylinders three inches in diameter. I planned someday to buy a lathe and turn the leg cylinders into something more artistic.

Tonk lay down on the floor in the archway between the dining room and kitchen with a sigh.

I opened the fridge. "What would you like?"

"I'm not picky. I'll have whatever you're having, if that's not too much trouble."

"No trouble."

While Valerie cracked eggs into a bowl I rummaged around for what I could find to put into an omelet. Omelets are the perfect way to feed a lot of people while getting rid of miscellaneous food. There's almost nothing you can't put into one: onion, bell pepper, sausage, cheese, garlic, tomato – I've even made one with leftover meatloaf. This time, however, I was going high-class. I'd found some frozen shrimp and provolone cheese.

Sensing that things had changed between us, I asked "I guess the fact that you're here this morning means you're not out arresting someone. Strike out with the crowd?" while I cut up the shrimp.

He didn't answer me immediately, debating with himself how much he wanted to reveal. I could feel his tension as he worked it over in his mind, perhaps making little lists of pros and cons, until he reached a decision. "Sort of. You ready for a bombshell?"

"Shoot."

"At least five people told me they saw a firefighter, definitely a man, near the car just before it exploded."

Valerie stopped whisking the eggs. I had already told her about this on the phone earlier, but it was still a shock for her to hear it again. After a moment she resumed whisking, though more slowly and deliberately than before.

"And it was Michael in the car?" I asked.

"It's going to take the coroner awhile to identify the body, but there was identification in the pocket which says it was him and we both saw him walking to it." He got up from the table and came into the kitchen. "Mind if I get some juice?"

Valerie opened the door of one of the cabinets revealing shelves of glasses. "Help yourself. Michael was the married guy Patricia was seeing?"

"Yeah," Bobby said as he selected a glass with Mickey Mouse printed on it from the shelf and put it on the countertop. He went to the refrigerator and pulled out a carton of Tropicana orange juice.

"Who was he calling when he walked back to his car?" I asked.

"You noticed that too?" He crossed the kitchen, "I checked with Verizon. He dialed the office of his insurance agent. The call was completed, but there was no message left. The car probably exploded before the machine finished its outgoing message." He poured a glassful of juice. "So," he drank, "know of any good suspects in the fire department?"

"The people said they saw a firefighter?" I asked, "Like a guy in gear?"

"That's what they told me."

"From what town?" The fire departments stitched the name of the town they served, or at least the initials, on the back of their coats.

"No one knew for sure."

A firefighter. I thought about that while I stirred the shrimp and a little oil around in the pan with a wooden spoon. "It doesn't have to be a firefighter at all. It would be good camouflage to wear gear at a large fire scene. Lots of guys running around in all directions; even other firefighters probably wouldn't question you. Anyone can snatch the coat of the guy operating the pumps; they don't usually wear them and just hang them from some grab bar. If it was returned quickly no one would be the wiser. Or you can buy gear online if you want; you don't even have to prove you're part of a fire department to do it, or maybe at night a Halloween costume would do."

"But it could be a firefighter," Valerie said. She took a second pan from the pot rack hanging over the stove and set it on a burner.

"Three murders all committed with fire? It certainly could be. I'm just not sure how suspecting a firefighter is going to lead you to the killer. There are hundreds of firefighters locally More if you count retired guys and some of them probably got to keep their gear as souvenirs. Do you also want to include guys who had some type firefighter training in the Army or Navy?"

"Still, better hundreds of suspects than everyone in the state," Bobby pointed out.

"I think you do better looking at Beverly," I said. I cut the provolone cheese slices into thin strips, tossing a few to Tonk as I did so. Valerie frowned at me; she hates when I spoil him. "The only reason to kill Beverly I can see is that the killer is one of her patients, and he told her something about Patricia's murder. He was afraid she'd tell someone, and so he had to kill her to protect himself. Get that list of patients, and you're looking at a hundred suspects tops. Probably even less because many of her patients were women."

Bobby was shaking his head before I even finished. "It's not going to happen. You were there. There's no way that lawyer is going to hand over that list, even if I had proof the killer was on it, which I don't, and I'm a million miles away from having enough evidence to get a warrant. There's just no way that nut is going to crack."

Valerie poured the eggs into the pan, and then covered it with a lid and adjusted the heat. "What if you go back to the motive? I mean, Patricia and Michael were involved with each other. Someone jealous of either of them could want both of them dead. What about Michael's wife?"

Bobby took a drink from his glass. "She was angry at him, but I don't think angry enough to kill; besides which she wasn't a patient of Beverly Dell and she never left her car the whole time Michael's car was there. We were standing right next to her. She couldn't have done anything to blow it up. And what about the male firefighter seen near the car?"

"Then how about an ex-boyfriend of Patricia's?"

"Her last boyfriend is dead. Suicide," I said.

"What? When?" Bobby asked in surprise. "Where did you hear that?"

I told him about my discussions with Patricia's sister, her neighbor, and her coworkers. "Her sister told me he committed suicide sometime last year after Patricia broke up with him. One of her neighbors said he looked young, and a coworker told me his name was Dan."

Bobby produced his notebook from somewhere and started writing. "Dan. First name or last?"

"I don't know for sure. Probably first, I guess."

"Maybe she had a different ex-boyfriend." Valerie said, and then had a sudden dark thought, "What if it wasn't suicide?"

Bobby threw his hands up and looked at her, "Shit, I don't know. You're asking me if I think this killer could have killed not three, but four people? Maybe. I don't even know who her last boyfriend was. I don't even know if he was local. I only know his first or possibly last name was Dan and that he looked young."

"But how many young people named Dan could have committed suicide in the last year?" Valerie persisted.

"In Southern New Hampshire, or should I include Northern

Massachusetts as well? Vermont? Connecticut? And we don't know it was suicide – we don't even know for sure he's dead – that's just what Patricia told her sister. Furthermore, suicide isn't often listed as suicide in the police records. A guy drives his car off a cliff you're going to put it down as a motor vehicle accident, even if excessive drugs or alcohol were involved. Believe me; it's easier to tell someone's parents their child died in a car wreck than they committed suicide. Pretty much you have to hang, poison, or shoot yourself in the head to be listed as a suicide."

We stood around thinking about that for a moment and listening to the eggs sizzle. I took the lid off the eggs, threw in the shrimp and added the provolone, then put the lid back.

"Even if I could locate this person," Bobby continued, "and convince either a judge or his relatives I had the right Dan, get the body exhumed, and get a coroner to look at it, so what? Are they going to be able to prove it was murder? Does knowing it was murder lead me closer to the murderer? No, if one of Patricia's exes is the way to go then I'll just go farther back in her phone records. He'll turn up there somewhere. It will take time, but if the killer's in there, I'll find him."

"But how many more people will die?" Valerie asked sadly.

"Yeah, I know." Bobby crossed the dining room to stand in front of the bay window looking into the front yard. "I can't believe this is happening here. Up until this the biggest crime we had here was some guy who stole stuff from his neighbors while they were away at work. Fifteen houses he hit. Like every house in the neighborhood got robbed but his. That's part of how we found him." He drank the rest of the glass of juice. "Part of me thinks it would be better if the killer was done killing and just faded away. Catching him isn't going to bring back Patricia or Beverly or Michael, and if he isn't done, if he's lining up on someone else while we're standing here making breakfast, I don't see how we're going to stop him in time."

That was a pretty heavy side order of shit to go with our omelet, but I noticed for the first time he had used the pronoun we, and my heart got a little lift. Maybe he was coming to understand what was driving me; I couldn't let this go.

I took the lid off of the pan and folded the omelet carefully in half with a spatula. "If anyone cares," I said, "breakfast is served."

Thirty-Four

After a quiet and gloomy meal Bobby thanked us for breakfast and left to lock himself in his office with Patricia's phone records, adding Michael Carston's into the mix as well. I offered to write a quick computer program that would use a scanner and optical character recognition to tabulate the numbers for him, but he refused. As he left I told him I would keep him informed of anything I found, and while he didn't tell me to back off, neither did he tell me he would keep me in his loop. It seemed a separate but parallel investigation was the best I was going to get. With Michael's murder in Amherst, that police department was going to get involved as well. I hoped they would make some progress where Bobby and I had not.

I was bone tired and dragged myself upstairs to bed. Sleep was close, so close, but I tossed and turned, unable to get there. Maybe the room wasn't quite dark enough, or maybe I had repressed memories of being sent to bed early without supper as a child, or maybe those were just excuses. Whatever the reason I couldn't sleep, I wasn't too worried. That night I would be able to; I was sure of it.

I got up and puttered around in my shop for most of the day, and avoided thinking about the murders as much as I could, which of course wasn't very much. In the evening after dinner with nothing better to do I went down to the fire station. A bunch of old timers, Russell Burtran, John Pederson, Max Deaks, and Roger Fiske were there playing poker. I sat in for a few hands, throwing some theories and questions around mostly just to see what they thought of them.

"What do you think about the fact that Beverly was gagged but Patricia wasn't?" I asked John while he shuffled.

He paused, then squared up the deck with a sharp rap against the tabletop and started dealing. "How the hell should I know?"

"What I'm thinking is what if the guy was her patient, and she was talking to him, trying to get him to let her go, and he got tired of listening to it and gagged her."

He thought about that for a moment, but before he could answer Fiske said "What if she were conscious as he carried her out to her car and he was worried about her screaming her head off on Main Street? Patricia's house was in the middle of nowhere."

John nodded a little.

Fiske was probably right. I fanned out the cards, found a pair of twos, anted in, drew three cards, all garbage, and folded.

A few hands later I asked, "Any of you know anything about starting fires with diesel fuel?"

Then later, "Why is it I could find out where Michael worked on the internet, but the killer apparently couldn't?"

I asked other questions, got no useful answers, and as the evening wore on those I did get were more clipped and monosyllabic. They were becoming irritated with me. Still when Burtran and Deaks got up to use the bathroom I broke out the photos from the fire that had killed Patricia and spread them out on the table.

"Jesus, Fallon," Fiske said in exasperation, "would you just let it go? The poor girl is dead and you're not going to solve it here. I just want to play some cards." He got up and went over to a cooler that they had brought in over by the meeting room door, opened the lid, and pulled out a beer. He cracked the tab on the can, lit a cigarette, and stepped outside.

John, however, was looking at the pictures. He tapped the one of the padlock used on the chain on Patricia's ankles. "I know that lock."

"What do you mean?" I asked quickly.

"Maybe ten years ago we had problems with stuff getting stolen out of the Fire Department. A generator, an ice auger, a chainsaw. It was happening in lots of departments. The State Police thought maybe an ex-firefighter or a ring of them was behind it. We started locking up all the spare equipment, anything that wasn't on the trucks. You remember that, Max?"

Max and Russell had come back from the bathroom. Max spun the picture so he could look at it. "Yeah. They never caught anyone, and it was all a big pain in the ass. The locks were cheap crap, probably bought through someone's brother-in-law in the state house. They were fussy to get open, and some of them jammed solid. We couldn't get to the equipment when we needed to."

"It never made any sense to me, stealing gear from a guy who might need it someday to save your ass, but it happened," John shook his head. "And it was mostly petty shit too. Sure, a portable gennie is worth about a grand, but you can get an ice auger at Home Depot for under two hundred bucks. Just a fact of life, I guess," he shrugged.

"What happened to the locks?" I asked.

"Across the state? I can't say," John said as he started shuffling the cards. "We threw most of ours out, though I think a couple of firefighters took some for personal use. Your kid used one as a bike lock, right Rus?"

Russell picked up the photo and looked at it but said nothing.

Fiske came back in, and I gathered up the pictures and put them away, and kept quiet the rest of the time I played.

While I'm more than capable of counting a single deck of cards and can calculate the poker odds accurately in my head, my heart wasn't in the game and I lost more than I won. As I saw it, the couple of hour's distraction had cost me just over twelve dollars and was well worth it.

I went home afterwards fully intending to go to sleep, planning to sleep through the whole next day in fact, but it all came to an end that night, with a speed and brutality that nearly cost me my life.

Thirty-Five

The call was for a basement fire in a house under construction on Oak Hill. It was a big Adirondack, one of those structures that make me feel as though I should leave a trail of breadcrumbs to keep from becoming lost in the endless series of enormous rooms. Tom was driving, Russell was in the officer's seat, Paul and I were in back. It was déjà vu all over again.

"Fallon, you're with me on the line," Russell called from the front seat.

"Right behind you," I finished fastening the air tank to my back and pulled it free from the clips.

"Paul, I want you to lay four inch down the driveway. We're going to need water supply for this one."

"Consider it done."

The truck sped down about two hundred feet of unpaved driveway, gravel crunching under the heavy treads. The house

228

loomed ghostly in the wintery light of a new gibbous moon. Three windows along the foundation line at the front of the house were blowing smoke and flames. This basement fire was rocking.

As we slid to a stop I noticed there were no cars parked in the turnaround in front of the house, and the detached four-car garage was just an unfinished stud frame. I believed the house was unoccupied during the construction, and wondered if it was worth going into the structure, risking our lives on an unknown basement fire for an empty building. That question hung in my mind for only a moment. As the officer of the truck it was Russell's call to make. Like the military, without our chain of command, we're nothing.

I jumped to the ground and pulled the speedlay line from under the pump panel, and ran to the front door paying out hose as I went. Paul opened one of the side compartments and hauled out lengths of four-inch diameter hose in fifty foot rolls. The next truck on the scene would connect to this length of hose down the driveway and feed its water to our truck. Tanker trucks as they arrived would supply that truck and in turn supply us without having to maneuver down the narrow, unpaved driveway to the house.

Russell met me at the front door with a Halligan bar, which looks something like a crowbar on steroids. It has a straight prying tool on one end and a right-angle prying tool on the other with a stout steel spike shooting off ninety degrees to that. In a talented hand, it can deal some serious damage. The door in front of us appeared ready for the challenge, constructed from massive boards of Brazilian Ipe banded together with black scroll-worked metal plates.

Russell's first blow with the spike glanced off the door leaving only a small scratch in the finish. I thought maybe we would need a battering ram like we were laying siege to a medieval castle, but his second blow sunk deep into the wood near the lock. He pulled the tool free with a squealing sound like

229

a rainforest crying out in pain and drove it in again. The side of the jam cracked and the doorknob fell off, and the door swung away from us and banged into the entryway wall.

Heavy smoke rolled out the doorway and we both crouched down and pulled our masks over our faces and spun our tank valves open. The hose became heavy in my hands as Tom started the pumps and filled it with water.

The entryway opened into a living room was every bit as massive as I had expected it to be. It looked like it would have been entirely possible to play an arena football game in there. Much of the floor was unfinished plywood subfloor. Big stacks of pre-finished flooring awaiting installation divided the room into alleys and made the room feel like a warehouse. Smoke rose from the subflooring which sagged slightly in a few places, and I again considered the wisdom of being in there, then followed behind Russell as he set off across the living room, hugging against the room's exterior wall where the floor would be strongest because it was supported by the foundation wall underneath.

The center of the room was dominated by a flagstone fireplace that could take at least a six-foot log in its maw. We passed this on the left, going through an arch into what would eventually be the dining room beyond, comfy and intimate seating for at least forty, and then entered into the kitchen through a double swinging door.

The kitchen was nearing completion with rose granite countertops, Italian marble floor tiles, and immaculate red oak cabinetry with brushed nickel hardware that glowed in the beam of my flashlight. Gaps remained in the walls and countertops where appliances would go when they were delivered. An island and seating counter combination filled the center of the room. I had always wanted a kitchen with an island.

Russell moved to a door in the far wall which likely opened into the basement stairway access and tried to open it, but something, perhaps heat stressing the frame, had jammed the door closed. I took off a glove and held my bare hand against the door face. It was warm, but not hot. The basement wasn't in flashover yet, but it was getting there.

I stood behind Russell and a little to the right with the hose at the ready as he drove the pry end of the Halligan into the gap between the door and the lock plate and leaned on it. The heavy oak door groaned but didn't budge. I set my feet, planning to throw a thousand gallons of water at anything that came up the stairs at us when he got that door open. Behind me I heard an enormous crash; I thought one of the stacks of hardwood falling through the weakened subfloor.

"Now or never, Rus." I said to his straining back.

"Uh-huh." He grunted back at me.

It was at that moment my mind suddenly put all the pieces together. If someone had asked me later, I would have told them I had not even been particularly thinking about the murders. Something about the hunch of his shoulders as he worked the bar, or maybe the way the smoke hung dense in the air, or maybe it was the crew we had with us. It all took me back to the fire in which I had found Patricia's body, and of course I remembered the funerals, both of them. It all seemed so clear to me now. Clear, and desperately, horribly tragic.

"Your son was named Daniel, wasn't he?"

Russell stopped working the bar and looked back at me. "What?"

I repeated myself, louder this time, "Your son's name was Daniel."

"What does that have to do with anything?"

"It was you, Russell." Not a question, a statement.

He made no comment, but stood listening.

"Patricia Woods, Beverly Dell, Michael Carston; you killed them all."

He looked at me but said nothing for a long time. I imagined an array of expressions crossing his face as he tried to find the right words, of course invisible to me behind his respirator mask. Then he turned away and renewed his attack upon the door, "What the hell are you talking about, Fallon? We've got a fire to fight here."

"Your son was dating Patricia." Russell stopped working again, listening. "You think he crashed his car and killed himself because Patricia broke up with him? Is that why you killed her, for not loving your son?"

He suddenly dug into the door with a fury, splinters of wood flying from the jamb. He was yelling something, but I couldn't tell what, though I did catch the word, "Bitch."

"Patricia broke up with Daniel to date Michael Carston. You think he came between them so you killed him?" I shouted at him.

No answer, but he let the Halligan fall from the door jamb to hang loosely from one gloved hand and leaned his back against the door, breathing heavily.

"But why did you kill Beverly Dell? What did she have to do with it?"

For a long time I thought he wasn't going to answer me, but then he did, "She wouldn't help him!" He cried.

I closed my eyes and remembered. "Daniel was her patient. The one she told me about, the one who committed suicide."

"Week after week I saw him getting worse. I told her that

her therapy wasn't helping him. She insisted he was getting better, that he was going to be OK. I should be patient, she said to me, therapy took time. Look at what she did to my son. My only son!"

All the dots connected, revealing a picture I wished I had never seen.

He leaned heavily on the Halligan like it was a cane. "You're too damned smart, you know that?" He spat it at me, like it was a condemnation.

"You know what really clinches it for me?" I said. "The night at the fire as I tried to get Patricia out of that house, you told me to get *her* out of there. You knew it was a woman, even though there was no visibility in that house at all. I had to actually put my hands on her to tell, but you knew. You knew because you had chained her to that bed. Fuck, Rus, how do you do that? How do you do that to another human being?"

"You couldn't possibly understand."

"No sane person could!"

I didn't know what was left to say to him. We stood there, facing each other as the house came apart around us. I realized the Halligan was an excellent weapon in his hands, and I could have picked a better time and place to confront him, in fact would have been hard pressed to think of a worse one. Still, I was not completely unarmed myself. The hose line in my hands, backed by over one hundred pounds per square inch of water pressure with an essentially endless supply behind it, could be used to drive him back like a riot cannon. I wasn't looking forward to a fight with him, but neither was I unprepared to defend myself.

Somewhere in the living room another pallet of wood fell through the floor.

His shoulders sagged. He looked around the room at the thickening smoke, his years of experience doing the math for him. At any moment the floor might collapse and we'd end up having our fight in the basement. "Let's get out of here."

He started walking towards me and I retreated, keeping the hose nozzle pointed at him, edging my way along the wall through the swinging double door into the dining room, back the way we had come. Hampered by the weight of the charged hose line as I backed up, he was casually, innocuously closing the gap between us. Ten feet. Five. My hand tightened on the valve control.

When he swung the Halligan at me from a range of maybe three feet it wasn't a lightening move designed to crush my skull or break my ribs. He swung it in an almost casual arc, one I could easily avoid by simply stepping to the side, which I did. The cracking of joists beneath my feet told me that was exactly what he had been planning all along. He had forced me away from the wall towards the middle of the room where the floor was going, going, gone.

I dropped the hose line, thinking perhaps without its additional weight the joists would hold long enough for me to get back onto the more solid ground nearer the wall. Instead I felt the floor go soft, and then tilt precariously towards the center of the room behind me. A section gave way with a splintering of wood and the shriek of tortured nails leaving a hole more than ten feet across boiling smoke and fire.

I reached out towards Russell who avoided my grasp, and then watched impassively as I fell through the hole into the basement below.

Thirty-Six

The fire department has an annual supper for all members past and present. It's a chance for the crew to meet the old timers, who regale us with stories of firefighting without modern equipment, of going into a building wearing a long leather coat and high boots while smoking a cigar armed with only a leaky canvas hose. We take all of it with a grain of salt, but it makes for fine entertainment while we pack away steamship round and mashed potatoes and green beans and salad with creamy Italian dressing, with apple cobbler ala mode for dessert.

It was at one of these that I met Jonas Gault, who, he liked to remind me, had been Chief of the Dunboro Fire Department while I was still just a glimmer in my parents' eyes. Also a carpenter, Jonas and I became fast friends. He would sit on a rickety stool in the corner of my shop sometimes while I tinkered, offering bits of fire department history and woodworking lore, and the occasional spare hand for tricky jobs. He told me about a complete set of captain's chairs he had made once. I recalled my first and thus far only attempt at scalloping the seat for a captain's chair had resulted in a seating surface that would have made the Marquis De Sade clasp his hands together in rapturous joy.

When I learned through guys at the department that Jonas lived alone near the edge of town in a veritable shotgun shack with only a pittance Social Security check to sustain him, I volunteered to come by and do some odd jobs – patch up the roof, replace a broken window, that kind of thing. Jonas readily agreed to the help, but insisted on paying for all the materials himself.

One Sunday morning, after a quick repointing of the mortar on his chimney which only took me a couple of hours, I offered to take him to breakfast at Norma's and he accepted. Long after I had run out of things at his house that needed doing, we continued to have breakfast together often.

I remember on one particular breakfast amidst the clatter of dishes and rattle of newspapers in Norma's that he leaned slightly towards me across the table. "You have time for a story?"

I tipped back in my chair and pushed my almost-empty plate of pancakes aside. The piece of pancake on the fork pulled away from the plate, tethered by lazy loops of syrup. "All the time in the world."

His fingers flexed on his coffee cup, and the sides of his eyes and mouth turn down. With the tightening of the muscles of his face, I got a glimpse of the younger man he had been. "This was about forty-five years ago, and I'm the new Chief of the Dunboro fire department. A woman comes home from grocery shopping, parks her car in her garage, and walks to the front door of her house. She touches the knob and it feels hot. She looks in the windows and sees smoke in her living room. Without hesitation she runs to the neighbor's house and calls the fire department."

"OK so far."

He nodded just a little, almost imperceptibly, "By the time we get there, two small windows at the top of the foundation line have broken out and are blowing smoke and flames."

"Fully involved basement fire."

Again he gave the miniscule nod, "Right. The house is a two-story garrison with two-car garage under. No big deal, I figure. I'll send a crew into the basement through the garage and they'll fight the fire from there. They get the hoses set up, and into the garage they go. For about five minutes I'm on the radio with the tanker crew setting up the water supply, and the next time I look up nothing has changed; I don't see the fire going out. No steam, no lessening of smoke."

"Where's the team in the garage?"

"Good question. Where is the team in the garage? I send a runner to get me an update. It turns out they can't find a way from the garage into the basement. They're down there in the smoke making like Marcel Marceau feeling along the walls, but they can't find the door. The homeowner tells me there is no doorway. When they finished the basement they didn't want the smell of the cars getting in, so they bricked it over."

"Super."

"Uh-huh. I call back the garage crew, and by this time the basement is rocking. It's been burning down there at least thirty minutes and perhaps as long as an hour."

"Is the living room floor still good?"

"The carpet hasn't melted, and that's a good sign, but for how much longer? I have a powwow with three of my most aggressive entry guys. Do they think they can take a hose line down the basement stairs and fight this fire from the top down? They think they can, and we decide to give it a go. With a hose line they go through the living room, across the dining room, and to the door at the top of the basement stairs. At that moment, two things happen. One, the basement door disintegrates and the fire comes up the stairs into the kitchen. Two, a fire has been quietly burning through a basement window and cooking the underside of an add-on deck at the back of the living room. The deck picks that moment to burst into flames, blowing the sliding glass door into the living room and cutting off their escape route."

He sort of half gestured with his hands holding his cup and coffee sloshed over the sides unnoticed. I picked the napkin off my lap and dropped it on top of the small puddle on the table. The coffee sucked up into the napkin causing a brown spot like a Rorschach Test.

"The back deck went up in this ball of fire you could see over the roof of the house – not good – and I sound for the evacuation. The guys in the kitchen, of course, know things have gone to shit all on their own. They abandon their hose line and flee through the kitchen door. One guy jumps out the dining room window, and receives about a dozen stitches for his trouble. Everyone assembles on the front lawn and we do a head count." He stopped and took a breath.

"And?"

"And, we're one guy short."

"Who?"

"I'm so frazzled at this point, I'm not even sure. I know the three guys who went in, and they're all there, but we've got a guy on the fireground unaccounted for."

"Where is he?"

"Who the fuck knows? I call for a sweep. Maybe he's trying to do something around the back of the house or out in the brush. I send people to search for him and we find his helmet."

He locked eyes with me to see if I understood the significance of this. I did. A firefighter pinned down somewhere, unable to get anyone's attention, will sometimes throw a piece of equipment out a window hoping someone will find it. It's a move of pure desperation, because you're almost always better off with your equipment than without it. Also the squash protector, as firefighters sometimes refer to their helmets, is an unusual choice – most guys will throw their flashlight. I had heard of cases where guys who were more or less completely buried had to throw their helmets as it was the only piece of equipment they could get off their bodies. I repeated my question. "So, where is he?"

"The helmet is lying on the lawn in back near the deck. All the second-floor windows are still intact, and he wouldn't have closed the window after throwing it out. The first floor is so heavily involved at this point, no one could be alive in there…" He trailed off.

I closed my eyes. The basement.

Basement fires are funny things. They're incredibly hot, and yet all the heat collects up against the joists of the floor above. If you stay down, flat against the floor, you can actually be surprisingly cool, relatively speaking. I pictured this unknown firefighter, who somehow managed to find a way into the basement, huddled in a corner, without his helmet, praying for a rescue before the house falls on him.

When I opened my eyes, Jonas was looking down into the coffee mug, squeezing its sides reflexively.

"How can you get to him?"

"I didn't know. I'm the new Chief on a department for all of a week, and I'm standing on the lawn watching this very common basement fire that has become a total and complete clusterfuck, and I – don't – know. Every thought in my head is contradicted by a dozen others. Every move I've made up to this moment has been wrong; what makes me think I can make a correct decision now? One of the guys wants to get his own pickup truck, parked by the side of the road, and drive it into the garage and through the basement wall to get a search team in that way. It seems like a good idea, but before he's gone two steps I call him back. Driving through that wall could bring the whole house down at this point, and even if it doesn't, it could kill the firefighter in the basement. It would risk losing more firefighters to rescue a guy who the odds say was already dead. I can't believe I've been on this fire for less than ten minutes; it feels like hours and I'm exhausted."

He stopped again and took a drink of coffee. He put the mug unsteadily down on the table as if it was too heavy to continue holding up.

"So?" I prodded.

"So what?"

"So, how did you get him out of the basement?" I paused. "Or didn't you?"

"Didn't have to. It turns out the firefighter had broken the strap on his helmet, and was in the back of the fire truck getting a spare when the roll call was taken. He wasn't in the building at all."

"So you didn't lose anyone?"

"Not in that fire. Lost the house, though." He tapped at the table with his index finger, emphasizing his words, "The point is it didn't have to go that way. If I had cut a hole in the living room floor with a chainsaw we could have fed water through the hole and put the fire out. Or I could have sent a crew down the stairs early and maybe that would have worked. I've never been on a fire scene before or since and felt so many of my decisions were wrong."

"But you didn't know the garage was cut off from the house."

"No, I didn't. But I still feel that way. I've lost other buildings, and I've, knock wood," which he did, rapping one oversized knuckle of his arthritic right hand on the tabletop "lost firefighters. And of all the fires I've been a part of over the years, that's the one I carry with me. It's a reminder that even when things are going well in a fire fight, just when you think everything is under control, you can find yourself in the shit faster than you can blink an eye."

Thirty-Seven

I was in the shit all right.

I had landed badly, on the tank on my back, on top of the debris pile from the collapsed floor. Pain like a harpoon lanced out from my tortured spine and sent lightning bolts juddering down to my hands and feet, which felt numb and tingly. I realized at some point my hood liner must have become twisted around underneath my helmet, because I could hear the bacon-grease sizzle of some patch of skin on my neck as it burned. Looking up was like looking into the eye of a hurricane of fire spinning through the hole in the floor into the room above.

I managed to roll myself off of the pile onto my hands and knees, probably looking much like a turtle, a crippled turtle at that, trying to turn itself upright. I then crawled and flopped myself away from the burning pile on limbs that only hesitantly responded to instructions from my brain. Lying in a clear spot on the bare concrete floor face down panting into my mask, I managed to get a gloved hand underneath the cowling of my helmet to straighten out the hood liner. The damaged skin screamed at me as I pulled the liner over it, though I had no way of knowing how bad the burn actually was.

I allowed myself another thirty seconds of lying motionless on the floor. If I was going to have any chance of getting out of this alive, I was going to have to rally every reserve I could find. Scrabbling around on the floor like a half-dead crab wasn't going to cut it. I counted off the thirty seconds, slowed my breathing, and pushed the pain into the corners of my body like someone clearing a room of furniture for a dance party. Ready to boogie?

I rose with a groan to a stooped standing position, surprised and heartened by the fact no bones seemed broken and my flashlight was still working.

The heat wasn't too bad, probably no more than three or four hundred degrees, which is practically tepid by firefighter standards. The holes in the floor were venting the worst of the smoke and superheated gases into the house above. It was a mixed blessing, however, because even as the holes made the basement cooler it made the rest of house more unstable. Enough holes in the floor and the entire structure would come raining into the basement like a house of cards, certain death for anyone who hadn't managed to get out of Dodge before it happened. An enormous crash echoed from across the basement somewhere out of sight in the smoke and darkness, probably another pallet of wood coming down. I realized as my startled heart thudded in my chest that I might not have to wait for the whole house to collapse, a pallet of wood would be just as fatal if it landed on me.

The basement had high ceilings, at least nine feet, which meant unless I found a ladder somewhere down here the stairs were my only way up and out. I headed off in that direction, knowing as I did so that Russell had had no luck prying the door open from the other side. Maybe he hadn't been trying too hard. I was certainly more motivated.

The stairs lay only a short distance away, fully ablaze, but still structurally sound, hopefully. I scampered up them quickly, keeping my weight over the stringers. As I ran I dropped one shoulder and simply hit the basement door with whatever momentum I had accumulated. The door didn't give at all, though I think my shoulder did.

I ran my flashlight around the doorjamb, looking for anything that could be holding it closed. Nothing caught my eye. Up at the top of the stairs the heat was nearly unbearable even through my gear. I recalled one of the instructors at the fire academy mentioning that when your facemask started to melt, it was too damned hot. There's a good safety tip. Mine looked okay so far. I ran the flashlight around the jamb again, this time catching a quick metallic reflection halfway up one side. I looked closer.

It was the point of a nail, a big one, maybe 12d or 16d, a framing nail. The door had been nailed shut from the other side with I had no idea how many nails.

Had Russell been planning this all along? Had he led me into the fire to kill me? It was a question I promised myself I would ask again later, if I survived.

I whammed my hand against the door. It was solid wood. With an axe or some type of breaching tool there was no question in my mind I could have gotten through. Barehanded in the condition I was in, it was utterly out of the question, and the stairs beneath me were becoming more uncertain with each passing second. I dejectedly moved back down into the basement.

So what was plan B for my great escape? Find another exit. A bulkhead door would have been outstanding, though I had no idea if one even existed. I found a foundation wall and moved along it, an inverted river of fire running in the joist spaces over my head. I came to a window. It was very short, only perhaps ten inches tall, and just about nine feet off of the floor. Could I stack up something to get up to it and worm my way through?

The idea was tempting, but as I looked around within the range of my flashlight I saw absolutely nothing to stack. There were the piles of hardwood, but as energetically as they were burning I thought trying to climb up one would be more like a Joan of Arc impersonation than an escape attempt. I took one last longing look at the window and moved on.

The basement was gigantic, roughly rectangular, and utterly devoid of another exit of any sort beyond the high narrow windows of which I counted six, three along the front, and three along the back.

I came across the heating plant, a big cubical propane burner and hot air circulator in one corner. It had already been set and plumbed in. I tried to wrench it free; it was immovable. Too bad, I could have used it to get up to one of the windows. There was a small trickle of water running down the wall near the heating plant and a puddle behind it. A crew out there was putting water onto the fire and some of it was running down here. They were probably using a technique called 'surround and drown' in which the structure is determined to be so unsafe that all the fire department can do is stand around throwing water on it to put it out.

Did anyone realize I was down here? Was anyone even looking for me? If Russell had simply walked out of the house back to the truck, he could have told Tom and Paul anything – I was around the rear of the house doing something, I was working on a kindled brush fire back in the woods, anything. I couldn't get out, and by the time anyone came in looking for me it would be too late.

What was plan C, Houdini?

I took precious moments trying to think of something and came up empty.

Against my better judgment I left the foundation wall, probably the safest place in the case of imminent structural collapse, and moved towards the center of the basement. It was the only place I hadn't looked. It was all I had left.

I came to a stone fireplace on this level, part of the same chimney structure that fed the fireplace I had seen on the ground floor. There was probably another one on the second floor as well, most likely in the master bedroom. A fireplace in the master bedroom was a hot commodity in the upscale construction market. I ducked inside and opened the damper. It opened about four inches and stopped. A cat could have gotten out through that slot, but I could not.

I could see a slice of the moon way up the chimney through the animal screen past the flue cap at the top. Oh, to be a bird.

I let the damper slide closed.

Just as I ducked out of the fireplace I got an idea. It was not a sure thing, but compared to the available alternatives it seemed like genius.

I ran across the basement to the heating plant. I wrestled with the access panel until I found the clips that held it in place and pulled it free. It was a fair piece of sheet metal, more than three feet on a side. The word "TRANE" was printed in block letters six inches high on the panel face.

I ran with it back to the fireplace, ducked inside, and placed the panel in the opening behind me. It was large enough to block it completely.

Now when the house collapsed, and running through the basement I had heard creaks and groans from the structure that told me it would happen soon, I would be safe inside here. I had seen whole houses burned to the ground, leaving nothing standing but the chimney. They survived fires all the time. Well, some of the time at any rate.

I settled against the rear wall of the fireplace, wondering

what it would sound like when the house caved in. I also wondered if the relatively thin sheet metal would hold out the falling debris, or if giant timbers and hot coals would smash through it and crush me inside the fireplace. Maybe I should have tried to get another panel off of the unit to make a double layer with this one. I sensed there was no time to do anything about that now, and besides, only the access panel was designed to come off without tools. Removing another panel would probably have required at least a screwdriver.

Suddenly, there was a deep rumbling sound I felt in my bones. It reminded me of standing on the subway platform as the Broadway local pulled into Penn Station. This was followed by a sound almost beyond description. Deafening. Cataclysmic. End of the world stuff. Something slammed against the sheet metal panel like a battering ram. It wedged up flush against the stone fireplace face and buckled, but held. Ash and small embers sifted through the chinks in the uneven stones to settle on the legs of my bunker pants. I brushed them off. The rumbling dissipated and then everything was quiet except for the occasion shifting of the burning pile now stacked outside my tomb. The metal sheet gave off incredible heat. I had unwitting built myself a stone oven like one that might be used to cook pizza or fire clay.

I took the flashlight off of the clip on my jacket and wedged it into a space between two stones of the fireplace face. Now with a little luck and geometry on my side, the front of the chimney would be washed with the cone of my flashlight beam. Would anyone see it? It was night outside, so perhaps they would. It was also possible they were using the twin fifteen hundred watt halogen lamps mounted on the fire truck to light the work area, in which case my flashlight would have all the visibility of a candle held up in front of the sun. No reason to think negatively, right? I and the chimney had survived the collapse. I would wait, and they would rescue me.

A bell went off right behind me and I bolted upright, banging my helmet against the damper. It was the low-pressure alarm on my air tank. How much time did that leave me? It depended a lot on the particular firefighter. Some guys could breathe up a whole tank of air in just fifteen minutes. Some guys managed to make them go almost an hour. I took cold comfort in the fact that, back in firefighter training, my tanks had lasted as long as anyone else's in the entire class.

There had been one training class in particular in which they had had us do hard physical labor while breathing from a tank. We carried fifty-foot rolls of four-inch hose and twelve-foot extension ladders back and forth across a parking lot. It served the dual purpose of getting us used to breathing on and working with the tanks, but it also allowed us to realize how long a tank would last for each of us. After the bells had gone off, they made us keep working. They wanted us to know what breathing out of the end of a tank felt like.

As the tank emptied it became harder and harder to pull air from it. The pressure dropped from positive to neutral, and then negative, sucking our masks onto our faces as our lungs labored. Guys in the parking lot had finally ripped their masks off and dropped to their knees, their faces red, wheezing in gulping breaths.

That, they said, is what the bottom of a tank felt like.

And no matter what, if you find yourself in a fire on an empty tank, don't take your mask off. You're better off breathing nothing at all than the superheated poisonous air in a fire.

So I sat with the mask at first tightening against my face just a little bit.

It was a conscious effort to keep my hands down at my sides as the pressure dropped, trying to hold each breath as long as possible, trying to take the air in tiny sips and make it last. My chest heaved, pulling in each gasp as though through a straw a mile long. The instinct to take the mask off was immense.

I said it to myself like a mantra.

Don't take the mask off.

There's nothing out there for you to breathe.

Nothing at all.

Thirty-Eight

March 12, 2004 dawned clear, bright, and calm; in every way the perfect New England spring morning. Forty-three year old Mark Miller, a seventeen year veteran firefighter with twenty two years of diving experience went on a training dive with a partner beneath a partially-frozen Lake Winnipesaukee in New Hampshire. Both men dove and surfaced repeatedly, and then together decided to explore what appeared to be an abandoned boiler resting on the lake bottom. The partner took a picture of Mark with the boiler, the two then signaling to each other they should return to the surface.

The partner returned to the surface.

Mark did not.

He waited; looking for telltale bubbles that would indicate Mark's position. None were seen.

He returned to where they had piled their additional gear prior to the dive to see if Mark had surfaced elsewhere without his partner noticing and gone there. He had not.

At this point, realizing something had most probably happened to Mark, the man had a passerby call 911, while he himself continued to look for bubbles.

It was estimated that 128 personnel from local departments, federal agencies, and area dive shops were ultimately involved in the search.

The body was not recovered until the next day.

Two homeless people squatting in the abandoned Worcester Cold Storage and Warehouse in Massachusetts knocked over a candle while having a dispute. Unable to extinguish the flames, they fled the building. They did not report the fire. It was December 3, 1999.

Arriving on the scene to a report of smoke, the solid brick building, which had no windows above the second floor, made it extremely difficult for the fire department to initially assess the extent of the fire. Believing there to be homeless people inside, firefighters began to explore the six-story building. They became disoriented in the rabbit's warren of rooms and hallways inside the structure, blanketed in thick smoke that reduced visibility to nearly zero, and were overcome by a fire which was rapidly accelerating out of control.

When the command came to evacuate the building, six firefighters: Paul Brotherton, Jeramiah Lucey, Timothy Jackson, Joseph McGuirk, Thomas Spencer, and James Lyons III did not come out.

The fire, which ultimately reached four alarms, took the concerted efforts of hundreds of firefighters from the surrounding towns six days to extinguish.

The bodies of the firefighters were not recovered until two days later.

Nine firefighters in Charleston, South Carolina were killed on June 18, 2007 when the Charleston Sofa Super Store partially collapsed during a rapidly spreading fire that started in a loading dock at the rear of the structure. The nine firefighters had had over 130 cumulative years of service between them. Two, James Dayton and William Hutchinson, had more than thirty years of fire service each.

On April 15, 2001 nineteen-year-old Bradley Golden was killed in a training fire set in an empty house during his third week on the fire department.

In July of 1953, fifteen firefighters were killed in a wildfire in the Mendocino National Forest.

Thirteen firefighters were killed in the Strand Theater in Brockton Massachusetts in 1946.

Twenty-seven were killed in explosions aboard two ships docked in Texas City in 1947.

Twelve died in the collapse of a drug store in New York City in 1966.

Twenty-one were killed in a stockyard fire in Chicago in 1910.

And let us not forget the three hundred and forty-three who perished on 9/11.

Despite advances in safety equipment and training, firefighters alone continue to die year after year in numbers that do not decrease. This is not true of coal miners. This is not true of combat soldiers. This is not true of spelunkers, mountain climbers, high-steel workers, skyscraper window washers, racecar drivers, aircraft pilots, lion tamers, snake charmers, or any other vocation you can think of.

We get burned, electrocuted, run over, drowned, crushed,

buried alive, blown up, poisoned, suffocated, impaled, severed, and mutilated, all for, at least at the volunteer level, seven dollars and fifteen cents an hour and all the smoke we can eat.

We wear T-shirts with slogans like 'Find them hot, leave them wet." We joke about running into buildings when everybody with half a brain in their heads is running out.

And those we leave behind when we answer the call? The mothers and fathers and wives and husbands and sons and daughters? They delude themselves, and we help them.

We know what we're doing. We'll be careful. We'll be safe.

Until maybe the day comes when an official-looking car pulls into the driveway, and the Chief comes to the front door, bell cap wrung repeatedly in his hands into an unrecognizable twist.

We're not coming home. We're never coming home again.

Oh, God, Valerie! I'm so sorry!

Thirty-Nine

My next conscious thought, if you could call it that, was of
me having a discussion with God. This wasn't a biblical
burning-bush kind of God, but more like the God as portrayed in
the Simpsons. We were just two guys shooting the shit, walking
along an avenue of clouds between pillars of alabaster marble.
The sky was completely, homogeneously white, and the light
bathing us seemed to come from all directions at once. We cast
no shadows. I never got a good look at his face beyond his
flowing white hair and beard. He had a pretty good paunch
beneath a simple white tunic belted with a length of rope.
Golden sandals adorned his feet. My God was like Santa Clause
going to a toga party at BU. There was a leash in my hand, at
the other end a chocolate lab I had owned in grad school named
Spiff.

We were discussing sin, specifically the sin of murder. My
lead-in question was quite simple: how could he allow it to
happen? If he could stop it by removing the hatred and fear and
greed and gluttony from our lives which causes us to commit
murder, why didn't he?

It's not that simple, he replied. He created us with free will, what we choose to do with that free will is up to us. Like a parent to a child, he instilled us with goodness, but at some point he lets us go to make our own way, our own choices, whether those choices are good or not.

"But," I persisted, "if a parent has two children, and we're all supposed to be your children," I paused here and he nodded at my basic premise, so I continued "doesn't that parent have an interest in seeing that the children don't kill each other even after they've moved out of the house?"

We came to an edge of the cloud path beyond which was an enormous field of flawless grass, each individual blade a perfect emerald green. Socrates and Nietzsche were playing badminton. I was kind of worried Spiff might poop on God's lawn, but Spiff, guided by some higher power, didn't seem to be interested in even watering the grass.

God tried a different tack. We are, to him, like fish in a tank. He put the fish in the tank, but then he just watches them, not interfering in their natural order.

"But doesn't the person who owns the fish tank want the fish to live? Doesn't he have an interest in keeping the fish from killing each other?"

God sighed. I think I was trying his patience. This is all, he said, part of a greater plan.

"Ah," I replied, "the old greater plan gambit. Probably one I wouldn't understand even if you told it to me."

"Probably not," he agreed.

"I imagine that's the same thing Ken Lay told his employees at Enron. You can't understand why I've taken seven hundred and sixty million dollars from the company and put it into my own bank account, but trust me, it's part of a greater plan. Incidentally, that whole Enron thing is another bit of needless suffering you let slip by."

God frowned at me. Let me tell you, that was not a great feeling.

"I know, I know. More of the whole greater plan thing." I shrugged.

At that moment Nietzsche hit a vicious overhead slam that Socrates whiffed his racket at ineffectually, the birdie striking him directly in the forehead.

"Good shot, Frederick!" I called out to him. The two men looked at me like I had let my dog tinkle on God's sandals. They eventually continued the game without comment.

I turned back to God. "OK, forget it. We'll just have to agree to disagree on that one. I have a different question. The bible talks about how you created the world in six days, and with the calendar of events it seems like the world is only about six thousand years old, and yet we have archaeology and strata studies which indicate it is a hell," I paused, amended myself, "heck of a lot older than that."

"Oh, that," he laughed, "I fake it."

The quality of the light changed over me, taking on a bluish tint. I was lying on my back on the cloud floor. My neck hurt. The leash was gone from my hand. The shadow of God loomed over me.

"You fake it?" I asked the shadow.

"What?" the shadow replied.

A second shadow moved the first aside. "Jack? Honey, can you hear me? Can you feel this?" There was pressure on my hand, something squeezing. I thought maybe I could return the squeeze, but it just didn't seem important that I do so in the grand scheme of things, so I decided not to. Then because of some odd reflex, like an infant grasping an adult's finger, I did anyway.

"Oh, Jack!" the shadow cried. It came rapidly closer, became focused. Valerie, face taut, eyes red, cheeks streaked with tears, full blown Maybelline nightmare. She came closer still, blurred back into an indistinct shape and passed to my left, burying her face in my neck, sobbing.

"Holy crap, Jack!" John's face entered the frame, mostly in focus. "I'm glad as hell you didn't die on my watch. People are going to talk about this one in fire stations across the country for the next hundred years!"

"What happened?" That little bit was harder to get out then I thought it would be. My ribs felt tired. My lungs felt achy. My head felt achy, along with my back, my neck, my shoulders. It would probably be easier to list the things that didn't hurt which at that moment seemed to be only three of the toes on my left foot.

"Russell came out and said you had fallen into the basement. We tried to get a crew down in there, but –"

"Russell said?"

"Yeah, he came out covered in soot with a cracked facemask. We tried to get to you, three different crews. No one could get near it. Then it was like the whole building just imploded and fell into the basement. We were sure you were dead!"

"Then how did you find me?"

"Your flashlight!"

I had only dim memories of doing something with my

flashlight after the building fell.

"We saw the light, and every guy on the scene jumped into the cellar hole, digging in the sludge and hot coals with shovels and rakes and their hands until we pulled you out of there."

I could almost see it; feel the pride of teamwork humming through his voice. They had jumped into hell and pulled me out of there alive. I had no recollection of it at all. I must have run out of air before they got to me. Was there any damage? I did a quick mental inventory and everything seemed to be in place, but would I even notice the gaps? If the single brain cell in my head that had understood quantum mechanics had died, how long would it take me to find out? Would I even care?

I lifted an arm from the sheet, noticing for the first time the IV stuck into the back of my hand. I let my arm rest across Valerie and patted her on the back. She burst into a fresh round of wracking sobs.

"Where's Russell now?"

"We don't know. He-"

The door to the room swung open and Bobby leaned his head in. "I heard voices. Is Jack conscious? I have some questions for him."

"You're not coming in here. He needs rest." A woman standing next to the bed spoke for the first time. She had olive skin, dark eyes, Mediterranean features, her hair bunched up under surgical cap with one thick lustrous curl of mahogany hair spilled out hanging to her shoulder. A stethoscope hung over her neck. She wore scrub greens with a blue rectangular nametag pinned to the chest over her heart that read "Teresa Millar M.D." in small white letters.

He came into the room, the door closing behind him. "Sorry, doctor, but they can't wait."

"There are about two hundred people out in the corridor hoping for an update," John said. "I'll go out and tell them you're back among the living." He patted me on the shoulder, which unexpectedly sent a small twinge of pain shooting through my neck.

Two hundred people. Small town living. Hot damn.

"Come on, Valerie. People out there will want to see you too." He gently disengaged her from me, and led her out. Valerie took one more look over her shoulder at me to make sure I still existed, her sight cut off by the door as it swung closed.

I heard a cheer from outside the room, and halfway expected to hear them break into a round of *For He's a Jolly Good Fellow*, like we were in the last five minutes of *It's a Wonderful Life*.

"I have just a few questions for him, and then I'll leave, doctor." Bobby moved into the spot by the side of the bed John had vacated.

The doctor frowned at him. "Five minutes." She said, and folded her arms across her chest. Casting a lingering and obvious glance at the watch on her wrist, she made it clear she would hold him to it.

Before Bobby could get rolling I interrupted him, "Where's Russell Burtran?"

"That's what I wanted to ask you. What happened in there?"

I told Bobby what I knew about Russell and what I suspected, about confronting him in the house on Oak Hill, his confession, and how I ended up in the basement. It took far longer than five minutes, but once I got rolling the doctor became engrossed in the story and was willing to let me run it out. "So where is he now?" I asked again.

"We don't know. After his apparent change of heart about killing you, he took off as soon as rescue operations began. He stole the fire Chief's pickup truck from the scene. We haven't found it yet. He's not at home, and his car is still at the fire station, so we don't know where he went. Any ideas?"

I thought about it.

In the silence that followed I could hear a tapping sound. Apparently the doctor's foot – she had gone back to clock watching.

Why had Russell run away? Did he think I would be rescued? Did he think I was dead? There was no way he could know either way for certain, in which case him running away could only mean one thing.

"I think I know where he went."

"Where?"

"I'll show you." I threw off the covers.

"Uh-uh, no way." The doctor attempted to pull the covers back over me. "You're severely dehydrated, and you've been through oxygen deprivation. You're at least mildly anoxic, and we're going to run some cognitive tests before you can go anywhere."

"Sorry, doctor, as far as I've come with this, I've got to see it through to the end."

I swung my legs out of the bed, startling slightly as my bare feet hit the cold tile floor.

Forty

I made it exactly two steps before I fell over. It started as a slight feeling of lightheadedness that began as soon as I stood up, but almost immediately became a spreading weakness across my shoulders and down my back. I tucked my head and hunched over, determined to power through it, and took my first step. The IV, having reached the end of its length, tore loose. I looked down in surprise at the spreading spot of blood on the back of my hand and took my second step, knowing even as my foot hit the floor that my knee was buckling, that it wouldn't hold me up. I looked up at Bobby and told him quite clearly I thought I was going to fall over, though later Bobby insisted all I said was something that sounded like "Gah," and I would have cracked my head open on the floor had he not been there to catch me.

Bobby and the doctor got me back into the bed. The doctor slapped a gauze pad on my hand and reseated the IV, this time in the crook of my elbow.

She leaned over, her face very close to mine. From this distance her eyes, which I thought were very dark brown, actually looked black, like she had giant outsized pupils. "You are going to stay in that bed Mr. Fallon until I tell you otherwise. Is that clear? Or do I need to put restraints on you?"

There was probably a snappy comeback I could have made, something flirty with a hint of sexual innuendo, but I was too busy just trying to keep from passing out, and so simply nodded my head dumbly.

"Good," She nodded once. "You," she pointed a finger at Dobby, "out."

"But he hasn't told me where Russell is."

"You had your five minutes. More than that in fact. If you have more questions, come back this evening."

"But-"

"No buts." She grabbed a hold of his uniform collar and began pulling him from the room. It looked almost comical because she was at least a foot shorter and more than a hundred pounds lighter than he was, and while simple physics dictated that he could have easily stopped her, he looked nonetheless completely helpless as she hauled him away.

"Where is he, Jack? Do you know?" He called to me as the room door swung closed.

I drew in all the air I could manage, which wasn't much, to answer him. "Try the cemetery."

That was it. My head was spinning, a cyclone of water running down the drain, and I was going with it.

"The cemetery." I muttered again, my head lolling over to one side.

They found the Chief's truck parked with the keys still in it and the driver's side door open on the crushed stone roadway that cut through the cemetery.

He had stopped by his house before going there. The police knew this because they later found his abandoned fire gear on the floor in his living room and a lockbox open on the bed in the guest bedroom, only a rag stained with gun oil and a few loose bullets rolling around inside. The .38 revolver registered in his name was missing.

Driving as close to the graves of his son and wife as he could, he had abandoned the truck at that point, and then set off across the cemetery on foot in a straight line, kicking over framed photos and knocking over flower vases on other graves as he went. He had dropped hard to his knees in front of his son's headstone leaving two deep oval impressions in the earth, put the barrel of the short-nosed .38 revolver in his ear and pulled the trigger.

He left a note, if you could call it that. It was stuffed into one pocket of his jeans, written on a gas receipt in simple block letters with a pen from the center console of the Chief's truck, and contained only the two words "I'm sorry."

It wasn't much of a note, even considering the gas receipt had little clear space for writing and the pen from the console was very nearly out of ink. It didn't convey the pain and anger of a man whose entire life had collapsed. A man who, unable to lash out at demon fate or an uncaring God or whatever else you wanted to attribute his misfortune, had struck at those he felt were responsible with a violence and bitterness which surprised us all who thought we knew him.

It wasn't until much later that I learned of this. I was busy playing the role of eyelid inspector for about the next thirty-five hours, and when I finally decided to return to the world of the conscious, it was night. I looked down at the IV in my arm and then followed the slender plastic tube up to the bag on the rack by the headboard. It was empty. Tracing the line of my other arm down to my hand I was surprised to find I held another hand within my own. Valerie had pulled one of the blocky wood-and-vinyl room chairs over next to the bed and fallen asleep in it, legs pulled up underneath her, head tilted at a bad angle against the back of the chair, one hand stretched out and held in mine, the other thrown over the short chair back. It was a position I knew would leave her an achy pretzel in the morning. Moonlight fell though the Venetian blinds and painted lines across her face.

I was just considering waking her when a nurse came in on ninja rubber-soled shoes. She efficiently swapped my empty bag for a full one, then noticed me watching her and leaned in close. I caught the scent of coffee and vanilla.

"Do you need anything?" she whispered.

"I don't think so." I whispered back.

She stood up and adjusted the flow valve on the drip, then gave me a little finger wave as she left.

I looked over at Valerie again in the moonlight, tried to put myself in her shoes. How would I feel if I lost her? Just probing the edges of that minefield was more dangerous than I cared to contemplate.

I adjusted my grip on her hand; let my index finger slide down her wrist. I could feel the beat of her pulse through the pad of my fingertip. Don't let there ever be a day I can't feel that, I prayed to whatever anthropomorphic God inhabited my philosophy.

Valerie's eyes fluttered open.

"Jack."

Pulling her gently towards me I slid over to one side of the narrow hospital bed. She climbed carefully aboard and snuggled against me, my side basking in her warmth. I felt her breathing hitch as she started to sob.

"Shhh," I whispered to her "no more tears. I'm here. I'm OK. I'm not going anywhere, I promise."

I meant it too, right down to the core of my soul. But is it a promise any of us can be certain we can keep?

I didn't get out of the hospital for another four days, and when I finally left I remained as weak as a small kitten. It frustrated me, because while lying in the bed I felt fine, but even trips to the bathroom became an obstacle as onerous as a trek across the Andes, barefoot. Dr. Millar promised me I would get better, though it would take time. We also discussed doing some physical therapy, which brought to mind the possibility I might ultimately end up with some level of disability, which was something I wanted to avoid even thinking about. We left that one hanging in the indefinite future.

While I was there I received a lot of visits from other firefighters, who would sit uncomfortably in the guest chair talking about sports or the weather, check their watches frequently, and often leave after exactly thirty minutes on the dot from the moment they had walked into the hospital room. Just because we're firefighters doesn't mean we're all bosom buddies or anything.

My best friend from graduate school, Steve, called from New York and my sister called from Long Island to make sure I was alright, as did my parents from Florida who offered to come up to see me. I assured them that was not necessary and I was doing fine. Though earnest in their offer I got the feeling they were glad they wouldn't have to make the trip up from Fort Lauderdale. Snowbirds dislike coming back north before their appointed migration time, almost regardless of the reason.

Once I woke up to find Rachael sitting in the chair beside the bed reading a Grisham paperback. She thanked me for finding her sister's killer, to which I responded it was more like her killer had found me. She also told me she was going to drop out of college and join the fire academy in Concord. We talked about that for a bit, what little I knew about a career in firefighting. It seemed like she was making an emotional decision rather than a thoughtful one, but I didn't see it as my place to dissuade her. When I started to doze off she kissed me on the cheek, thanked me again, and left.

Bobby also came by several times to give me updates on the investigation, a gesture I accepted as the olive branch it was intended to be.

Connecting Patricia to Daniel had proved more difficult than he would have thought.

There were never any phone calls between them Bobby could find. If Patricia had ever had an email account, or even a computer, no one knew anything about it. Patricia's sometimes running partner and neighbor hesitantly identified Daniel from a photograph with a shrug and a maybe. No one at Patricia's workplace could identify Daniel from the photo; none of the local eateries remembered seeing them together.

Daniel did show up in Beverly Dell's records, which Tolland released after the death of Russell Burtran. Her notes indicated during sessions that he spoke often of a woman he loved who loved another man, though he never mentioned either Patricia or Michael by name. Furthermore, there was ample proof of Michael Carston's involvement with Patricia, including lingerie purchases, flowers, a little jewelry, and numerous matching dates in their respective calendars.

Of course, none of this connected Russell to anything or proved he had murdered anyone.

He had not been definitely tied to the purchase of the

handcuffs used on Patricia, which most likely been in cash from one of any number of sex shops near Boston. His verified purchase through credit card receipts of a similar type of chain as had been used on Patricia from Home Depot was likewise proof of nothing. Home Depot sold a mile of it every month. The lock was interestingly of the same type as had been used in the stationhouses years ago, but it was impossible to prove the lock used on Patricia had been given to Russell. They were never able to locate the key to the lock in any of Russell's possessions. Examination of the cable ties used on Beverly had been inconclusive. The accelerants used in the fires that killed Patricia, Beverly, and Michael had been so generic as to be untraceable.

Finally, though I spent hours at the dispatch center, old-style headphones with sweaty, hard, plastic ear cones pressed to my head, listening to the tape of the 911 call reporting the fire at Oak Hill, I was unable to convince myself it was Russell making the call. The message was simply too brief, the caller speaking too softly:

Dispatcher: 911, what is the nature of your emergency?

Caller: There's a fire at a house on Oak Hill in Dunboro.

Dispatcher: What is the address?

Caller: It's the big house near the top.

Dispatcher: I am notifying the fire department. Do you know if there is anyone in the residence?

Caller: …

Dispatcher: Sir, is there anyone in the residence?

Caller: (hangs up).

The question of whether or not he had led me to that house

intent on killing me consumed many of my conscious hours as I lay in the hospital bed. If so, it meant he felt I was getting close to him. That I had little idea I was actually closing in on him up until the moment I accused him made his actions difficult to understand. And yet even though I couldn't prove it now because all of the evidence was destroyed, the basement door had been nailed shut. Had Russell done that? Vandals? It was a mystery I would be unable to solve.

They had his confession, admittedly only heard by me at the Oak Hill fire, the two words scrawled on the gas receipt, and the fact he had fled and then killed himself at his son's grave, though essentially circumstantial, seemed very damning. It was ultimately on the weight of that evidence Bobby closed Dunboro's first two murder books and Amherst closed one of theirs. The police felt they had found the right man.

On the whole, though, everyone would have been a lot happier had Russell chosen to leave a more detailed suicide note.

Bobby also voided the parking ticket.

By the time I was discharged from the hospital the news outlets had all lost interest. The new hot story was about some starlet drunk on Mohitos and flying high on prescription pain killers who had plowed her SUV into a crowd of people waiting, irony of ironies, in line to see the opening of her new movie. No one had been killed, and she had immediately checked herself into a secluded spa citing exhaustion. Lawyers for the victims were lining up like horses at the gate before a race.

I had missed my fifteen minutes of fame lying in a hospital watching Judge Judy on television and eating chocolate pudding with Valerie, and I couldn't have been happier.

I was sorry that while I was in the hospital Beverly's funeral had been held in Phoenix. In no condition to travel, I had sent flowers along with my regrets and condolences. If I was going to find closure there, it was going to have to come from somewhere else.

Forty-One

Russell's funeral was held on the following Saturday in the Burtran family plot of the town cemetery. It was a small gathering, without any immediate relatives. There was talk maybe Russell had had a brother in Pennsylvania somewhere, but in the end no one knew where he was or how to contact him. His fire department family attended, twenty-seven of us dressed in our Class A uniforms with shiny brass buttons and polished patent leather shoes, looking more than anything else like a parade in search of a route and spectators.

Russell was buried on top of his wife, a practice which has always kind of creeped me out. His half of the dual headstone had been carved with the date of his death and the epitaph "beloved husband and father." Alongside his wife ("beloved wife and mother") and Daniel ("beloved son") they certainly had all their beloved bases covered nicely. I wondered if somehow that was the default inscription.

So ended the Burtran lineage on that crystalline fall day in Dunboro.

I stood while the priest intoned the usual banalities – ashes to ashes, valley of death, etcetera – but became weaker and weaker, slumping over farther and farther, until I was forced to step away from the group to sit quietly on the edge of a nearby headstone. Jonas came over and perched on it next to me, his Class A uniform billowing enormously on his age-withered frame, jacket hung on scarecrow shoulders, thin wrists sticking out of gaping cuffs, like a young boy putting on a suit jacket owned by his father.

"You OK?" he asked.

"Just tired."

"This is my wife's stone, you know?"

I leaned back and saw the inscription, clean block letters chiseled into the grey granite surface, "*Elizabeth Rebecca Gault, the love of my life*" with the date of her death some ten years earlier.

I began to get up but Jonas grabbed my arm and pulled me back down. "She wouldn't mind."

He smiled at me and I smiled back. We remained sitting there for the rest of the service.

No one spoke for the dead.

The reception afterwards was held in the meeting room over the firehouse. We sat around somberly on folding chairs while the uneaten spaghetti dinner got cold and the salad wilted. Many of the guys held beer, some of them something stronger; all of us just sitting around staring into our drinks. The little conversation that took place was brief and muted.

I'd heard of cases where a fire department has had to deal with the reality of an arsonist exposed in their midst. This was about forty million times worse.

Valerie, who had helped set up the food along with other fire department wives, came over and sat on a chair next to me. She took my hand, our wedding rings clinking together. "Can I get you anything?"

I held up my empty cup, "Some water?"

"Sure," she took it and went into the kitchen area.

Roger Fiske came over and placed a heavy hand on my shoulder. "You got the wrong man," he growled.

"What?"

"Russell never hurt a soul, and he was a better firefighter than you'll ever be," his breath washed over me in an alcohol fog. "His wife and son were gone, and you fucking hounded an innocent man to his death."

He saw Valerie returning and left without another word, the palms of his hands slamming against the breaker bar on the meeting room door, banging it against its stop on his way out.

"What was that about?" Valerie asked as she handed me the cup of water.

I shook my head, bewildered, "I don't know."

Jonas spoke loudly from a chair near the front of the room. "Back in the winter of 1978, we had a wicked ice storm. Most of the town was without power for nine days."

A couple of guys looked up from their cups and in his direction.

"The department was stretched to its absolute limit with a solid week of trees and wires down calls and car accidents. We initially broke the department into teams of four, and then down to teams of two as we went to twelve-hour shifts. Well, I was teamed up with Russell."

There were a few murmurs from the group. A couple of the old timers smiled – they had apparently heard this story before. It was new to me.

"We went to a car accident, single car into a tree, over by Baxter's Bridge. The car had plowed into the tree fast, the whole front end wrapped around the trunk, the hood pushed in, steam hissing out of the ruptured radiator, the entire frame buckled back. And as we pulled up, we heard singing. There was a woman in the driver's seat, and she was singing a medley of Elvis songs at the top of her lungs. *Heartbreak Hotel, All Shook Up, Blue Christmas, Hound Dog, and Don't Be Cruel.* We figured she must have brained herself something awful on the steering wheel or the windshield to be singing at a car accident, so I radioed for an ambulance and Russell grabbed a pry bar from the tool box and went over to the car. He pried the door open and leaned in to look at her. She wasn't hurt at all; she was drunk, holding onto a bottle of Smirnoff by the neck with one hand, thumping out the bass beat on the dashboard with the other. By this time I had run up and was standing behind him. "Are you alright?" he asked. Her eyes seemed to focus for the first time as she looked around her. "What the fuck did you do to my car?" she yelled at him, and she whacked him in the head with the bottle right on his helmet."

A couple of guys laughed, but it was short lived.

"I remember when Russell drove Engine Two down to Lowell to get the pump rebuilt," Max Deaks began, "He's going down Route 3 at about sixty miles an hour when one end of the two-and-a-half inch hose stored in the upper bed came loose. Before he knows it, he's laid more than fifteen hundred feet of hose on the highway at rush hour."

"What'd he do?" Someone asked.

"What could he do? He stopped the truck dead in the

middle of the road and flipped on his emergency beacons. He got out, and gathered up all that hose. Traffic is crawling around him; drivers are honking their horns. Two Nashua police cars go by and buzz him with their sirens. He just smiled, flipped them off, and kept picking up hose."

"Jesus," Winston laughed, shaking his head, and then he looked over at Tom sitting next to him. "Remember that fire four years ago at the dog breeders? Russell went into one of the rooms and there were like 50 puppies in playpens and boxes and dog crates all over the place. The smoke was getting thicker and the fire was getting closer, and he was looking at all these dogs, and he just started scooping them all up. He came out on the front lawn, and he had puppies down his pants, and in his pockets and up his sleeves, in his jacket, he was carrying like five in his helmet. He was pulling puppies out of everywhere like a magic trick."

The laughter got louder and wider spread.

I understood what they were trying to do. They were trying to remember Russell for the years he had been one of them, and not the horrific betrayal he had done to them at the end. For more than forty years Russell Burtran had been a firefighter and laid his life on the line. The person he had become, the things he had done, they couldn't reconcile that with the man they had worked with and sweated with and bled with.

At that moment I felt alone. I reached over and pulled Valerie to me, held her close. Whatever he had done before, he had tried to kill me, and for that and Patricia, Beverly, and Michael I couldn't see him as anything other than a monster. If ever, in one of my more generous moments, I felt like forgiving and forgetting I would always carry the puckered line of scar tissue on my neck from the burn as a reminder.

"So Russell said to Dawkins, 'Honest, Sheriff, that's not my firetruck.'" Deaks squeaked out, his face red with the effort before dissolving in fit of guffaws.

This was followed by a burst of laughter, many of the men leaning forward and pounding on the table.

This was how the department would survive. They would remember, and they would forget, and they would heal, in time.

And even as I stood apart from them, that was alright with me.

Embers

Afterword

As a twelve year volunteer firefighter I have drawn heavily from my experiences in the fire department and stories told to me by other firefighters. Many of the training scenes are from my own training classes, and Jack's first fire is actually my first fire, and yes, the homeowner told me to go fuck myself when I asked him to move his car. The story that Jonas told Jack about losing a firefighter at a basement fire was told to me by a retired Chief from one of the towns in western New Hampshire. I regrettably don't recall his name or the town, and if he recognizes the story as his own and wishes to contact me I will certainly give him credit. He, or others, may reach me at psoletsky@gmail.com.

Now turn the page for a special preview of *A Hard Rain*, the second Jack Fallon mystery.

One

The storm hovered, stagnant, just off the coast of New Hampshire, circulating lazily in a clockwise fashion, scooping up vast draughts of the Atlantic Ocean and pouring them all across the state. Rivers and ponds overflowed their banks, dirt roads became impassable mires, mudslides had closed at least three sections of highway, and trees unable to find purchase in soil reduced to the density and consistency of quicksand were falling over hourly, often taking phone and power lines with them in their acquiescence to gravity.

It was one goddamned awful mess.

Our small town of Dunboro, New Hampshire was, quite rapidly, turning into one homogenous smear in shades of dark grays and muddy browns. The rain fell, and fell, and fell, from a sky the color of hammered pewter by day and the dark of a dusty coal bin by night. It had been doing so for over ten days now, three inches in the last twenty-four hours, approaching thirteen inches since we had last seen the light of the sun.

I shrugged my shoulders inside my jacket which felt like it weighed about fifty pounds. Designed to protect me in a fire, it was only moderately waterproof, and after two hours in the seemingly endless downpour it had become sodden. I tipped my head forward and watched the mass of water that had accumulated in the brim of my helmet spill off and spatter into the puddles on the ground at my feet. This, I told myself, was the glamorous side of being a volunteer firefighter.

The Dunboro volunteer fire department was overburdened and stretched thin. Several roads, like the one that I was currently guarding, were flooded and impassable, and in total darkness because most of the streetlights in town were out. There were power lines down all over. Basements were filling up, and we were helping out with portable gas-powered pumps wherever we could spare a man. If there was a bright spot to be found in all of this, it was that the damp had permeated everything, and there was no longer anything in town capable of catching fire.

The glare of headlights filled the road ahead of me and I turned on the heavy-duty flashlight that I was carrying on a strap over one shoulder and waved it back and forth across the approaching car, signaling the driver to stop.

When he pulled over and rolled down the window I leaned in to talk to the dark haired man behind the wheel. "The road's out up ahead." I informed him.

"Out? I just came through here this morning," he complained.

"There's been a lot of rain since this morning," I replied,

just as I had for the last dozen motorists trying to get through here. "There's at least four feet of water across the road ahead. Where are you trying to get to?"

"Four corners."

I noticed the vehicle was a dark green Dodge Durango with a lot of ground clearance, but nowhere near enough for the road ahead. I hoped he wasn't going to give me an argument, the cheap bravado of oversized SUV drivers who are sure that they can muscle through anything. Thankfully, it turned out that he wasn't; he accepted my directions without argument.

I stepped aside and the driver did a three-point turn majestically in about seven points, the car clearly larger than he was capable of maneuvering, and went on his way. I returned to standing in the middle of the road drowning an inch at a time.

It seemed to me that I had taken showers that were drier.

Checking my watch I was surprised to find that it was only early evening. I felt certain that I had been standing there for hours and as dark as it was it must be considerably later. I searched the sky for any hint of light, any thinning of the clouds, and saw nothing.

A wave of exhaustion suddenly washed over me and I leaned forward, my hands on my knees. The strap on my shoulder slipped and the sway of the heavy flashlight almost tipped me onto my face. Leaning over opened a gap in my jacket collar at the back of my neck, and rainwater from my helmet brim rushed right in. Nice.

These sudden periods of weakness, I thought of them as personal power failures, I carried with me as a reminder of my recent brush with death. I had been trapped in a basement fire and rescued after my respirator tank had run out of air. The injuries I had suffered, the perplexing and conflicting symptoms I displayed, had baffled the physicians, though I did seem to be improving slowly.

With immense dedication to my physical therapy I had gotten rid of the cane that I had needed during my convalescence four weeks ago. The day that I had stopped using it I had run it through the band saw in my workshop cutting it into a dozen short canelets. I admit that it had been childish on my part to do so, but it had felt so damned good to be done with it.

If I had still had it with me I would have been leaning on it.

I probably wasn't in quite good enough shape to be standing out here for six hours at a pop. The doctors had not yet cleared me to perform normal firefighting duties, but John Pederson, the chief of the department, and I had talked about it and he had consented to my request to let me stand a few shifts on road detail. Rattling around at home had been starting to drive me nuts. John hadn't really been in a position to refuse help from anyone, with the department fielding endless calls for assistance. His own two sons, ages fourteen and sixteen, were standing guard on other flooded roads elsewhere in town. When all hell broke loose, child labor laws got a little lax. If I got into trouble, I could always use the radio on my belt to call for relief, except that the repeater on top of Follett Hill had failed two days ago and much of the town, including the spot that I now stood, was smack dab in the middle of a communications hole.

I got really dizzy for a moment and was forced to kneel down suddenly in the roadway, my right hand flat on the blacktop. The flashlight hit the ground next to me, its tough plastic case absorbing the impact without damage. I took deep and even breaths, trying to avoid hyperventilating, my mouth set in a firm line, willing myself to grind through it. If water was still running down my back I couldn't feel it. My skin felt clammy and a little bit tingly as if most of my body was asleep.

At a gleam of light off the roadway I looked up and saw another pair of headlights approaching. I forced myself back to my feet, the dizziness swelling like a soft warm balloon in my head and either I swayed on my feet or the town experienced a minor earthquake. I fumbled with the flashlight, turned it on, and waved it in the general direction of the approaching car.

It kept coming.

A shot of adrenaline to my bloodstream slapped a little more spine into my back. I waved the flashlight more energetically, adding my other arm into the action as well.

And still the car came. I had no way of knowing if the driver even saw me.

I moved to the side of the road and stood behind a stout oak, waving the flashlight and peeking at the approaching car around the tree trunk.

The car, a dark Porsche, sped by, accelerating as it headed down the road towards where the pavement vanished into the murk. It threw up an enormous wave when it hit, its momentum damping quickly, coming to a stop half submerged, right to the level of the windows.

I sloshed over to the car, muck filling my boots, and found a woman sitting in the driver seat chest deep in water and crying. For just a moment, less than a fraction of a second, in the reflection of my flashlight she looked just like Sharon Bishop.

That was impossible of course, but it took longer than I would have expected to force the image from my mind. The woman in the car had blonde hair, either dirty blonde or just plain dirty, plastered to her head. Her light colored top that had become mostly see-thru and she wore no bra, her nipples pink and erect. Yet even as disheveled as she was, she was achingly beautiful, with a perfectly symmetrical oval face and an alluring tilt to her eyes. She would turn the head of every man within fifty feet. Just like Sharon.

The dashboard indicators were still lit, though the car had stalled, so I reached past her and turned off the ignition. "Miss. Are you alright? Are you hurt?"

She ignored me, sobbing louder, pounding her hands against the wheel. She got two weak hoots out of the horn, and then nothing. The electrical system must have shorted out.

I unlocked the door and pulled it open, hauling against the minor suction as the water level inside and outside the car reached equilibrium. I reached across her and unbuckled her seatbelt. "You're alright. Let me help you out of there. It's just a car. It can be fixed."

She stopped sobbing like someone had flipped her off switch and glared at me with wet, angry eyes that underneath glowed with a searing light of crazed terror. "Do you think I care about the fucking car? All I had to do was get out of town. Now he's going to find me and kill me for sure!"

"What?"

She slapped at my hands when I tried to help her up and clawed her way past me out of the car.

Another pair of headlights illuminated us, another car coming down the road. The last thing I needed was for that car to plow into this one in the dark.

I turned away from her and started waving the flashlight at the approaching car, holding my other hand up. There was a splashing sound behind me and I glanced back over my shoulder to see her thrashing through the thigh-deep water, moving away from me along where the road would have been had it not been flooded. "Miss, I – stop!"

I checked the other car, which was gliding to a halt where the pavement ended, then looked back at her again. The woman was going at a pretty good clip, putting distance between us, just a smudge of lightness, ghostly in the car headlights against the darkness that surrounded her.

The car honked at me and the window whirred down. The driver, a woman, leaned out, shielding her eyes from the rain with the flat of her hand. "What's going on? Do you need any help?"

"Hey!" I called out, but the fleeing woman was gone from my sight.

The night and the rain had swallowed her whole.

23640789R00161

Made in the USA
Middletown, DE
30 August 2015